NEVER MISSING, NEVER FOUND

ALSO BY AMANDA PANITCH

Damage Done

NEVER MISSING NEVER FOUND

AMANDA PANITCH

Random House 🏠 New York

Text copyright © 2016 by Amanda Panitch
Jacket photograph of girl copyright © by Rekha Garton/
Moment Open/Getty Images

Visit us on the Web! randomhouseteens.com

Educators and librarians, for a variety of teaching tools, visit us at
RHTeachersLibrarians.com

Library of Congress Cataloging-in-Publication Data
Names: Panitch, Amanda, author.
Title: Never missing, never found / Amanda Panitch.
Description: First edition. | New York : Random House, [2016] |
Summary: "Stolen from her family as a young girl, Scarlett is now
moving on from the past and starting her summer job at Adventure Time
amusement park. When a girl goes missing from the park, it's clear that
the past is not done with Scarlett"—Provided by publisher.
Identifiers: LCCN 2015029365 | ISBN 978-0-553-50764-5 (hardback) |
ISBN 978-0-553-50766-9 (lib. bdg.) | ISBN 978-0-553-50765-2 (ebook)
Subjects: | CYAC: Missing children—Fiction. | Kidnapping—Fiction. |
Secrets—Fiction. | Human trafficking—Fiction. | Families—Fiction. |
BISAC: JUVENILE FICTION / Social Issues / Dating & Sex. |
JUVENILE FICTION / Family / Siblings.
Classification: LCC PZ7.P18933 Ne 2016 | DDC [Fic]—dc23
LC record available at http://lccn.loc.gov/2015029365

Printed in the United States of America
10 9 8 7 6 5 4 3 2 1
First Edition

For my sister, Rebecca,
and my brothers, Adam, Noah, and Sam:
the first ones to hear my stories

NEVER MISSING, NEVER FOUND

PROLOGUE

I didn't choose to join the illustrious society of missing girls. I didn't grab an application, dot my *i*'s with hearts (it was third grade, okay?), and sign my name with a flourish in my newly acquired cursive. I was taken.

My breath puffed into clouds and the cold cut through me clean, like a knife, and yet when the car idled to a stop next to the sidewalk, I chose *not* to get in. It didn't matter. I was a short, skinny little kid, and it was easy enough for the man to get out of the car, tuck me under his arm like a football, and whisk me away.

And I didn't choose Pixie. If the woman upstairs had given me a choice, I would have asked for a nice girl. A girl to stroke my hair when I cried and make up stories with me to chase away the dark. I wouldn't have chosen this skinny girl with the rat face and ever-darting eyes. Still, after a month of scrubbing floors and crying into my dirty mattress—my only friend the dim, flickering bulb swinging overhead—I took the girl she gave me.

I made almost no choices in that basement. None that mattered. I secretly chose to call the woman upstairs Stepmother, after the evil stepmother who made Cinderella scour the fireplace until her knuckles bled, but it wasn't like that turned me into an actual Cinderella and sent me a fairy godmother to sweep me away. Stepmother chose the clothes Pixie and I wore, the chores she'd make us do, the food we ate, and the times we woke up. The only real choices we had were how much food to eat and what time to go to sleep, and as eating too little or going to sleep too late made us painfully hungry or tired the next day, they weren't real choices at all.

At the end of my time with Stepmother, I made one choice. That choice mattered. That choice changed everything—took my path and Pixie's path and untangled them in one swift rip.

After so long without the ability to choose, making choices feels ... I don't know, like a superpower. Five choices can change the world.

Or at least myself.

CHAPTER ONE

In the first issue of the Skywoman comics, the good citizens of Silver City are in trouble. An eeeeevil villain has diverted the course of a fiery meteor and has, for no good reason, decided to plop it right on the city itself. Everybody's weeping and tearing at their hair and pounding the ground with desperation, but there's nothing they can do (like go to another city, apparently).

Until Skywoman shows up in a swirl of baby blue and gold. She swoops through the air and forces that meteor back on track. Then she decapitates the eeeeevil villain for good measure. Everybody cheers and kisses the ground they were just beating.

In the basement, every time I closed my eyes, that's

what I pictured: Skywoman, sailing down from the sky, smashing the bars of the basement's window in one great sweep, and lifting me out by the nape of my neck, as if I were a kitten. She never came. Because she isn't real.

The theme park bearing her image is, though.

I think it would embarrass her, honestly.

The employment office of Five Banners Adventure World, home of Skywoman and the League of the Righteous, is more trailer than office, plunked at the far side of the vast employee parking lot, where it creaks on its wheels every time a gust of wind blows through. I sit in one of the trailer's tiny cubicles, my dignity cupped in my hands as I speak to one of the park's assistant managers, who doesn't look a second older than me.

"I just love working with people," I lie as enthusiastically as I can manage. "Making people happy makes me happy. I love to problem-solve." Did I hit all the buzzwords the job listing mentioned? "I don't have any retail experience, but I've done some babysitting." I thrust my hands out in front of me and unfurl my fingers, revealing my dignity, the gleaming and golden center of a flower.

The assistant manager, who wears a lime-green polo so bright it hurts my eyes and clashes with her blond hair, smiles. "You sound like you'll be a great fit here, with your zeal for helping people," she says. "Congratulations, Scarlett. You've got the job."

"Yay," I say.

"You look like a medium-size women's shirt," she says,

apparently not much impressed with my display of zeal. That's fine, because my zeal stems mostly from a desire to pay for my gas and car insurance. It's not like I really use my car to go anywhere, but I need to have it, because as long as I have it, I *can* go somewhere if I want to. Without it, I'm trapped. "What size pants are you?"

I tell her, and she stands. "Great, I'll be right back," she says. I wave a silent goodbye to my dignity as she goes. Anyone who works at Five Banners Adventure World over the summer needs to be prepared to exchange her dignity for the allotted two lime-green polo shirts, two pairs of khaki pants, a brown belt, and a name tag that screams SCARLETT! in bubble letters. Bonus points for knowledge of Wonderman, Skywoman, and the gang, the group of superheroes around whom the park is based. I love comics, so I win all the bonus points.

It's worth the temporary loss of dignity to be here, surrounded by Skywoman and Wonderman and their crew. I spent so many years imagining them that the thought of seeing them walking around every day, of talking to them— well, the people dressed up as them—is so exciting. What I really want is to be one of the girls who get to wear the Skywoman costume, but you're required to put in a season of work at the park before you can transition to the Costumed Character Department. This is my one season. And then I'll get to make kids' days, smile wide and tell them that nothing will ever hurt them. That's not true, of course, but it's a good thing for someone to believe. At least for a little while.

The assistant manager bustles back in, her arms overflowing with tacky clothing. She dumps them in my arms and grabs a set of forms off the desk. "You just have to sign here," she says, pointing out the signature lines with a pointy crimson nail. She flutters lashes coated so thickly with mascara I imagine it must be a struggle for her to open and close them, like lifting miniature weights with every blink. "To say you received each part of your uniform, that they're all in good condition, et cetera, et cetera."

I run my new shirts through my fingers. They stink of industrial detergent and the fabric is rough against my skin. My fingers tingle with the ghosts of old calluses. "There's a stain up by the neck here," I say, and Stepmother's voice echoes in my skull, *r*'s rolling with her Eastern European accent. I was never able to pin down exactly what country she'd come from, just the general area. *Not good enough, girl. Do you know what happens to girls who are not good enough?* "And a thread's ripped out here."

The assistant manager snorts. "If that's the worst you get, you're lucky." Her name tag screams MONICA! "My first year I got a pair of pants that were ripped right through the crotch. I had to sew them up myself, and my supervisor told me they looked unprofessional. My pay got docked for that."

I check both my pairs of khakis for rips through the crotch. All the crotches are intact, thank goodness. Though if I have to sew them up myself, my sewing will be perfect. Perfect, neat, *good* little stitches. Maybe I can teach this

Monica how to sew. She'll marvel at my talents, ask me how I got so good.

I've been quiet for too long. I should probably express sympathy or something. That's what a normal person would do. Like my sister. "That stinks."

"It's cool," Monica says. "Everything else is great here, really. Job is great, people are great, lots of fun perks." Her voice sounds rote, memorized. This is probably the speech she gives to all the new peons. "Do you have any questions? Orientation is next week."

"I think I'm good," I say, and I stand. "I just show up here for orientation?"

"Yeah. It'll be in the arena, inside the park, but there'll be signs pointing you there from here." She hands me a stack of papers, glossy brochures and forms emblazoned with the dual insignias of Skywoman and Wonderman, who are positioned front and center on the top brochure. As they should be, of course. They're the heads of the League of the Righteous, or LoR for short. They can save anyone. Or so I thought when I was little. Before I turned eight.

They couldn't save little Scarlett. Or Pixie.

I shiver, a trail of cold water rushing over my spine.

To distract myself, I think hard about Skywoman's first epic battle with her archenemy, the Blade. The Blade murdered Skywoman's parents back when Skywoman was simply Augusta Leigh Sorensen, setting Augusta on her heroic path in the first place. Skywoman unleashed her lasso made of clouds, which swirled over her head under its own power.

Even after so many years, Pixie has a way of working herself into every facet of my life. She's there when I eat breakfast, when I sit down to do my homework, when I feel the sun wash warm over my face. Always reminding me she'll never get to do any of those things again.

I swallow hard and concentrate harder on the battle going on in my head. The Blade's always-sinister yellow eyes, flashing like a cat's. Her claws shearing through Skywoman's lasso and then lunging at Skywoman's throat.

"Are you okay?" Monica asks. She smiles sympathetically at me, as if she knows exactly what I'm going through. She doesn't, of course, but I appreciate the effort, and so I try to smile back.

"Yeah, sorry. Just got dizzy when I stood up. Guess I should've eaten breakfast."

"It's the most important meal of the day!" Monica chirps. "You got everything?"

I pile my uniforms, my forms, my brochures, my everything, into a precarious leaning tower in my arms. "I think so," I say. "Thanks. I guess I'll see you next week?"

She goes to shake my hand but drops her arms and laughs when she registers my leaning tower. "No problem," she says. "See you next week."

My first job. I've chosen Five Banners, and Five Banners has chosen me back. This is the second choice I've ever made that has meant anything.

I dump my papers and uniforms in the passenger seat of my car. The air feels warm and humid, and it smells like wet leaves and pavement; it must have rained while I was inside filling out forms and working my way through my assorted interviewers. Roller-coaster loops stretch high up in the distance. The rain couldn't have been that bad, because every so often the tracks loose a roar and a faint shriek that translates to a successful ride. If there had been thunder or lightning, all the coasters would have closed and all the people who wanted to ride the coasters would have gone to ride the massive line at Guest Relations instead, with its hills of yelling and loops of children's tears and the splat at the end when the Guest Relations rep flatly denies your refund request.

Because no refunds. No refunds ever. On anything. That's Five Banners' corporate policy.

By the time I get home, my forms have scattered all over the floor and my uniforms are in a crumpled heap in the passenger-side well. I blame the town's traffic lights, which have yellow lights about as long as an eyeblink to try to milk money from all the Adventure World–going tourists. I don't mind so much, though. It's kind of like a game, making sure I stop in time. A good way to distract myself from the fact that I'm steering thousands of pounds of sharp metal and flammable liquid with the touch of my hand.

After pulling into the driveway, I reach down to collect

my belongings, groaning just for the sake of groaning, and jump when something thumps on my window. I look up to see my little brother's face smushed against the glass, his nostrils open wide and his breath clouding the rest of him in fog.

A smile breaks across my face, and I lean over to click the lock open. Matthew scrambles in and immediately starts cleaning up my stuff, beaming the way only a seven-year-old can. If I believed in God, I'd thank him (or her) every day for creating baby brothers.

I take the pile of uniforms and forms from his lap. He grins up at me, exposing a space where one of his front teeth should be.

"Thanks, dude," I say. "Did you just lose that today?"

He kicks his feet. I'd frown very strongly at anyone else who smeared footprints on my dashboard. Matthew can kick all he wants. "Yeah," he says. "Did you get the job?"

"I did get the job." I raise my eyebrows. "And guess what that means?"

He punches the air. "Free tickets!"

"All the free tickets you can eat," I promise.

He scrunches his nose. "I don't want to eat them."

"Oh, really?" I pretend to consider. "What in the world would you do with them, then?"

"You're being silly," he says. A lock of brown hair flops over his eye, and his lips purse like he's still not sure whether to believe me.

"I am," I say. His face splits into a wide smile. "Now

help me carry this stuff inside and we'll have a snack."
Food is the way into Matthew's heart. Food is also the way
into my heart. It's how you can tell we're related.

Though we've lived here in Jefferson for four years
now—the majority of Matthew's life and almost all the
time since I called my parents from the police station, my
teeth chattering so hard they thought it was static—I still
think of this house as "the new house."

It's objectively nicer than our old house in Illinois; our
New Jersey house is a neat two-story with cherry-red shutters and bright white siding my dad pummels with the
pressure washer the first Sunday of every month, and a
lawn so even and green that, in combination with the red
shutters and red door, it makes for a festive, Christmasy
mood all year round. It's objectively friendlier than our
old house too, which was located at the end of a very long
driveway at the end of a very long street, where neighbors
were few and far between. Our New Jersey house is smack
in the middle of a cul-de-sac, crammed side by side with
houses that are crammed side by side with more houses, so
close that neighbors can shout from window to window if
they need to borrow a cup of sugar or need someone to pop
over and watch the kids.

Still, it's firmly part of the After, and anything in the
After is new. Even Matthew, though I can't imagine my
life without him.

Matthew precedes me into the house, doing a weird sort
of dubstep move that works only when you're seven years

old and delighted. Sometimes I wish I were seven years old again. And that I'd never turn eight, because eight was when the man grabbed me off the sidewalk.

"I want *cookies* for a snack," he says.

I dump my pile of stuff onto the hall table. "How about celery with peanut butter?"

"Okay, but how about cookies?"

"Okay, but how about celery with peanut butter and raisins?"

"Okay, but how about celery with peanut butter and chocolate chips?"

"That just sounds gross." I wrinkle my nose. "Celery with peanut butter and raisins. Final offer."

He pouts and runs ahead of me. "Fine."

The new Jefferson kitchen is blinding in its whiteness and shininess and sunniness; every time I walk in, I have to blink and tell myself that no, Scarlett, you haven't just stepped through a portal to the future. As my vision clears, I notice my sister at the table, her hands cloaked in oven mitts, sliding the last cookie off a baking sheet and placing it onto a piled-high plate. Wisps of dark hair stick to her forehead, forming crazy curlicues in the sweat.

"Hello, Scarlett," she says, her voice cold and distant. You'd think the sugar would sweeten her tone even a little bit, except she probably hasn't tasted her product. If I'd made those cookies, I'd have eaten all the dough, and it would have been worth it, even after Melody told me how much I'd regret it next time I stepped on the scale. "I told Matthew he could have a cookie earlier. I had to make some for the bake sale tomorrow."

I have to bite my tongue not to ask "Which one?" Melody is sixteen, a year younger than me, and involved in so many school activities it makes my head spin just to think of them: student government (vice president!), chorus (second soprano!), field hockey (varsity!), French club (*la trésorière!*), creative writing club (cofounder!). Even now, during summer, she has all sorts of things to do and baked goods to make. I honestly have no idea how she manages to do all that she does. I can barely manage to hold myself together enough to make it to school every day. Even this new job is pushing it.

"He shouldn't be eating cookies before dinner," I say.

It's too late: a cookie is already half-chewed and half-down Matthew's gullet. Little traitor.

"It's just one cookie," Melody says, turning around to put the baking sheet in the dishwasher. "I think he'll live."

I stare at her back and fantasize about her turning around with a big white smile, a hug, and a "How was your interview?" I wouldn't even care if she got flour and sugar all over me. That could be showered off, but the glow she'd give me would last for days. Weeks, maybe.

"I got the job," I say. Not that she'll care.

"That's good," Melody says, turning back and flicking a sticky curl from her forehead. She rubs her hands together; bits of flour and sugar and whatever else goes into chocolate chip cookies flake off and drift to the floor like snow.

"You'll have something to put on your college applications now." She gives Matthew a peck on the top of his head, and love washes over her face for a moment; it makes my chest hurt just to see it. Matthew doesn't even acknowledge it, consumed as he is with his third cookie. "I have to shower and take these to Sarah's. Can you watch Matthew? Dad should be home any minute."

I deftly pluck a fourth cookie from Matthew's hand. He groans, and I almost relent. Almost. "Yeah, I can watch him."

"Good. Thanks. See you later." Melody sweeps out of the kitchen without a backward glance, shiny sheet of hair swinging behind her.

After I'd made the call from the police station, the cop, the nice one who had wrapped me in a blanket that smelled like old milk, sat with me to wait for my parents. Plural, because once upon a time I had a mother, too. They came as soon as they could; I could hear the screeching of their tires in the parking lot through the open window. My heart thumped as I heard their footsteps coming down the hall, and then they turned the corner and I saw them: my dad, hollow-cheeked, threads of silver winding through his beard; my mom, her face lined and eyes weary, carrying toddler Matthew; and Melody, trailing behind them, hands clasped before her, mouth trembling.

My dad burst into tears and fell to his knees, pulling me into his arms and holding me so tightly I could barely breathe. My mom couldn't stop patting my head, like I was a lost dog. She had this funny look on her face, half disbe-lief, half astonishment, and she had to put Matthew down and rest her other hand against the wall to keep herself from falling over. Matthew kept tugging on the bottom of her shirt and asking her who I was, but she didn't answer.

Melody just stared. Even when I looked at her and said, squeezing the words over the lump in my throat, how happy I was to see her again, she just stared. Even after I made it out of the hospital, my butt frozen from sitting on cold metal table after cold metal table, and I told her how happy I was to go back home and sleep in my own bed, she just stared, eyes colder than the hospital's tables.

Nothing has changed since.

CHAPTER TWO

I have no friends. When I told that to my dad a while back, he reacted with horror, patting me on the shoulder and assuring me that of course I had friends, that I was perfectly normal and everybody liked me. I squinted at him in surprise, because I hadn't been seeking pity or attention. I'd simply been stating a fact.

I had friends once—Maddy and Nicole, my best friends from elementary school, neither of whom I've spoken with since I returned home—and I could have friends again, if I smiled at the girls at school and asked them questions about themselves. I've tried a couple of times, started the process, but always put a stop to it. After a certain amount of time, the girls would start asking about my past, asking about when I moved to New Jersey or why I got nauseous at the smell of tuna fish. I'd clam up, and they'd withdraw, and I'd think that it was for the better. Because the closer we got, the closer I'd get to slipping up. Revealing what had happened to me. To Pixie.

But third grade. Maddy and Nicole. My dad woke me up on my last normal morning with the whap of a pillow and a kiss on the forehead, and bid me goodbye with a big, arm-swinging hug. My mom handed me my lunch, crinkly in a brown paper bag, and warned me not to trade my sandwich for Maddy's Oreos, because she'd know.

The school day itself was ordinary, achingly so, and because I went over the details a thousand times in Stepmother's house, I know it by heart. There was a spelling test I passed with an 88 (*photosynthesis* and *extinction* got the best of me), a short video on Abraham Lincoln and the Gettysburg Address, a lesson on the multiplication of fractions, and lunch, where I traded my sandwich for Maddy's Twinkie (it wasn't an Oreo, so the trade was legit).

On my walk home, I almost didn't notice the car sidle up next to me.

"Hey there," the man inside said. "Don't panic, honey, but I have some bad news. Your mommy got sick, and she and your daddy had to rush to the hospital in the ambulance."

My heart climbed up my throat. "Is she going to be okay?"

"They don't know," the man said. His voice was deep,

and half his face was covered in a shadow of stubble. "But they sent me from the hospital to bring you back there to see her." He paused, then continued ominously, "Hopefully, we'll make it in time."

Don't talk to strangers. Don't listen to strangers, even if they say they know you. "My house is right near here," I said, already moving away, my fingers locked tight around the straps of my backpack. "I should go home first."

"They told me you needed to come right away." He licked his lips nervously, and I blinked, and somehow he was standing outside the car. "I didn't want to have to say this, but it doesn't look good. She might die, honey."

The word "honey" looked wrong coming out of his mouth; there was something about his fat lips and the way his eyes didn't move as he spoke.

"My next-door neighbor will take me," I said, my heart thumping so hard it made me feel sick. "But thanks. I have to go now."

I turned, and suddenly he wasn't standing next to the car but was in front of me, and his arms were locked around me, and my backpack was dropping to the ground the way my insides were dropping to my feet.

"Sorry, honey," he said, and his hand was over my mouth, and something smelled sickly sweet, like stomach medicine mixed with the dregs from a box of sugary cereal. "I tried to make this easy on you."

And then everything was black.

• • •

First days scare me: first days of school, first time shopping at a new store, first time trying a new food. I don't like the unfamiliar, because all bad things start with the unfamiliar. So I'm not exactly looking forward to the Five Banners orientation.

It's not so bad, though. The day passes in a blur of bright colors and glossy paper and stupid catchphrases. (This year's Five Banners corporate motto: Safe! Friendly! Clean! They love their exclamation points, Five Banners.) I learn a lot about the park's history and the League of the Righteous. I learn nothing about how to operate a cash register or what to do if an item doesn't ring up or how to deflect creepy old men from hitting on me. (Make up a fake boyfriend and trot him out when you need him, Lara in Rides advises; best to make him tall and strong and very, very jealous.)

The next day—my first day at Adventure World—is misty, and cool for June. The sun shines palely, as if through a sheet of gauze, and I shiver as the chill pricks me.

I stand in my front hallway, checking the contents of my clear Five Banners fanny pack, making sure I have all the identification cards and employee documents that grant me access to the park—you'd think I was trying to fly to Pakistan or Somalia. My dad hovers beside me, cup of coffee in hand. A column of steam stretches toward the ceiling. "They didn't give you a jacket?" my dad asks. "You look cold."

"I'm not cold," I lie. I kind of hoped the neon-green polo would keep me warm through the sheer radiance of its color, but no such luck. And the pants sag on me, even with the aid of the belt. "I'll be inside most of the day anyway."

Employee ID card, check. Driver's license, check. Phone, check. All set. I take a deep breath. "Well, off I go. Hopefully, I won't get fired on my first day."

"You won't get fired." And then my dad is hugging me with one arm, cup of coffee held carefully to one side, and he is warm, and I am warm too. I close my eyes and commit this hug—they're so few and far between, after all—to memory. "You'll be the best damn cashier Five Banners has ever seen. They'll be begging you to stay next year, but you'll have to tell them, 'Sorry, folks. Off to Harvard to become a neurophysicist.' "

I can't help my laugh as I pull away. "Is that even a thing?"

"It doesn't have to be a thing. You'll make it a thing."

My laugh dries up. "If any of us are going to make it a thing, it'll be Melody."

"Don't worry about Melody. Melody has her own problems." He smiles down at me. "Besides, Melody hates math, and I hear neurophysics involves lots of math."

"Fine," I say. "As long as it doesn't involve geography, then I'm in."

"No geography. Just geometry. Lots of hypotenuses and angles and x's and y's."

"I can handle that." Math is easy. Math is good. If you do everything right, you get the right answer, and the right answer is the same every time, whether you get it in the morning or at night or your teacher hates you or whatever. Literature is open to too much interpretation. Something like "the grass is green" can mean anything except that the grass is colored green. "If I don't leave now, I'll be late. Give Matthew a kiss for me."

"Good luck. You'll do great." He retreats to the kitchen, coffee cup now clutched tightly in both hands. He doesn't look back.

Today the parking lot is positively bustling. We are a sea of phosphorescent algae in our glowing green shirts, shifting and flowing around the cars in waves. I drift along in the crowd, feeling the voices rush over me. There's a concert going on today, apparently, which means a lot of drunk guests, and security guards taking overtime. Wonderman's Fall, one of the most popular roller coasters, is down for emergency repairs. Two guests fought yesterday over the last souvenir cup at Orcaman's Reservoir, and an ambulance drove straight through the flower garden featured on the front of the Five Banners Adventure World brochure, sparking a design crisis. Fascinating stuff.

As I near the employee entrance, though, one word pushes its way to the front of the gossip, shoving all the mundane words about souvenir cups and gardens to the ground and trampling them under its feet—"missing." Missing. *Missing.*

"Hey, what happened?" I ask a fellow green shirt.

"You didn't hear about Monica?" The girl's enormous doe eyes flick to my name tag. "You're in Merch"—she must notice my confusion—"Merchandising," she clarifies, "so you've got to know her."

"It's my first day," I say. "But I interviewed with a Monica."

"Blond hair? Tons of mascara? Nails out to here?" She motions somewhere vaguely in front of her.

"Well, not quite out to there, but yeah," I say. Blond hair, long nails, warm smile. "I think."

The girl leans in. Her breath smells like pretzels. "Monica went missing," she says, her voice hushed, like she's afraid someone will overhear. It's too late; we've gathered a crowd of other green shirts, mostly Merch tags, like me. They join in, a Greek chorus of whispers: *Working late this weekend, till midnight, the only manager on the east side. Sent all her workers home and then never counted her tills. Supervisor next morning went to go check it out, all pissed, and found the tills half-open, money everywhere, a trail of nickels out the door. Nothing on the cameras. No witnesses. No word for two days now.*

She's gone.
She's gone.
She's gone.

The green shirt inside the employment office clocks me in and prints out the receipt with my day's assignment on it, but all her movements sag, and even I can tell she's just going through the motions. I wonder if she's always like this—saggy, tired, glum—or if she knew Monica. Her nails are long and crimson too, so I assume she did, then realize how ridiculous that assumption is, like there's a secret guild of long-nailed girls.

"You're at headquarters," she informs me, then tells me how to get there.

"Thanks," I say, trying to sound extra perky, because that's what normal people, people like Melody, do in times of crisis: try to cheer each other up. "And don't worry about Monica. It's better to be missing than dead."

Her head jerks up and her lips part, but I'm gone before she has the chance to speak.

I push my way through the clouds of whispers and enter the park through the employee entrance. There aren't real people in the park yet, just employees sweeping the cobblestoned streets and straightening signs in windows. People are walking in groups, as if they're schools of fish, afraid a shark will pick them off if they venture out by themselves.

Before opening, the park smells like stale popcorn and rain on stone. Sounds are harsh and abrupt: the whap of a flap opening over a stand selling superhero capes and plastic visors, the screeching of the chains lifting the metal grate over the park's hamburger joint, the rush-roar of a coaster doing its first warm-up lap of the day.

"Yesterday we had to close the Dragon King at five o'clock, with the lightning," a passing green shirt tells his colleague. "You can't imagine the crying and the . . ."

I make my way to headquarters, which has the distinction of being the park's south-side merchandising hub. In the comic books and the cartoon, the League of the Righteous headquarters is full of computer screens reporting on the movements of the LoR's sworn enemies, like Slugworth and the Blade.

This LoR headquarters, on the other hand, overflows with coffee mugs plastered with Wonderman's face, rompers with Skywoman's logo on the front, and Orcaman key chains. There are even fake computer screens reporting on Slugworth's movements; they're on sale for $49.99, plus tax. I stop to examine them. According to the splashy package, you can record your own voice-overs for Slugworth's actions. I'm tempted to do one of my own, just to delay the actual start of the day. I can still turn around. I can still go home and bury my face in my blankets and not have to meet strange people and do new things.

But then I'll never get to be Skywoman.

I push my way through the packed aisles, shoving aside fallen stacks of T-shirts with my feet. Normally, I would automatically pick them up and hang them evenly spaced on the rack, but my hands are fidgeting too much with nerves right now.

Finally I find myself at the cashier's station. There are three registers. All three are empty. I blink at them. Nobody magically appears.

"Hello?" I say. "Is anyone here?" If I wanted to, I could totally sweep a stack of Wonderman pajama pants and personalized Skywoman doorplates into my arms and take off. If I wanted to. "Hello?"

The back wall opens, fluttering a display of bath towels, and a boy falls out. "Hello there," he says. I stare, dumbstruck. The secret door is a hiding place on par with the concealed chute to Wonderman's secret garage, where awaits his prize vehicle, the Wondermobile (which can transform into a plane, a submarine, a boat, or a rocket ship, depending upon his—or the plot's—needs on any particular day). "You must be Scarlett."

I stare some more. The boy is probably my age, red-haired and freckly. The collar of his polo is rumpled, unlike mine, which I ensured this morning was perfectly straight. "Yes," I say. "How did you know?"

His eyes crinkle at the corners. They're warm and sharp and the color of weak tea. "You're wearing a name tag," he says.

"Oh. Right." I try to sneak a look at his name tag, but it's hidden behind the register. "They sent me here. It's my first day."

"No way," he says. "I swear I've seen you before."

I don't recognize him from school. I don't recognize him from my neighborhood.

Could he know me from Before?

No, I tell myself firmly. Illinois is a long way away; the odds are minuscule. It's more likely he caught my face on one of the MISSING posters or on the news after I was found. "A feel-good story," all the anchors chirped, smiling and exposing big teeth so white they had to be fake.

"Well, it's my first day, so I don't know what to tell you."

I try to sound as breezy as possible. A balmy wind blowing over a tropical beach—that's me.

"Do you go to Riverside?" He cocks his head, smiling.

"No, I go to Holt."

"Huh." His eyes rake my face again, and I feel myself flush. "I could swear I know you."

Maybe he did move here from Illinois, where I was a news item for years, a name scrolling across the ticker at the bottom of the screen. Maybe his bedroom walls are plastered with photos of missing girls. *Probably not,* I admonish myself. That isn't something that would pop into a normal person's head. Melody would never think such a thing. So creepy. "Well . . . it's my first day. So."

His hair flashes copper under the fluorescent lighting. "Well, in any case, it's nice to meet you, Scarlett." He sticks out his hand. "I'm Connor, south-side assistant manager, at your service."

"It's nice to meet you, Connor." I shake his hand. It's milky white and rough, covered in calluses and scars. "So what should I do?"

"We're going to train you on register. You haven't been trained on register, right?"

"No. It's my first day." I'm beginning to feel like one of the Skywoman windup dolls stacked in the corner, where you pull the string on the back and elicit one of three prerecorded phrases. *It's my first day, gentle citizen of Silver City!*

"Okay, good. The other cashier should be here any minute."

Somewhere distant, a bell bongs. I count the chimes. *Seven. Eight. Nine.* Connor shakes his head and sighs. "Park's officially open," he says. "She's officially late. Oh, there she is. Hey there!"

The other cashier does not look capable of ending any sentences with exclamation points. Her skin is pallid, especially against the glow of her shirt, and her otherwise unremarkable face is distinguished by a most serious lack of eyebrows. She's taken it upon herself to defy fate and has drawn in new ones; they start at different points on her forehead and stretch, crookedly, to the spot roughly above her nose.

"Good morning," I say. "I'm Scarlett."

No Eyebrows grunts in response and swings her till onto the counter with a clatter. "I got held up in Cash," she says. "You can ask Rob."

"It's okay, I believe you," Connor says easily. "Once you get set up, you'll be training Scarlett on the register today."

No Eyebrows grunts again.

"Great," Connor says. It seems he's fluent in Troll. "Let me set you up."

His fingers fly over the touch screen so fast they blur. Connor notices me watching and grins. "We used to have competitions to see who could type their info in the fastest," he says. "I always won."

"Lies!" a voice thunders from the front of the store. I jump, expecting someone as huge as Slugworth, but the owner of the voice reveals himself to be short and squat, more hobbit than giant. "Don't listen to him, new girl. Don't you see his nose growing?"

The hobbit also wears the name tag of an assistant manager. Over the top of his collar poke the edges of a tattoo that, judging from the bloody tips of the spikes, depicts something delightfully gory. Holes yawn in his earlobes where gauges would be if not forbidden by the Five Banners dress code. "You're Scarlett, I see," he says. "I'm Rob, the counterpart to Connor here."

"Basically, he's my evil twin," Connor says.

"Basically," Rob agrees. "Your evil, far-more-better-looking twin."

"I don't think that's grammatically correct," I say, squinting.

"See?" Connor says. "Grammatically incorrect. Therefore, I am both the better-looking and the smarter twin. You're my new favorite person, Scarlett."

"You should be honored," Rob tells me gravely. "He only has a new favorite person every seven minutes."

I pretend to check a nonexistent watch. "I'll enjoy the next six and a half minutes, then."

Connor waggles his eyebrows. "They'll be the best six and a half minutes of your life."

Rob has a surprisingly high, light laugh. "More like six and a half seconds."

Connor socks him on the shoulder. "Dude," he says. "How would you know?"

Rob grins. His teeth are oddly small, as if they belong to a baby. "This is good," he says. "We need this. To keep our mind off . . ."

The air sags, grows heavy. "I'm sorry," I say. "I should've figured you knew her."

"*Know* her," Rob says abruptly. "She's not dead."

"It's better to be missing than dead," I say encouragingly.

Nobody seems to know quite what to say back to that. No Eyebrows picks at her nails. Connor says, finally, "Yeah. We all knew her. Know her."

"I'm sure she'll be found soon," I lie. She'll never be found. Even if they find the girl they think is Monica, even if the doctors give her the okay and she has pointy crimson nails and slathered-on mascara, she'll never be Monica again. She might act like her, pretend to fill her life, but she'll never be the same. That's just what happens when you join the club.

"Yeah," Connor says. "We hope."

Rob looks away. "We should go finish the schedule."

"We should indeed," says Connor. "Scarlett, we'll leave you in the very capable hands of Lizzy here. Give me a shout if you have any questions." He leans in and whispers darkly, "Not Rob. Never Rob."

"Okay," I say. Lizzy, unsurprisingly, grunts, and Connor and Rob disappear through the door set craftily into the back wall.

"So," I say brightly. "How about this register thing?"

Lizzy looks at me with dull blue eyes. I'm thinking she must not have heard me somehow, though she's not more than three feet away, when she speaks. "She looked like you, you know," she says, and though she doesn't specify who "she" is, we both know.

"I interviewed with her," I say, bouncing a little bit to hide my unease. "We didn't look that much alike. She's blond; I have black hair. She's way paler than me too. So, um, how about that register?"

She stares at me, eyes flat. "No," she says. "You have black hair, and she might wear more makeup, but you look the same. You do."

The club. It rubs off on you, leaving the smell of desperation, a certain starved glint in your eye. You know there isn't anything you can do to avoid it. Or at least I like to think so, because that means there wasn't anything I could've done to change what happened to me.

Lizzy and I don't speak again, and she doesn't offer to teach me the register. I wait for her to teach me, so patiently none of the customers can see my stomach rolling with nerves; it's the same way I used to wait for Stepmother to finish what she was saying or regain her train of thought.

And then a cry splits the silence. It comes from what sounds like right outside the store, and my heart jumps into my throat. "What was that?" I ask Lizzy. She shrugs, squinting at her hands under the counter. Her wrists are wiggling; she must be texting.

All right, then. It's up to me. I creep through the empty store, sticking my hand into my pocket. Weapons are expressly forbidden on Five Banners premises, and there's a metal detector set up outside the employee entrance, but it's not like they strip-search us. It's not like it was hard to smuggle in my trusty canister of pepper spray, which hasn't left my side in five years.

My fingers relax when I find the source of the cry. It's a kid, a little boy in a bright red Wonderman T-shirt, probably four or five years old, huddled against the outside of the doorway. Only a little bit younger than Matthew, but, a quick look around confirms, there doesn't seem to be an accompanying adult. My heart softens, and I crouch down at his side. "Hey there," I say. He snuffles at me, his face red and swollen with tears. "Is your mom or dad here with you?"

At that he lets out another wail, and I pat his tousled blond curls in what I hope is a reassuring way. I like kids. I *love* some kids, like Matthew. But they scare me too. They remind me of what I was like at that age. So young. Unsuspecting. Unready. "Don't worry. It'll be okay." I take his sticky hand in mine and stand. Safe. I need to keep him safe.

"Scarlett. Hey! Scarlett." It's Connor, weaving his way through the crowd, his eyebrows bunched into a question mark.

"He's lost," I explain.

"I should've suspected." I make my own eyebrow

question mark, and he clarifies. "I'm the park's magnet for missing kids. Somehow they always find me." It's good he takes that moment to crouch down and look the kid in the eye, because my mouth's gone dry and I don't think I can respond. "Hey there, buddy. Don't you worry. We're going to find your mom or dad, okay?" Connor beams at him, and it's like the sun shines just a little bit brighter.

The kid's lip stops quivering long enough for him to say, "My mom."

"Your mom? Great. We'll find your mom for you, buddy. Can you tell me your name? No, let me guess. Your name is Wonderman, isn't it?"

That makes the kid crack a smile. "No."

Connor scrunches up his face, scratching his chin. "Orcaman?"

The kid giggles. I find myself smiling too. "No!"

"Skywoman, then."

"No!"

Connor shakes his head in mock frustration. "Well, you're just going to have to tell me, then, because guessing is too hard."

The kid sniffs. His face is already losing some of its puffiness. "Colin."

"Colin! That's an excellent name," Connor says, patting Colin on the shoulder like they're teammates in some kind of sport. I wouldn't know—I don't watch any. "It's almost like my name. My name's Connor. *C* names are the best, right?"

"Yeah!" Little Colin pumps his fist in the air.

I stand there and watch, with increasing amusement, as Connor teases out what Colin's mother was wearing (a blue shirt and pants like a mermaid, whatever that means), where he last saw her (outside Wonderman's Fall, a nearby coaster), and if he knows her phone number (no, but he thinks it has a five in it). "Don't worry about it, dude," Connor says. He stands and looks me in the eye, as if he's talking to me instead of the kid. I've always been tall for a girl; we're nearly the same height. "You're safe now. Let's go to Guest Relations. We'll find your mom and get you home."

My breath catches in my throat, and for a moment I feel weightless. Connor's eyes crinkle, and I feel it, I do: safe.

Colin breaks the connection by stomping his foot. "But I don't want to go home. I want to ride on Wonderman's Fall."

"We'll see about that." Connor grins at me. There's no way this kid is tall enough, but we'll just let him believe it for now. "Thanks for finding him, Scarlett. You saved the day."

For the rest of my "register training" shift with Lizzy (during which three customers come through and I gain no knowledge of the register), I bask in the glow of Connor's words and his eyes and his smile.

CHAPTER THREE

After the man pressed the cloth against my face, I woke to find myself in the backseat of a car. I sat up, and the world spun. I slumped against the wall and closed my eyes and let my head pound. *Pound on the window,* a small, bright part of me urged, but I could barely move, much less raise my fist. *You need to get out. You need to get free.*

"Don't bother trying to get out," the man said from the front seat. His voice echoed in the confines of the small space, and I cracked my eyes and let the light blur around me. I had to see his face so they could catch him when I escaped, or they'd never catch him, and I would always be looking for him over my shoulder.

"I'm real sorry it had to be like this," he said, his voice

growing softer, gentler, smoother against the jagged flashes of pain in my skull. "I tried to make it easy. You should listen to me. God knows you'd better listen to *her.*"

The "her" didn't even register. "Please let me go," I said. My words were thick and stumbled on their way out. "Please." That's what my mom always told me: say "please" and I'd have a much better chance of getting what I wanted. "Please. Please."

My eyes were still open and I was staring out the window and all I could see was trees, bare stalks of bark luminous against the black of the sky. I tried to move my head, tried to see his face, but my neck wouldn't listen.

"Go back to sleep," the man said, and I swear his voice was kind. The way my doctor's voice would get, soft and syrupy, before he'd swoop in with a needle. "We'll be there soon, and *she* will be happier if you're calm."

I tried to protest, but my eyes closed of their own accord, and soon all I could see was those trees, but this time they were phantoms scratching at the sky, and they were all screaming with the same voice.

The man was the one who woke me up the second time. I blinked slowly, groggily, and felt him shaking my shoulder. I was still in the backseat, slumped over the strap of the seat belt, my forehead cold and damp against the window. "We're here, honey," he said. "Can you get up? Don't worry if you can't. The sleepy-time stuff I gave you is probably still wearing off. I can carry you if you can't walk."

The thought of being cradled in this man's thick, hairy

arms made my eyes pop open. The fog cleared from my head like a cloudy windowpane rubbed till it squeaks. "I can walk," I said, fighting against the slur in my voice. "I can get out."

He opened the door for me. I gritted my teeth and focused, lifting one foot and placing it on the ground. Once I'd managed that, I swung my other foot over, lifted it, and put it on the ground. I gritted my teeth so hard I thought they might turn to sand. Now I had to hop out and run. Run to a house where someone would save me.

"You're taking too long. She's waiting," the man said, and he scooped me into his arms. My nose knocked against the bone of his shoulder and I bit back a cry of pain. My feet dangled helplessly a foot or two above the packed dirt. Over his shoulder I could just see a row of houses stretching off into the distance, a normal suburban street.

"I can do it," I said, my voice muffled against his shirt. He smelled like smoke.

"You just rest," he said.

The houses around me blurred, then came into focus, then blurred again. I didn't know if it was tears or exhaustion or whatever it was that the man had given me. For a second it looked like my street, but that couldn't be; we had to have driven several hours. And the lawns were nicer than mine. I could have grown up here, though, and it probably wouldn't have been much different from growing up on my street. Neat little houses, brightly colored shutters, the occasional toy strewn on a lawn. Maybe this *was* my street. Maybe the man was bringing me home.

I blinked hard, watching the world blur, refocus, blur. No. That was crazy talk. Home was far away. I needed to get back.

The man carried me up the driveway and pressed hard on the doorbell. From inside I could hear the tinny strains of some nursery rhyme playing. Despite myself, I felt my muscles relax just a tiny bit. Someone who chose a nursery-rhyme tune as a doorbell chime couldn't be a bad person.

The door opened. "Hurry, I don't want anyone to see you," someone—a woman, *she*—hissed, and I bounced up and down as the man hurried inside. The air in the house was toasty warm, and it smelled like baking bread. Someone whose house was warm and smelled like baking bread definitely couldn't be a bad person.

Everything was blurry again, so I couldn't see much besides a watercolor wash when the man deposited me on what felt like a sofa. My face pressed itself into the back and wouldn't move. It smelled faintly of smoke, like the man.

"As we agreed," he said.

"Yes, yes, I know." There was the sound of tearing paper, and the man made a noise of approval. "And here's a bit extra for your discretion."

"Thank you." A footstep squeaked on the floor.

"Wait," the woman said. Her voice was low, gravelly. "I don't want her drooling on my couch. I didn't say to put her there. Do you know how much that couch cost?"

The man sighed. He sounded tired. I did not feel sorry for him. "Where do you want her?" The couch tipped beneath me, and my stomach rolled over. I was back in the air.

"The basement," the woman said. "Like the last one." She heaved a gusty sigh. "Hopefully, this one will work out better."

I got a view of white carpet and a flash of silver hair before the basement door was opened, and I was lost.

At exactly twelve-thirty, two hours or so after we rescued little Colin, Connor strides back into the store. "If it isn't Adventure World's own true-life Skywoman," he says.

Heat creeps down my neck. "I didn't do anything except go over to him when I heard the crying," I say. "Did you find his mom?"

"No, I dropped him off at the costumed-character center. They like to start their training early," he says seriously. When I roll my eyes, he laughs. "Of course. She was already waiting at Guest Relations for us, hysterical. No mermaids on her pants, by the way."

"Darn."

"So, other than your heroism, how's your training going?"

"Okay," I say. I don't want to tell the truth in front of

Lizzy. However rude she's been, I'd rather not hurt her feelings.

"Well, it's your lunchtime," he says. "And coincidentally, it's my lunchtime too. You probably don't know where to go, so I'll grace you with my presence on the walk over. If you ask nicely, I might even let you eat with me. You're very welcome."

"Okay," I say, because what else can you say to that?

He leads me through the store's aisles and out into the day. Sun peeks through the fog overhead and wavers palely in reflections on the damp cobblestones. "Rainy mornings that turn into clear afternoons are the best," Connor says.

I wait for him to elaborate. Crowds of kids decked out in superhero and supervillain attire roam past, chattering in chipmunk voices. The sound of the roller coasters forms a dull roar in the background, like the rumble of a crowd. "Why?" I finally ask.

"Because everybody thinks it's going to rain all day, so nobody comes to the park," he says. "But once it clears up, we get to spend a whole nice afternoon doing nothing."

"How industrious of you," I say drily. "They should make you employee of the month."

Connor gives me a cheeky smile. "I've been employee of the month," he says. "Four times, in fact."

Before I can think up something witty to say to that, he veers off to the side. We're in one of the park's squares, a bright, cheery area full of food stands and benches full, in turn, of sweaty tourists sucking down water, and there's nothing off to the side but hedges and a fence. "Over here," he says. He fiddles with one of the fence's panels, and a door creaks open. "Magic."

My legs have sprouted roots and tied me to the ground. The hidden door in the back of headquarters is one thing; this is another. The former leads to a back room with managers, people, in it; this door could swallow me and spit me out anywhere.

"Where does it go?"

He lifts a shoulder in an easy shrug. "You know how whenever we walk from place to place, people tend to stop us and ask us directions or what time the dolphin shows are or where they sell cotton candy?"

"No," I say. "It's my first day, remember?"

"Oh, right," he says. "I keep forgetting. Probably because you're so good at your job."

"Probably." If my job is standing around and doing nothing.

"Well, anyway, they do," he says. "So our lunch is an hour, and if we spend a half hour stopping and answering people's questions, that only leaves half an hour to eat the delicious, grease-soaked food Five Banners fuels us with. So we take shortcuts. Secret passages, if you will. That sounds a lot more fun, doesn't it?"

"It's dark," I say. A secret passage. That won't be full of people. Maybe Monica disappeared in a secret passage.

"It's just a dirt road." Connor swings the door open wider so I can see: it is, indeed, a dirt path winding around the outside of the fence, and there are, indeed, no people. "Come on. We'll have so much more time to eat."

It's not like I never go places by myself. There's an old cabin I like to visit way back in the woods around my house—it's old and half rotted through, but it gives me a place to think without other people looking at me or talking at me or thinking at me. That's different. I know those woods, and I could easily run away at any hint of danger. I can't run away if I'm trapped in a secret passage.

I try to take a step forward, but I can't. When I loosen my legs to take a step backward, I find I can do that, though. "You go ahead," I say, making my voice as breezy as the breeziest breeze that ever breezed. "I'll meet you there."

Something flickers in his eyes. "You don't even know where you're going," he says. "Are you . . ."

"The whole thing with . . . you know," I say. Guilt weighs heavy in my stomach. A fellow society member deserves more than serving as my excuse. Because even though it's true, she's not the only reason I don't want to go back there. I have the memory of that man's hands digging deep into my armpits. "I just want to stay around people, you know?"

Connor rolls back his sleeve and flexes his skinny, pale bicep. Freckles dot his arms and make a maze that leads under his sleeve. I want to follow it. I want to find the center.

I realize my cheeks are hot at the same time I realize Connor is speaking. "What?"

His smile dims a bit. "I said, you don't trust me to protect you? I fought off the Blade once. True, she was very drunk and I was escorting her backstage, away from all the children she'd traumatized, but still."

I force a laugh. "It's cool if you go, really," I say. "I'll meet you there."

He steps toward me, and the door swings shut behind him. "What, and force you to miss out on even a second of my glorious company? Don't be ridiculous."

"Gee, thanks," I say, but something happy fills me, something golden.

Sure enough, we're stopped every few minutes by a guest with an inane question, but Connor is always upbeat and never loses his pitch. I fall quiet (not like I could've answered any of their questions anyway) and watch the master perform: his eyes flash, his arms windmill, his head tips back in a near-constant stream of laughter. How can he talk when he's always laughing?

And, sure enough, when we make it to the Canteen, half our lunch break is already gone. "I'm sorry," I say. "You could've been eating by now."

"Don't worry about it," Connor says. "I'm watching my weight anyway." The twist in his lips keeps me from taking him seriously.

I've never had a boyfriend for the same reason I don't have friends. I've been kissed a couple of times, every once in a while when I'd go to a school dance, and once, clumsily, during a game of Seven Minutes in Heaven, and it never felt like all that big a deal—it was just somebody else pressing his lips against mine, the same way he might press his hand on my shoulder to move me out of the way.

I don't think a kiss with Connor would feel like someone pressing on my shoulder.

The Canteen is a corrugated metal shack, rusting in spots, set back against the fence near one of the major roller coasters. It's hidden from the guests, obviously, or it would be painted a cartoonish color and boast a name like Wonderman's Fueling Depot (a real restaurant on the north side). The roller coaster rattles it every time it swoops overhead. I do not want to eat here, but Connor is already opening the door, and I'm following.

The inside looks much like I would've expected from the outside. The one long room is scattered with picnic tables that I can just tell are splintery. Against the wall are two vending machines that sell soda and sugary snacks. The smell of old grease is thick in the air. A cafeteria-style hot bar on the far side of the room dispenses food, all of which seems to be slathered in glimmering orange fat. Oil glistens on the mozzarella sticks, on the soggy fries, on the fried chicken. My stomach lurches.

It's not even free. We don't get paid for our lunch break, and we are not allowed to bring our own lunches, so basically Five Banners is forcing us to hand them back an hour or so of our day while they cackle and flip the minutes through their fingers like a stack of dollar bills.

"Grab some food and we'll meet over there." Connor

points at a table in the corner. The table is covered with a blue plastic tablecloth, and the blue plastic tablecloth is covered with crumbs and smears of grease. "It's my usual spot."

"Okay," I say, and I begin roaming the displays of food, eventually selecting a wilted salad (the dressing is gleaming and orange) and mozzarella sticks for the calcium, for my bones. Connor is already sitting at his table, staring intently at the burger before him, when I finish paying, so I weave my way through the tables and green shirts toward him. I have a headache by the time I get there and sit down; the noise of everybody's chatter bouncing off the metal ceiling is deafening, not to mention the coaster's roar overhead. The second I sit down, he shoves his burger in his mouth. *He waited for me*, I think, touched, and somehow that makes the glaring lights overhead feel softer, the splintery wood feel like . . . well, less splintery wood.

"A salad?" Connor says between bites. "Mistake. The cooks backstage aren't known for their skills with vegetables. I'd recommend the burger. In fact, the only thing I would recommend is the burger."

"I'm a vegetarian," I say. I'm not a vegetarian. I don't know why I said that. I stuff my mouth with a forkful of warm lettuce before I can lie to him again.

"Nice," Connor says. "I could never be a vegetarian. I grew up on a farm."

I swallow; the half-chewed lettuce slides down my

throat in one solid lump. "I'd think that would make you more likely to be a vegetarian, not less."

"We farm vegetables," he says. "And horses. Not that we eat the horses, just the vegetables. But you know what they say about seeing how your food gets made. . . ."

"Do you still farm?"

"Yeah," Connor says. The burger lies half-eaten on his plate as he gestures around him. "When I'm not here, I spend most of my summer driving a tractor and baling hay." I don't even know what that means. "That's how I get my tremendous muscles."

I open my mouth to ask what baling hay is, but before I can get the words out, a whirlwind descends upon our table, a whirlwind of shiny hair and chiming jewelry and flowery smells. I'm immediately thrown back to Stepmother's house, sitting at the feet of one of the girls—Violetta—as she braided my hair with hands so limp she kept dropping the strands. She wore the same perfume, the same arrangement of necklaces and bracelets that chimed against each other with every movement.

When the dust clears, neo-Violetta is sitting across from me, her chin propped in her hands. "Who's this?" she asks.

I blink. I can't tell if she's talking to me, or to Connor, or to the wall. "I'm Scarlett," I say. "It's my first day."

"She's a star," Connor says to neo-Violetta, a mouthful of half-chewed french fries garbling his words. "You'd better get in on the ground floor now so you can say you knew her when."

Neo-Violetta laughs. Her laugh is strong and clear, warm and friendly, with the feel of something familiar. "Scarlett, hello. Nice to meet you." She extends her hand. I meet it above the table at an awkward angle; as we shake, my elbow hits the table's surface and skids in a spot of orange oil. "I'm Katharina. I'm in Merch too."

Her name tag marks her as a regular peon, like me, not a manager or assistant manager. "Nice to meet you," I say.

Katharina is beautiful, far more beautiful than the original Violetta. Her proximity to Connor makes my stomach curdle, though that might just be an effect of the grease. Her hair ripples to her waist in purplish-black waves, and her eyes are huge and liquid. Her olive skin shimmers— actually shimmers—against the neon green of her polo. Nobody looks good in the polo. Nobody except Katharina, apparently. It's so unfair—my skin is practically the same color as hers is, yet the polo washes me out.

"So, Scarlett, I knew this was your first day before I even sat down," she says.

"Was it the salad?" I ask. "Connor already told me nobody gets the salad."

"Well, yes," Katharina says. "That salad's probably been sitting on the counter for a week. But, no. It wasn't that."

Connor clears his throat. "We should get back, Scarlett," he says. "Especially if we're going to walk through the park again."

I stand to go, leaving most of my food untouched. I'm not sure why Connor is so eager to get out of here—we still have a good few minutes—but I'm happy to play along. Something about Katharina, perhaps her mental proximity to Violetta, makes me itch. "It was good to meet you, Katharina," I say. "I hope I'll see you around."

"I knew you were new because I know everyone." She twists one long, silky lock of hair around her finger and lets it go; it falls right back into place. "If I don't know you, it basically means you don't exist."

I'm not sure exactly what to say to that. She's staring at me with an expression of utter seriousness, like someone's just died. Or gone missing. "Okay, then," I say. "I'll keep that in mind."

She looks at me for a moment longer, then bursts into that familiar laugh again. "I was joking, obvi," she says. "So you're training today, huh? Who with?"

I can't remember her name. "She doesn't have any eyebrows, and she's not very nice," I say.

Katharina's eyebrows go up in shock, as if they're mourning the loss of their fallen comrades. "You gave her to Lizzy?" she says to Connor. "How could you? She doesn't even have *eyebrows*." Like it's a character trait.

"I don't have any say in staff assignments," Connor says defensively. It's the first time I've seen him today that he doesn't have a smile on his face. "Cynthia does them, and I can get fired if I don't listen. It's not my fault."

Katharina shakes her head at him. "Shame, shame on you," she says, then turns back to me. "Don't worry, Scarlett. I'll help you."

"Aren't you on the north side today?" Connor piles his fries atop the remains of his hamburger, then smashes it all down with a napkin. Ketchup oozes onto his tray.

"Randall's managing the north today," she says. "Randall loves me. I'll swap with Lizzy."

"I can't approve that, you know." Connor is staring down at the mess he made of his lunch. "You'll have to talk to Cynthia." To me, he says, "Cynthia's the south-side Merch supervisor. My and Rob's boss."

"Cynthia loves me too." It might be my imagination, but I think there's a hint of challenge in Katharina's tone. "Don't you worry, Scarlett. I'll save the day."

"You do have very nice eyebrows." And she does: thick (but not too thick, *obvi*), black, and perfectly arched. I don't think I've ever really noticed somebody's eyebrows before today.

"We need to get back," Connor says, abandoning his lunch and standing. "Scarlett, or we'll be late."

"Don't want to be late on my first day," I say.

"See you soon," Katharina says. Somehow, I just now notice, she's obtained a salad, a real salad, with dark, fresh greens and tomatoes that are more red than pink and carrot shavings and ranch dressing, and a bowl of soup.

As we walk back and answer more park guests' stupid questions, I can't get the smell of grease out of my nose.

When Connor and I reach headquarters, we hit the cash registers only to discover that No Eyebrows is gone. I feel a rush of relief, but Connor's brows furrow in confusion. "Where'd she go?" he mutters. "If she's on a smoke break and left the register unattended, I swear to God . . ."

"Hey, Connor." I look over to see Rob falling out of the wall. "Cynthia had me send Lizzy to the arctic north."

"Godspeed, Lizzy," Connor says. "Did she say who—"

"Hey, hey." It's Katharina. "Miss me?"

I force a smile, though I know it probably comes out more like a grimace. It's not Katharina's fault that she reminds me of Stepmother's house. Of the basement. Of the lost years. "Hey," I say.

"She swapped Lizzy for Katharina," Rob says. "God knows why."

"Shut it, jerk face," Katharina says, smiling that enigmatic smile. "I bet Scarlett knows nothing about using the register, does she?"

"She's been training with Lizzy all morning," Connor interjects. "She's not stupid, Katharina. I'm sure she's picked it up by now."

They both look at me. I want to sink down, down, down into Wonderman's underground garage and ride away in the Wondermobile. "Lizzy wasn't a very good teacher," I say. "But I've picked something up, sure."

"What do you do if you have a return?" Katharina says, folding her arms across her chest.

I look at the floor. Unfortunately, the answer is not written there. "I don't know."

"See?" Katharina shoots Connor a triumphant look. "You leave her to me. I'll take good care of her."

Connor's mouth twists, but he punches Katharina's information into the register. "Wish I could help, but Cynthia has me doing inventory for the next few hours. Give me a shout if you need anything," he directs to me. I nod, and then he and Rob are gone.

Whatever other impression I might have of her, I have to admit that Katharina is a good teacher. And I'm a quick learner, of course—you learn to listen carefully when doing the wrong thing will earn you a beating. By the time an hour or so has passed, I know how to check someone out, how to input discounts, how to process a return or an exchange, and what to do if I can't find a price on something and it's the last one in the store or I'm really busy (pick an item you think looks like it might be the same price and scan that instead; this rule is not in the Five Banners Merch handbook, for some reason). "I feel like a cash register god," I say.

"You're welcome," Katharina says. She leans up against the counter, breaking another rule in the Five Banners handbook. We are supposed to be flagpoles, stiff and upright at all times. "How's your first day been so far?"

"Slow," I say. "I haven't really done anything yet. I thought there would be more . . . people."

Katharina nods. "It's still early in the season, even if

it is a weekend," she says. "Wait till all the schools let out. We'll have all four registers at this station full and lines out the door."

"Can't wait," I say. I'm not sure if I'm lying. "How long have you worked here?"

"I just started this year." Katharina stretches, reaching her arms toward the ceiling. Her fingertips nearly brush one of the CHECK OUT HERE signs dangling above. "I moved here a few months ago." She relaxes and clasps her hands before her, a surprisingly demure gesture. "Do you like it here so far?"

"I like the people," I say, and by "people" I mean "person," and by "person" I mean Connor.

"The people here are great," Katharina says. "Of course, everyone's been all mopey over Monica, so it's hard to really get a handle on them, I bet."

I blink. "She's missing," I say. "I think it's understandable people would feel a little 'mopey.'"

"She probably just ran away." Katharina's eyes gleam. "Don't you think?"

My stomach swims with uneasiness. "I don't think anything," I say. "I barely knew her."

"So you did know her," Katharina says.

"I interviewed with her," I say. "Other than that, no."

"So you did know her," Katharina says again. "What do you think happened? Do you think she ran away? Or do you think, maybe, she was kidnapped?"

"I don't think anything!" My voice comes out louder

than I meant it to; a guest browsing the racks of key chains jumps and sends a bunch of them cascading to the floor. "I should go clean that up."

Katharina grabs me by the shoulder. I twist, but her fingers dig in, so I go limp. I'm used to being man-handled, tossed around like I'm inanimate. If you don't struggle, it's over faster. "I knew her," she says. "I worked under her sometimes. She was lazy. She wasn't a very good manager."

I try twisting again, but her fingers only dig in deeper. This isn't how it's supposed to go; she's supposed to see that I'm no threat and release me. "Let me go," I say. My heart is battering my ribs.

"We just all have to stay positive." I don't know if she's talking to me or to herself. She stares off into the distance, her eyes unfocused. "She'll turn up. You know what they say: never missing, never found."

I turn to ice and slip from her fingers. The muscles of my shoulder throb. "Who says that?"

"Everyone," Katharina says. "Haven't you heard it before?" She sighs. "You're right," she continues. "We should clean up those key chains before somebody slips on them and sues."

Everyone. Everyone. No, that's not something *everyone* says. That's something I've only ever heard one person say. And that person is long gone.

Katharina and I finish the rest of my first day in near

silence. She attempts small talk every so often, but I can't respond with anything but wooden, one-word answers. No matter how many times I look around, no matter how many times I breathe in deep and tell myself it's all in my head, I can't shake the creepy-crawly feeling that somebody is watching me.

CHAPTER FOUR

At some point between the man opening the basement door and him depositing me downstairs, I drifted off again. I didn't know it then, but I should've stayed asleep. I should've slept for years and years, to be woken only by the touch of a police officer, rather than a kiss of true love.

I dreamed of my sister, Melody. Melly. More specifically, I dreamed of the time a year or so back when Melody had wet the bed. I'd woken to her pulling on my arm, her eyes bright and shiny with tears. "Can you help?" she said, wiping at her nose with the back of her hand.

I'd been sound asleep and dreaming of my third-grade crush, Gunnar, who was shy and had dimples and had once brushed my arm with his arm as we walked past each other in the hallway, which translated, obviously, into true love. But I blinked Gunnar away and forced myself out of bed. "What about Mom?" Our dad was away on a business trip, but our mom was home. "Did you wake her up?"

Melody's lip wobbled. "I shook her and shook her and she wouldn't wake up," she said. "Can you please help?"

I sighed. The first time we hadn't been able to wake up our mom, Melody and I had panicked, thinking our mom was dead, and called 911. After that, our mom had sat us down and told us that sometimes it was normal, not being able to wake up, and that as long as she was breathing, we should just let her be. She taught us how to listen for her heartbeat and take a spoon and hold it up to her nose to see if it fogged.

"Okay," I said to Melody. "I think there are clean sheets in the hall closet. I'll change them for you."

Melody grabbed my hand as she followed me down the hall. It was sticky, but I didn't pull away. She was my sister. "Thank you, Scarlett."

This time, in the basement, I woke up to the drip, drip, drip of water and immediately had to pee myself. I hoped that meant the drugs were wearing off.

God, but I had to pee. I had to pee so bad it hurt; my bladder was pulsing jagged little lightning bolts of pain through my abdomen. I sat up, lifting my shoulders from what felt like a mattress, with a creak that was only in my head.

The next thing I noticed was the dark, and the third

thing I noticed was the cold. My eyes were beginning to adjust to the gloom of the basement, helped along by the pale light filtering in through the one high, barred window. The slowly appearing shapes shook as I shivered. I was joined by a small table, two plastic chairs that might have come from a classroom, and a dresser in the corner. I stood up, stepping off my bare mattress and onto a thin, rough rug that protected me, at least, from the concrete floor.

I took a step toward the stairs. If I could make it to the door at the top, surely I would be free. "Hello?" I called, just in case. Maybe this was a mistake. This had to be a mistake.

I was halfway up the stairs when the door creaked open, and there *she* was.

In another life, she could have been my teacher or my pediatrician or the nice mail lady who gave me lollipops whenever she saw me come to collect the mail. Because she didn't look like a monster. For years after, I thought of her as a monster, and she *was* a monster, and it scared me to think of how well she wore her human disguise. It made me wonder if everybody in the world was like that, if that's just what happened when you became an adult: you grew horns and claws and slipped on human skin like a bathrobe.

"What's your name?" she asked me. Silver hair, tied back into a low ponytail, glittered in the light behind her. Her lips were a bright, bright red, her skin as white as the belly of a fish. Snow White all grown up and turned into Cinderella's evil stepmother.

"Scarlett," I said. My voice trembled only once.

The woman looked down at me over the bridge of her nose. "Scarlett is a ridiculous name for a child," she said. "You'll be Jane. Jane is a good, simple, elegant name."

"But that's not my name."

Quick as a flash, the woman was halfway down the stairs and I was reeling backward, my cheek stinging with a blow. "You won't ever talk back to me," she said, and it was the calmness in her tone that scared me more than anything. "You'll only speak when spoken to, and you'll only call me ma'am. Do you understand, Jane?"

My mind raced, unable to catch up to what was going on.

"Do you understand, Jane?" she said again, taking a step toward me.

I shrank back, cringing against the wall. "Yes, ma'am."

"Good." And she was back at the top of the stairs, moving gracefully, as if she were a dancer. "You'll start work tomorrow. And you best behave, or you'll end up like the last girl."

I couldn't stop the words from bursting out. "What happened to the last girl? Ma'am?"

A small, cold smile split her cheeks. "Trust me, Jane. You don't want to end up like the last girl."

And then I was alone, and I was back on my mattress, and it was warm and wet beneath me.

. . .

When I woke up the next morning, I stank like pee and I could hardly breathe for the fear. I would have been shaking, only I was as petrified as an old piece of wood and didn't think I could move.

I scrambled to my feet when the woman opened the door at the top of the stairs. "Come, Jane," she said. "I'll show you your duties."

I swallowed hard and forced myself up, step by step. The woman made a tsking noise deep in her throat when I got within smelling distance. "First you'll need to wash, of course." Her voice was measured, and each word ended abruptly. I didn't realize it then, but she was trying to suppress an accent. "I'll give you some of the girls' old clothes. They're clean and warm, though I expect they will be large on you."

I was silent, which was apparently the wrong move. The woman loomed overhead. "Are you not going to thank me, Jane?"

After that, the thanks couldn't come fast enough. "Thank you, thank you, thank you, ma'am."

"Good." She sounded, if not pleased, at least not angry. "Come."

I let her clothe me—sure enough, the clothes were too big, but they were clean and warm—and pour me a bowl of cereal. "Do not get used to me feeding you," she warned me, then shook her head as I tried to take a seat at the table. "Sitting is for guests. You are a worker now. You stand."

I stood and shoveled the cereal (dry) into my mouth as quickly as I could. It stuck to the inside of my mouth and my throat; every crunch echoed inside my head.

"Do you like your cereal?" the woman asked.

I knew enough by now, even after one night, to know that there was only one answer. "Yes, ma'am," I said between bites. Not with my mouth full—I knew she wouldn't like that.

She gave me an appraising look. "You seem smarter than the last girl," she said. "Maybe you won't come to a bad end."

I took another bite of cereal.

"I almost came to a bad end," she said. "When I had to leave my country. And I had to leave my country. There was nothing there for me but bombs and sad men.

"There was only one way for me to get over here, to this country, where I would be safe. The government did not want me, so I had to depend on bad men. Do you understand? No, you don't. You are too young. But you will understand one day."

I watched her through narrowed eyes as I ate. She was gazing out the window, eyes misty, but I suspected they'd snap back on me if I so much as moved a muscle toward the exit.

"Slowly I became more than that girl. I am who I am because I am hard. Do you understand me, Jane?"

I didn't, but I nodded anyway. Her lips stretched into an approximation of a smile. "I will make you hard. Neither of our families wanted us, did they, Jane?" Her laugh was a bark. "No matter. I will show you how we girls survive in such a world, Jane."

When I pull into the driveway, tired from my first day at Adventure World, Matthew is waiting for me on the front stoop. His face lights up as I turn off my ignition, and he races to my car as I get out. His smile is a beam of sunshine. If it wouldn't kill him, I'd stuff him and embalm him and keep him safe in my closet so he could be sweet and loving and seven forever. "Did you get my free tickets?" he says. "Can we go to Adventure World now?"

I ruffle his hair. "I just spent eight hours at Adventure World," I say. "I'm not going back now. Maybe next week." I could wear a cute sundress and cute sunglasses and parade my cute brother around in front of Connor. Connor would tumble immediately into love and we'd run off and get married and raise Matthew as our own. "Who's watching you? Is Dad home?"

"He's still at work." Matthew runs back to the stoop, disappointed, apparently, in me and my lack of free tickets. Little user. Maybe it's best he grows up after all.

"So Melody's home? Or the babysitter?"

Matthew disappears inside before he can answer me. I'm not a huge fan of his babysitter, a flat-eyed girl from the other end of the street who never laughs at any of his jokes, but I'd much rather shove twenty bucks at her and usher her out the door than have to put up with Melody and her stupid cookies and her distaste for my very existence.

So naturally, when I get inside and dump my clear fanny pack on the front table, a dramatic gesture meant to signify to the zero people watching that I'm simply too exhausted to cart it one more step, I hear the dulcet tones of Melody's DVD aerobics wafting from the living room: "One, two, three, four. One, two, three, four. Work that body, girl, work it!"

I stop in the doorway. Today is my first day as a working woman. Or at least, one where I'm working for pay. Time to grow up, maybe. "Hi, Melody," I say. "What's going on?"

Her movements are sleek, like a snake's, and sweat shimmers over her face. "What does it look like?" she puffs, squatting and stretching her arms over her head.

On days Melody doesn't have field hockey practice, she likes to work out anyway, just in case a pinch of fat was considering taking up residence on one of her hips. Sometimes she runs; sometimes she lifts weights on the machine in the basement. When she's stuck in the house watching Matthew, she digs up one of our mom's old aerobics DVDs from a million years ago and gets to sweating. "Nice seeing you, too," I say, going to move away. I'm dying for some celery with peanut butter.

Who am I trying to kid? I'm dying for a cookie. Two cookies. Three cookies.

"Wait," Melody says. I swivel back to face her. Maybe this is it: a meeting of the hearts. A change of the minds. A day that will go down in Contreras family history.

She spreads her legs wide, almost into a split, and leans over to balance on her arms. "How was work?" she asks.

"It was good," I say. "It wasn't too busy today, but everyone said it would get busy once all the schools get out. Everyone seems nice." I don't want to play it up too much, though, make it seem like I'm trying to make her jealous. She's never asked about my day before, never. "The work itself kind of sucks, though. It's just grunt work, you know, ringing people up at the register, stocking shelves, that kind of thing."

"That's not so bad," she says. She lunges, then stands back up, then lunges again. I hover in the doorway, waiting to see if she has anything else to say. Maybe we can be like the sisters I read about in books or see on TV, cuddling close and whispering our secrets into each other's ears. Like I used to have at Stepmother's. It's the only thing I miss.

"So. Did you hear about the missing girl?" she asks.

I flex my fingers to keep the blood moving. They're suddenly as cold as the floor of the basement. "Of course I did. She worked at Adventure World."

Lunge, squat, stand. Lunge, squat, stand. Melody turns her head to look at me as she twists and thrusts. "I heard she went missing while she was there," she says, panting. Her eyes are shining with interest, with excitement. My stomach turns. This is all a game to her. It's entertainment. "Did you hear anything today? Does anyone have any theories?"

"She's missing," I say icily. "That's all anyone knows." My fantasies of closeness fizzle and disappear with a pop, as they always do. And yet they always come back.

"Scarlett!" Matthew calls from the kitchen. "I'm hungry."

I back away, relieved for the excuse to escape. "Matthew's hungry," I say unnecessarily. "Have a good workout."

"Wait!" Melody calls.

I hesitate, but I don't stop. Once bitten, twice burned. Is that what they say?

I spent five years in therapy with the wise and fabulous Dr. Martinez after I fought my way out of the underworld. She slowly carried me from a place where I wouldn't acknowledge what had happened to me, where I would close my eyes and cover my ears anytime she tried to ask me a question, to a place where I could talk openly and honestly about what it had been like in the basement, with Pixie, with the girls upstairs, with Stepmother. I didn't exactly reach a sunny beach, but I did finally learn to see the sun peeking through the clouds. To stop looking over my shoulder every second of every minute of every hour of every day.

Anyway, I told Dr. Martinez about my troubles with my sister, how she would no longer speak to me, would flinch away when I tried to take her hand, and Dr. Martinez told me to avoid yelling, to avoid getting angry, because I couldn't help how Melody felt. She had to go through her own adjustment period too, and I couldn't expect things to go right back to the way things had been before I "left."

Dr. Martinez kept on telling me to be patient for one year, two years, three years, and then she stopped, because it became clear that whatever problem Melody had with me, it wasn't going away with time.

That's why I eventually convinced my dad to let me quit therapy. I told him—and Dr. Martinez—that I was fine, that I'd moved on. I would never really move on, and I think they knew that, but they believed me enough to let me go. But despite all I'd shared with Dr. Martinez, despite all the progress I'd made with my own mind, there were certain corners that I could never explore. Certain thoughts I can never, even now, let free.

The next morning I'm sent again to the south side, but not to headquarters; I'm to work at a store called Wonderkidz, which I'm guessing is a Wonderman-themed shop for kids. It's a clear, warm day, unlike yesterday, and the sunshine is bright and crisp in my lungs. It's so clean and fresh it almost makes me forget the specter of the missing girl staining the cobblestones.

Wonderkidz isn't far from headquarters, and I see Connor's coppery red hair glinting in the sunlight before he sees me. I raise my arm and wave it so enthusiastically I think something tears in my chest. He still doesn't see me, which is fortunate; by the time he turns around and his lips break into a smile, I'm restrained enough to give him a small, calm, collected wave. Cool. Enthusiasm is not cool. People like Melody don't do enthusiasm. "Morning," I say. "I'm off to Wonderkidz."

"I know," he says. "I'm the one who wrote the schedule on the whiteboard."

"With great power comes great responsibility. I hope you're using it wisely."

"I just hope you don't hate me at the end of your shift. Remember, it's not my fault. Blame Cynthia."

"That bodes well," I say. "Did you stick me with Lizzy again?"

His jaw drops in mock shock. "Like I would ever do that to you," he says. "What do you think of me? In all honesty, though," he continues, "you'll probably be begging to wash Lizzy's feet before an hour's gone."

I ask him to elaborate once we continue on, even threaten him with a plush sword hanging from one of the stands we pass, but he refuses. I want to tell him that whatever's in store at Wonderkidz, I've been through worse. That whatever trauma he's joking about inflicting upon me is an actual joke, because nothing could ever faze me again.

Within five minutes of entering the store, I want to claw my ears off and stuff the bloody holes full of cotton.

"Is that going to play all day?" I ask him.

The store itself isn't bad. It's small and open to the elements, with space for only two registers, and it's out of the way at the very edge of the south side, so people actually have to mean to come here. The walls and shelves are stacked with superhero-themed kids' stuff: plush replicas of Skywoman's cloud lasso, plush replicas of the Wondermobile, plush replicas of the eponymous Blade's blade . . . basically, plush replicas of everything you could possibly make a plush replica of.

It's the sound track that's the problem. There are four speakers, one in each corner of the store, aimed directly at the registers and blasting a skin-crawling, spine-tingling, teeth-gritting song from the Wonderman and Skywoman movies, sung—and screeched, definitely screeched—by a group of what has to be hellspawn, because those noises can't be coming from the throats of sweet, innocent children.

"All day," Connor confirms. "And just wait until it repeats. It repeats about every ten minutes."

"How could you do this to me?" I groan. "I thought I was your favorite person."

"You are," he says. "It's just that it was between you and getting fired, and, well . . . I'm not losing my job. I had to suffer through Wonderkidz too."

He logs me into the register and sets up my cashbox. I lean against the counter and cross my arms. "You don't have to do this."

"Oh, but I do," Connor says. He hoists himself up onto the counter, breaking the Five Banners rule that says no sitting on counters, but *whoa* a flash of white freckled belly and my cheeks are so hot I'm afraid the plush lightning bolts I'm leaning against might actually crackle and burst into flame. "Or I'll get fired. But Lizzy is coming in at lunch. I could conceivably beg Cynthia to switch her out for you come lunchtime."

"I will kill someone if I have to," I say, and I'm only half-joking.

"Let's not go that far," he says, which is good, because I don't ever want to have to go that far again. He folds his arms across his chest. "Answer three questions right and I'll let you switch."

I uncross my arms and prop myself against the wall behind me, leaning toward him. It wouldn't be so bad if I were to fall against his legs. I wonder what baling hay does to a person's legs. "Fire away."

"First question." His voice deepens and snaps like a weatherman's. "What is this year's official Five Banners corporate motto?"

Easy for anyone who's read the employee handbook. Which I have. "Safe! Friendly! Clean!"

"Correct. And, apparently, if you're safe, friendly, and hygienic, you can go ahead and steal as much money as you want." He looks up at the ceiling. "Kidding, obviously."

I follow his eyes. He's staring at a camera, its red light an unceasing eye. "Even if you weren't kidding," I say. "No stealing allowed. That's also in the handbook."

"No bonus points for that, smarty-pants," Connor says. "Though, nice try."

"I wasn't trying for bonus points."

"You so were," he says. "Okay, second question. How did Skywoman's husband die?"

"Trick question," I say immediately. "Her *first* husband, a cop, was killed when he attempted to apprehend the Blade after she'd murdered his commander and slipped into his commander's skin like one of the costumed characters here."

"Nice analogy." He leans in, eyes lighting up.

"Her *second* husband," I continue, "is not dead, as any Skywoman fan would know. Her second husband was one of the Blade's henchmen, spying on Skywoman. When Skywoman discovered his trickery, she tried to kill him, but the Blade swooped in at the last minute and stopped her with a kiss, the only thing that could possibly have stunned Skywoman enough to stop her in her tracks, and that gave them time to escape." I flip my hair over my shoulder. "As any true Skywoman fan would know."

"You're a true Skywoman fan, eh?" He sounds amused. "I should've known."

"Why should you have known?"

His eyes are narrowed in thought; they set off the creases that light up when he smiles. "Because I just should have," he says. "You seem like the type of girl who would like Skywoman. Are you one of the Sky-fanatics?"

"No," I say defensively, and it's true, because I terminated my membership in the online Skywoman fan club two years ago. Though at this point I have enough letters from Skywoman on official Silver City stationery, and secret decoder rings for deciphering their hidden messages, to start a Sky-fanatic branch of my own. "Why, do I seem like a nerd?"

He laughs and swings his legs. His feet thump emphatically against the side of the counter; on the upswing, they nearly brush against my side. "No! You just seem like the kind of girl who would like Skywoman. Like tough, and smart. Like you don't take any crap. Stop trying to distract me from my third question."

I raise an eyebrow. "If it's anything as easy as your first two questions, I'll be out of here at noon on the dot. Sorry, Lizzy."

His legs stop and slam against the counter. His sudden smile is the sun breaking through the clouds. "What instrument does my little brother, Zach, play in the jazz band?"

My mouth falls open. "That's not a fair question!"

"Really? I don't remember setting down rules." He raises an eyebrow. "Guess you forfeit."

"Never!" I chew on the inside of my mouth. "The trumpet."

"Nope." He swings himself down from the counter, launching himself forward and landing only a few inches from me, and leans in. Heat radiates through his polo and cooks me from the inside out, a human microwave. He smells like Axe and detergent and a trace of something musty, cigarette smoke maybe—not strong enough for him to be a smoker himself, but strong enough that he must live in a smoker's home. "Bari sax. Sorry."

Our noses are only inches apart. I could lean forward. I could catch his lips on mine. I could feel his heartbeat against my chest. I can already feel it, or at least I feel like I feel it. Maybe I'm just feeling my own.

Before I have the chance to do anything, he clears his throat and jolts away, hitting himself on the counter. Freckles glow on his red face like miniature suns. He coughs again. "Sorry," he says. He's looking at the floor, the walls, the ceiling, anywhere but at me.

Do I repulse him that much? I swallow hard and lean back. It's probably for the best anyway. I had an everything bagel for breakfast. I would have tasted like garlic and onion. "You should apologize for that last question. So not fair. I call redo," I say.

He smiles, but there's something distant about it. "No redos," he says. "That's also a Five Banners company motto. Didn't you read the manual?"

He doesn't duck in time to avoid getting smacked with a plush Blade.

"Maybe I'll still try to let you switch at lunch," he says. "Maybe. If you're nice to me. Kissing my feet wouldn't hurt."

"The stench would probably kill me," I say. "Which, come to think of it, is probably preferable to being stuck here all day. Go ahead, take your shoes off."

His laugh trails behind him as he leaves, fading into the screech of the singing hellspawn above.

The wait until lunch is the longest four hours of my life. Connor makes it slightly more bearable, popping in every half hour or so to pick something up or authorize a return or let me hit him with one of many assorted plush weapons. At a hard-fought one o'clock, he returns, and with a guest.

"Hi, Katharina," I say cautiously. Of course he'd bring *her* to cover my lunch. I haven't forgotten the feel of her fingers digging into my shoulder.

Her smile is bright and cheerful. "Hey, Scarlett."

"So, don't hate me," Connor says, "despite your loss at our entirely fair wager, I still went and tried to get you moved. You're welcome. But Cynthia—really sweet woman—told me I can't move someone without good cause."

"Are my bleeding eardrums not good cause?" I clamp a hand to the side of my head, stretching my lips into the most grotesque grimace I can possibly form.

He moves in closer and looks me right in the eye. I stare back, noticing, from the corner of my eye, Katharina staring too. "For your ears, anything." He's so close I can smell him again, though after all his running around in the heat, there's a salty tinge of sweat to the scent of Connor. "Except my job, and that's what Cynthia will take if I move you. Sorry. I'll make it up to you, I swear."

I feel a smile twist the corners of my lips, like paper

curling above a candle flame. "You'd better," I say. "I'll be waiting."

"Go ahead and wait," he says. "I dare you. Hold your breath."

I would be tingling inside if Katharina weren't still staring. "Well, if you're going to make it up to me, I suppose I'll come back after lunch."

"You'd better," he says. "Because I'll be holding my breath too, and I can only hold it for exactly one hour."

"You must be a star at pool parties."

Though Connor doesn't come with me this time, I still take his regular table. Rob joins me. "Did Connor say you could sit here?" he asks, and he seems entirely serious.

"He didn't say I couldn't sit here," I say. I'm already eating my pizza, after having sponged off an entire five napkins' worth of grease. I'm not moving now.

Rob glares at me for another few seconds, then relaxes. "I'm just kidding," he says. "You're Connor's new favorite person. Of course you can sit here."

"I can't believe I'm still his favorite person," I say. "I'm impressed. If I remember correctly, you told me he has a new favorite person approximately every seven minutes."

Rob stares at me a moment too long. "Yeah," he says at last. "Usually he does."

All the rest of the way through lunch and all the rest of my walk back to Wonderkidz, during which I'm stopped no fewer than six times to give directions, I can't keep a smile off my face.

"Hey," I say to Katharina, the smile still flitting about my cheeks and, I'm sure, making me look the fool.

"Hey," she says back. She is not smiling. She looks like she's taken a big bite out of a ruby-red watermelon slice and discovered too late it's a plush replica. "Have a good lunch?"

"Great," I say. "I ate with Rob. He showed me his tattoo." A mountain of skulls, dripping with blood and topped with roses and spikes.

"Gross, isn't it?"

"Terrible," I say happily. "Just imagine what it's going to look like when he's eighty-five."

"I have," she says. "So. You like Connor?"

The smile slips off my face and falls with a splat onto the floor. My finger freezes halfway through typing in the pass code to unlock my register. "Of course I like Connor," I say. "I like Rob. I like you. I like everyone I've met here. Everyone who has eyebrows, at least."

"No," she says, the very word a challenge. "I don't mean like him like that, and you know it. You *like* Connor."

"He's a nice guy," I say. Evasive maneuvers, stat. "I hope he doesn't have a tattoo like Rob's. Hey, have you ever thought about getting a tattoo? I've been thinking about it."

"You totally like him," she says. Her face is the sun; I can't look directly at it, or I'll get burned. "You don't have to be embarrassed. A lot of girls like Connor. He's a big fat flirt."

I want to ask her to elaborate, but if I ask her to elaborate, it'll be even more obvious that I like him. Evade, evade, evade. "If I were going to get a tattoo, I would probably get it on my ankle," I say. "Maybe a butterfly. Or hey, the Five Banners logo. Maybe I'd get a raise. Hey, look, customers!"

I've never been so glad in my life to see customers—excuse me, guests. It's a family, a man and a woman and their little son. "Let me help you," I tell his parents. "Whatever you need, I can help."

"I want a Wonderman," the kid says.

"Wonderman? We have lots of Wondermans!" I say. "Anime Wondermans, stuffed Wondermans, action figures, we've got it all!"

Katharina pokes me hard between the shoulder blades. I flinch. "Hey, Scarlett," she says. "Cover me for a second? I have to make a call." She's got her phone in her hand, already unlocked.

"That's fine," I say. Anything to get her out of here. Her questioning is starting to make me feel like I'm back at the police station. They questioned me for hours after they found me, trying to gather what had happened to me and how I'd come to be wandering alone and barefoot down the side of a major highway. I can still viscerally recall the shock on their faces when they saw the bottoms of my feet, which were torn and bloody. I hadn't even noticed. I'd felt nothing.

I match the kid with his perfect Wonderman, and he leaves smiling, which makes me feel like I've done a good thing. Their departure leads into Katharina's return. She's smiling now too. "All okay?" she asks.

"Fine," I say. "It was a success."

"Glad to hear it." She's still smiling, and it unnerves me because it's not a cheerful smile or a glowing smile, the way mine felt. It's more of a smirk than a smile, really, a twist to her lips that says, *I know something you don't know.*

I don't ask her anything. She might want me to ask her something, but I don't want to play into her hand, whatever it is. And she doesn't say anything, no loaded comments, no leading questions. She just hums and hums something tuneless that matches up suspiciously with the screeching hellspawn.

She stops humming and breaks into a wide smile when someone walks through the entrance to our store. "Cady!" Katharina says. "Glad you could make it. I thought you'd be on lunch now."

The girl—Cady—grins back at Katharina. "Of course," she says. "I could use a good surprise today."

Surprise? I study this new girl as she and Katharina jabber, throwing around names of park people and places. I hear Rob pop up, and the elusive Cynthia, but then I tune out.

Cady's small and thin, flat as a little kid, though she's clearly my age, or close. She's wearing a green shirt and the red-lined name tag that translates to assistant manager, like Connor and Rob, and her bleached-blond hair sticks up in spikes all over her head in a pixie cut. "Hey, I'm Cady," she says. "I don't think we've met."

"No, we haven't," I say. "I'm Scarlett. It's my second day."

She flutters her fingers at me. Rings are forbidden by the Five Banners dress code, but she's got on three of them, chunky silver ones. "How do you like it so far?"

"I like the people." Connor's smile flashes through my mind, and I worry for a moment that Katharina is going to go off on me and him again, but she doesn't. "I was into Skywoman a lot as a kid, so it's kind of cool to be working—"

"Hey!" Cady's smile is a sudden, bright flash, and it's definitely not aimed at me. I look over at the door to see Connor standing in the entryway. My heart skips a beat. It's like Katharina's prodding has brought my feelings bubbling to the surface, dinosaur bones rising from an oil pit after millions of years under the earth. I've read about crushes, and I've thought guys were cute before, but I've never felt it like this, like I want to burrow in between his arms and stay there for a while. Not so long that I'd feel trapped, but a while.

"Hey," Connor says, still standing in the doorway. I wait for him to come in, to blind us all with his smile, but he just stands there, hovering awkwardly with his hand on the doorframe, as though he's not sure whether he's coming or going. "Is everything okay?"

"Everything's fine," Katharina says. Her grin looks like a shark's. "Cady just wanted to say hi."

Connor finally shows a smile, but it's even less convincing than Katharina's. It makes me think of the way monkeys bare their teeth in submission. "Well, hi. I have a lot to do today. I should really go."

A lot to do today? He didn't have a lot to do today when he was asking me totally unfair questions about his brother.

"Wait." Cady trots toward him, her smile still bright, and then she's pulling his face to hers.

They're kissing.

They're *kissing.*

Cady and Connor are kissing.

Connor is kissing someone, and that someone isn't me.

I feel like somebody's kicked me in the stomach and sucked all the breath out of me. I feel like I'm going to throw up.

I look away because I have to look away or I'll fall over, and I see Katharina watching me. I struggle to compose myself, but there's only so much I can do against the way I'm feeling right now.

I look back when I hear Connor clearing his throat. He's pushed himself into the doorway as far as he possibly can without actually being outside. Cady has retreated a few feet and her smile is wavering now, like I'm looking at her through a glass of water. "Cade," Connor says quietly. "Maybe we should talk."

Cady shakes her head. Hoop earrings go swinging. "Nope!" she says. "I don't think we need to talk. I just . . . I needed to see you." Her voice trembles, and Connor sighs.

"Cade . . ." He reaches out and takes her into his arms again, though thankfully they don't kiss. He just holds her tight against him, and his eyes meet mine over her shoulder. I glance away.

"Cady and Connor started here on the same day two years ago and it was love at first sight," Katharina says for what must be my benefit, because surely both Cady and Connor know when they met. "Don't they make the cutest couple?"

All the words I have shrivel up and die in my throat. I nod weakly. The floor is very interesting today.

"We're—" Connor starts, but Katharina interrupts him.

"Cady was the last person to see Monica the night she . . . you know," Katharina says, again for my benefit. A choked sort of sob comes from Cady's direction, and Connor sighs again.

"The police called me out to talk again today," Cady says. Even choked up, her voice is small and pert and adorable, like her nose.

"Haven't you already talked to them?" Connor says. His voice is sober.

"Like three times."

I look back up to see Cady's freckles standing out in sharp relief against her paling cheeks. "I don't know what else they want. I told them everything. Do they think I don't want to help them find her? I love her. We were friends." She catches her bottom lip between her teeth. "Are friends. We *are* friends."

"Cade." Connor holds her tight against him. I clench my teeth together till my jaw hurts and turn to Katharina so I don't have to see how perfectly their bodies fit together. I expect her to look triumphant somehow, like she's won, but she's doesn't. Her expression is written in a language I don't know; I can't even read that alphabet.

"Don't worry, Cade," Katharina says. She's still looking at me, and now her eyes are burning. "You know what they say: it's better to be missing than dead."

After a month in the basement, I began to think of the woman as Stepmother. And I was Cinderella.

She woke me every morning with a yell as the sun's watery rays were just beginning to stream in through the basement's one small, high window. She made me brush my teeth every morning, and take a shower every other day so I wouldn't smell up her clean, clean house. I scrubbed floors and scoured tile and cleaned up after the girls. The girls weren't really girls; that's just what Stepmother called them. Really they were women, women who wore lots of makeup and lacy underwear and who sometimes cried in the bathroom when they thought nobody could hear, and nobody could, because by then I was nobody.

She was always watching me. Three times during that first week I tried to run out the door. One of the girls caught me, then one of the men who came to visit the girls, then Stepmother herself. She stripped half the skin off my back as I cried, and she beat me more for crying. "You will learn from this, Jane," she said over my yelps. "And you will be better for it. Stronger."

After the first few weeks I stopped trying, both because I didn't want to get beaten again and because nobody was waiting for me. That's what she told me, that my parents had given me to her because I'd been bad and they didn't want me anymore. That sounds ridiculous to me now, but back then I absorbed her words the way my hair absorbed the smell of the girls' cigarette smoke.

The girls were mostly nice to me. Not nice where they'd help me leave or answer my questions about what they were all doing here too. But sometimes they'd give me pieces of hard candy or ask me how I was doing or spritz me with their flowery perfume. None of them ever hit me.

I was good. I was a good girl, always a good girl, and finally Stepmother noticed. A month in and I hadn't spoken to anyone, not for real, nothing besides "Yes, ma'am" or "Excuse me, sir," and the words were clawing their way out of my eye sockets, pushing my eyeballs out so they goggled. "You've been good this month," Stepmother said. "I want you to continue to be good. How do you feel now, Jane?"

By then I'd realized that Jane *was* a good, solid, sensible name. And good, solid, sensible girls deserved company. Jane missed Melody. "I miss my sister, ma'am," Jane said honestly, because she did. She wasn't thinking about what that might mean for her. Or for another girl. It was just how she felt.

Stepmother gave me an appraising look. "I'll see what I can do."

Pixie showed up a week later, while I was sleeping; I went to sleep in the basement, curled up tight as a cat on my mattress, and woke to see a strange girl staring at me from across the room, her back up against the wall, her arms crossed tight over her chest. I blinked at her. She blinked back, slowly. She must have been drugged too.

"Hello," I said. "I'm Scarlett. But here my name is Jane."

Her eyes filled with tears. "I'm Pixie. Where am I?"

I got up and stretched. My back cracked, and Pixie jumped. "It's okay," I said. "You're safe."

She began to shake. "I don't want to be here."

"Shhh. Shhh." I made my way over to her, slowly, carefully, like I was trying not to spook a rabbit, and laid a hand on her shoulder. It seems absurd now that I wouldn't realize that I was the one who had put her there, but I didn't. In my mind she'd appeared out of nowhere, a gift from the universe. "It'll all be okay. Take a deep breath."

She took a deep breath, and it shuddered. She took another, and it shuddered less. "How did I get here?"

"It's okay," I told her, and squeezed her shoulder comfortingly. "You can be Cinderella too."

"Are you a missing girl too?" she asked.

"Yes," I said, and spared a sad, fleeting thought for my parents, who didn't miss me. Melody missed me, though. I knew she did. "I went missing more than a month ago." Every morning, I made sure to glance at the calendar

Stepmother had hanging in the kitchen, the one covered in pictures of doe-eyed kittens. "From near Chicago."

She took another deep breath, and it didn't shudder at all. "Okay. Okay." And then she laid a hand on my shoulder, like it was her turn to comfort me. "At least we're not dead. You know what they say: it's better to be missing than dead."

Everybody is staring at me. Connor and Cady have separated, at least.

"Scarlett, are you okay?" Connor asks, his brow creased in concern.

I'm not okay, I'm not.

"Yeah, *Scarlett*." Is it my imagination, or does Katharina stress my name? "Are you okay? You look like you're going to pass out."

My heart has stopped. My entire core has frozen solid into a block of ice, and if I say even one word, I will shatter into a million pieces. So I nod.

Katharina isn't the girl from the basement. Katharina can't be the girl from the basement. Because she's dead. Because I killed her.

CHAPTER FIVE

I don't speak for the rest of the day, a strategy I used at Stepmother's when I was afraid to say anything lest I throw up. Connor gives me a quick goodbye, his smile a ghost of its former self. Cady rushes out after him, and I bid her goodbye with a limp wave. Katharina doesn't speak to me either; it's like she knows what she did with that phrase. Like she knows how she undid me. I catch her watching me from the corner of her eye every so often, though, or at least I think I do. I might be imagining things. I might be going crazy. I might already be crazy.

Fortunately, my job doesn't really require me to speak. I greet guests with the same weak smile I gave Cady, and answer questions with nods or headshakes. I am a million miles away from Adventure World right now. I am a million miles above the ground, above even the peak of the Dragon King, the tallest, fastest roller coaster in the world.

Katharina leaves for lunch and doesn't come back. I don't know where she goes. They replace her with an androgynous young person named Marley, who has short buzzed hair and a nose stud, who seems perfectly content to spend the shift playing with the plush toys and the occasional game of catch with me.

It isn't until I leave for the day and go to clock out at the employment office by the entrance that I come crashing back down to earth. "Have a good night," the girl at the desk tells me flatly, clicking her nails against her desk. Those nails. I remember those nails. I assured that girl my first morning that it was better to be missing than dead, and I said the same thing later to Connor and Rob. Katharina must have heard somehow. Or maybe it was a coincidence. There are always these stories popping up about how a woman loses her engagement ring on the beach during her honeymoon and then, twenty years later, fillets a salmon for dinner and finds her old ring inside. Or twin brothers in Finland who die in separate motorcycle crashes on the same road on the same day, one in the morning and one at night. Coincidences are crazy things.

My stomach is still swimming when I get home,

though; if you cut me open right now, you might find an engagement ring bouncing around in my guts. I worked a longer shift today than yesterday, so it's after eight o'clock, which means Melody is off at one of her many friends' houses. I can't remember the last time she spent a night at home. She's always with her field hockey teammates or student council buddies or one of the French exchange students, doing bonding activities like braiding each other's hair or painting each other's nails or whatever friends do when they get together. I wouldn't know. Anytime I've gotten too close to someone, I've run away. What if someone found out what happened to my last friend?

"Scarlett," Melody calls from the living room. "Is that you?"

Huh. She's home. Maybe she's sick.

No. Melody doesn't ever get sick. Flawless people never get sick.

"Yeah," I say. "It's me." I go to the living room, expecting to see Melody finishing up one of her workouts or something, but she's perched on the edge of the couch, hands folded in her lap, dressed in a fluffy orange-patterned skirt and a tight tee. I ask, "Are you getting ready to go out?"

She dazzles me with a wide smile. "I was waiting for you," she says. "I thought you might want to go to the vigil with me." She says this like she's handing me a gift wrapped with a glittery bow.

I unwrap the gift. It's empty. "What vigil?"

"They're having a vigil for the missing girl tonight out at Riverside," Melody says, her smile wilting a little. "It was in the paper. I was thinking we should go."

"We?" There's never been a "we" with me and Melody. "Why?"

"Because you're my sister," she says, like it was silly of me even to ask. "To support this girl and say how much we hope she's found."

This girl. I bet Melody doesn't even know Monica's name.

I don't ask her, though.

"I have to go to the bathroom," I say, and flee. I need a second to think. Going somewhere with Melody, especially somewhere as emotionally loaded as a vigil, can't possibly be so simple as just going somewhere with Melody. She must want something, and that something isn't spending time with me.

I don't go to the bathroom. Well, technically I go *to* the bathroom—I clomp toward the bathroom and open and shut the door, but I don't go *inside* the bathroom. Once I've shut the door loudly enough that I know Melody can hear it, I tiptoe back down the hall and into the kitchen, where today's paper is still scattered across the kitchen table. I unstick it from the coffee rings adorning the wood like the Olympics rings and flip quickly through the pages until I find the article about Monica Jackson.

The article doesn't tell me much I don't already know.

It reiterates her full name, which I already knew: Monica Rose Jackson. It contains a black-and-white picture of her—her senior portrait, complete with a tense, hesitant smile and rings of eyeliner so dark it looks almost like she has two black eyes. I already know what she looks like, or what she looked like, anyway, before she went missing. Right now she could be buried in the dirt, gray bone flashing through tattered purple remnants of skin, or locked in a basement somewhere, reduced to skin and bone and enormous pits for eyes.

The article reminds me that Monica went missing after her night shift several days ago, leaving her register drawers uncounted. It doesn't tell me whether someone finished counting the drawers for her or if they were left there, gaping open to the night in some sort of monument.

Probably the former.

There are pleas from her family: a single mother, two little sisters, and an older brother who swears he's going to kill the son of a bitch who took his sister. A brief résumé of her life: cheerleader, student council member, and the secretary of Model UN. She wanted to go to The College of New Jersey and double-major in physical therapy and special education. The vigil will be tonight at nine outside Riverside High School; candles will be provided.

I wonder if there's a guidebook somewhere about how to write an article about a missing kid. My dad didn't save any of the articles or MISSING posters or record any of the TV broadcasts from after I went missing, but it wasn't like it was hard to type my name into Google and see what popped up. My life, too, had been reduced to a series of sound bites: four nine, seventy pounds, black hair, brown eyes. Loves comics. Allergic to shellfish.

"Scarlett?"

I jump, and the pages of the newspaper whisper to the floor. "Dad."

"I was just putting Matthew to bed," he says. "What are you up to?"

I kneel and gather the pages back into a loose packet. "Reading the news."

"About the missing girl?"

"She has a name, you know," I say, a bit more frostily than I intend.

"I know," my dad says. "Monica Rose Jackson. I know her name. I'm sorry."

I shake my head. "I didn't mean to snap at you."

"It's okay." He glances at the paper in my hands. I drop it on the table, where it falls apart again. Everything I touch falls apart. "Are you going to go to the vigil? I'll go with you, if you want."

"It's okay," I say, and then, seized with an uncharacteristic recklessness, I add, "I'm going to go with Melody."

"Really?" He sounds skeptical. "You and Melody?"

I raise my imaginary shield. "She offered."

He raises an eyebrow. "Okay."

The first choice I made in the basement, and the second choice I made in the Five Banners employment office. This is the third choice. Not just to go to the vigil with Melody, though that's a choice in itself. No. I choose to continue trying, to continue hoping, to continue swimming against the current in the hope that Melody will change. That she'll realize she's been wrong about me all along, that she's my sister and she loves me.

I'm wondering if I've made a mistake, if I should actually run up to my room and hide, when Melody comes in, her hands clasped together in midclap. "So we're going?" she says. "You'll drive?"

So much for hiding. "I can drive," I say.

My dad looks from me to Melody, from Melody to me. "Are any of your friends going, Melly?"

Melody shakes her head. Her ponytail sways side to side. "Nope, just me and my sister!"

It kills me how skeptical he looks. "We'll be fine," I tell him. How hard would it be for him even to consider that this is a new start? I know as well as he does that Melody plans to use my proximity to the Five Banners folks to learn as much as she can about the missing girl—Monica—and then probably toss me away afterward, like a used tissue. It's just that, maybe, as she's doing all that, she'll discover that she likes me after all, which would lead to braiding each other's hair and painting each other's nails. Not that I would want to put my hands on anyone else's gross feet, but still.

"Okay," my dad says. "Just be smart." He's looking sternly at Melody. "Be safe."

I interject what I hope sounds like a carefree laugh. "We will," I say. "How ironic would it be to go missing at a missing girl's vigil?"

He doesn't laugh, or even smile. "Melly."

She rolls her eyes and crosses her arms. Her own imaginary shield. "I'm not an idiot. I'm not going to do anything stupid."

"No one said you were," my dad says.

I should link arms with her. No, that would be too much. "We should go," I say.

She sweeps from the room without a backward glance. "Let me just pee."

"Scarlett, really." My dad, again. "Be careful."

"I promise."

I began to say it over and over, every time Pixie complained, every time she cried. "It's better to be missing than dead." "It's better to be missing than dead." "Pixie, it's better to be a missing girl than a dead girl."

Pixie was not a quick learner the way I was. She ran for it the first time we got upstairs, and Stepmother caught her and beat her with a belt. She ran again that afternoon, and Stepmother caught her and beat her again. She ran again that night, limping a little this time, and Stepmother caught her and beat her yet again.

That night Stepmother gave me some gauze and medicinal cream, telling me quickly what to do with them, and I cleaned Pixie's back as she whimpered, telling her to keep quiet, because Stepmother didn't like when we were loud. She didn't like the men to hear us down there. I talked to her as I cleaned. It was to distract me as much as it was to distract her; the blood and strips of flesh painting her back made bile burn my throat. "You know the League of the Righteous, right? I read all the comic books and watched all the shows." She nodded. "Who's your favorite?"

"Skywoman," she said faintly, the word breaking in the middle as I skated over a particularly deep cut.

"Me too," I said. "She's amazing. I wonder what's been happening since I've been in here." Pixie didn't answer, so I forged on. "The last one I read, she'd just cornered the Blade in the sewers. They left it on a cliff-hanger. I mean, of course the Blade's going to get away, but I want to know how. Maybe she'll suddenly learn to fly."

Still no response. "She's the coolest. My parents think comic books are for little kids, though. But they didn't want me anymore. What about yours?"

Pixie shifted under my careful hand. "I don't have parents."

"Everybody has parents," I said. "Humans don't reproduce asexually." Thank you, third-grade science unit.

"Of course I had parents *once*," Pixie said scornfully, like I was the one who was being stupid. "But I went into foster care when I was four. I don't even remember them."

"Oh," I said. I wasn't really sure what foster care was, but I didn't want her to think I actually was stupid. "Sorry."

"It's—" She sucked air through her teeth. "Sorry. That just really hurt."

"These ones here are deeper than the others," I said. I had to distract her somehow. "Tell me a story. About foster care." Maybe that way I could figure out what exactly it was.

"Okay," she said. "At my old foster mom's house, I used to have rabbits. I kept them outside, in a hutch in the backyard. My baby foster brother named them, so their names were pretty stupid, but I loved them."

"What were their names?"

She rolled her eyes and sighed. "Bugs Bunny and Baby Bunny," she said. "No making fun."

"I won't," I said obediently.

"Anyway, it turns out Bugs Bunny was a girl and Baby Bunny was a boy," she said. "Because Bugs Bunny got pregnant and had lots of cute little rabbit babies."

"Aw," I said. She didn't "aw" back or agree. I should have taken that as a sign. "That must have been so cute."

I couldn't see her face, but her voice lowered, and I imagined her smiling. "They were supercute," she said. "Their eyes weren't open at first, so they would squirm around, bumping into each other and Bugs Bunny's belly."

"Aw," I sighed again. Melody and I had found a nest of baby rabbits once, in the yard. We knew enough not to touch them, because that meant the mother would be scared off and would let the babies die, but we spent hours watching them from a safe distance. Even once we went inside, we'd play rabbit, which consisted of us curling up together beneath a couple of furry rugs and pretending we were baby rabbits. Sometimes we'd try to crawl around with our eyes closed and giggle as we bumped into things. It was a fun game. I'd give anything to play rabbit again.

"You know what happened next?" she asked.

"What?"

Her voice went flat. "My foster father drowned them all in the sink." I gasped. "He didn't want them to keep having more and more babies.

"I still got to keep Bugs and Baby, though," she continued. "Until I had to go to a different foster home. The new foster mother didn't want any rabbits, so she made me leave them behind."

My mouth gaped open, then shut, then open again. I'd become a dying fish. "I'm sorry," I said.

"He probably drowned them, too," Pixie said. "So you be happy that you got to have real parents, at least for a little while, and stop complaining about how they don't want you anymore. Because some of us didn't even get to have rabbits."

I tried to swallow, but my throat was dry. My hand mechanically kept working, cleaning her wounds from the inside out. I didn't know what to say. I didn't think she was right, but I couldn't just go ahead and *say* that.

That night she cried herself to sleep and I held her close, snuggled up for warmth side by side on that dirty old mattress. It was almost like having a sister again.

The vigil is packed. Melody and I pull into the high school parking lot only a few minutes before nine and take one of the last spaces, one of the dreaded few all the way in the back behind everybody else. I back in slowly, carefully, as Melody cranes her neck, looking for people she knows. She hasn't spoken to me since we left the house. It's okay. She still needs me, and it feels nice to have Melody need me, even if it's just for a little while.

It's a nice night, at least, if there ever is a nice night for a vigil. I can smell the candles, what must be hundreds and hundreds of them, before I get to the football field and see the swarms of pinpricks dotting the darkness. People are stuffed together, shoulder to shoulder, in the bleachers, like we're at the state football championships or senior awards night, except that everyone is crying. I don't know why girls even bothered to put on mascara or eyeliner if they knew they were coming here tonight, because there must be hundreds of dollars of makeup running in sooty trails down girls' cheeks.

"Ooh," Melody says breathlessly. "It's so pretty. We need to make sure we get a candle."

"Yeah," I say, without thinking.

There's a spot big enough for two people in the front row of the closest bleachers to the exit. I'm about to ask

Melody if she wants the spot when I see a flash of coppery hair, and the decision is made for me. I plop down in the seat, leaving Melody to hover above me.

"I think I see people I know over there. . . ." But she needs me, and so she can't leave. "Fine," she huffs, sitting next to me. "Ooh, it's cold."

"Scarlett?" Someone nudges my shoulder. Connor. I turn back and smile as somberly as I can when I see Connor, Cady, Katharina, Rob, and a group of others I can only assume to be fellow Five Banners employees. "Guys, it's Scarlett."

"Who's Scarlett?" someone asks.

"I'm Scarlett." I extend my hand into the morass of Adventure World-ers. Somebody shakes it. I don't know who. "I've been working at the park for a couple days now."

"So you didn't know Monica?" This comes from a tiny, pretty woman with miles of black hair and dark skin. Her eyelashes look longer than my pinky fingers.

"She doesn't have to know Monica to be here," someone says from the crowd.

The tiny woman winces and jerks, like someone's elbowed her in the side. "I wasn't saying that!"

This whole time Melody's been quiet, her eyes darting back and forth, her thumb picking at her fingernails. I almost laugh. She's nervous. I can't believe she's nervous.

"I know, it's okay," I assure the crowd. And I'm actually telling the truth. The small woman's question didn't come out accusatory or judgmental; she merely sounded curious. I turn my attention back to her. "I didn't really know her, but I met her. I interviewed with her." I take a deep breath. "She seemed very nice. I liked her."

"She was very nice. I worked with her for two years." This woman is the only one I haven't heard immediately correct herself into the present tense. I wonder what that means. If she's positive Monica is dead. "I'm Cynthia, by the way."

"Cynthia," I say. "I've heard that name."

"I told her you were responsible for putting her in Wonderkidz," Connor says to Cynthia, who I remember is his boss. "So it would be completely justified if she shoved you off the bleachers right now."

"It was nothing personal. Somebody has to do it," Cynthia says. I can't even look at her; I'm too busy focusing on the distance between Connor and Cady, or, to be exact, the lack of it. A splinter wouldn't fit in there. She's crammed herself right up against his side.

"Yeah," I say. "I know. It's okay." I glance over at Melody, who's still wringing her fingers. "This is my younger sister, Melody, by the way."

As everybody greets Melody, voices rich with what I assume is admiration for her shiny hair and sparkling, flawless skin, I think about how I want to ask Cynthia about Monica, about whether she thinks Monica is dead, but I know that's not an appropriate choice of topic, especially for Monica's vigil. Instead, I stay silent and take one of the candles being passed through the crowd. Someone lights mine, and I bring it to my nose and breathe deep the smell of fire and smoke.

Someone nudges me on the shoulder. I turn to see Connor, bumping me with his knee. "You look awfully pensive. What are you thinking about?"

There's only one right answer; I certainly can't tell him what's really going on in my head. "Monica," I say. "It's been four days since she went missing?"

"Four days," Cady says. Her voice is raspy, like she's been crying. I should feel sorry for her, but I don't. She has Connor to wipe her tears away.

"Four days," I echo. "I'm sure they'll find her."

Somebody—an older, heavyset woman, maybe Monica's mother or aunt—is on the field, speaking, but her microphone isn't working, and so I can't hear everything she says. I can just hear the snatches of sound bites that made it into the article: "cheerleader," "volunteer," "special ed," "special."

"Yeah, it's only been four days," Connor says. "She'll be fine. You know Monica. She's a badass. She's going to be fine."

I notice Cynthia doesn't say anything, only looks down at her candle, her eyes following the leaps of the tiny flame. Rob echoes Connor's words like the best friend he is. He's got his gauges in tonight; they're big and silver and reflect the orange of all the flickering lights.

It's Katharina, naturally, who dissents. "You guys, I

don't want to be a downer, because you know I loved Monica," she says. "And maybe this isn't the place to say it, but . . . it's been four days. It's time we start thinking about how she might not come home. That she probably won't come home. I mean, it's been four days."

Cady lets out a gasp that turns into a sob. Connor murmurs something in her ear, and Rob murmurs something in Connor's ear. Cynthia still says nothing.

That leaves me. "It's only been four days," I say. "There are plenty of stories about people who go missing for longer than that and come out okay."

"How long?" Katharina's eyes are trained on me. Like she's daring me.

Melody goes rigid next to me. Trying to look unconcerned, I shrug. "I don't know," I say. "Jaycee Dugard was found after years and years. Elizabeth Smart, too. That girl in Austria." Me.

Katharina chews on the inside of her cheek. "Can someone really be missing that long and come out okay? I mean, I know they can make it out, but would they really be okay?"

Monica's mother or aunt is now talking about the community's response to what happened: "overwhelmed," "supportive," "so very grateful," "so many casseroles." My heart is hammering at the walls of my throat like it wants to evacuate. Every time Katharina moves, she wafts the scent of Violetta in my direction.

"I feel nauseous," I say. "I think I'm going to throw

up." A cry of alarm goes up from the people standing in front of me, and they part easily for me to make my way out. I push through the crowd, careful to keep my candle sheltered, but when I make it to the back of the bleachers, I realize it's gone out anyway.

At my school, the back of the bleachers—the space under the structures—is generally full of rule breakers of all stripes: the smokers, the druggies. I've never been one of the rule breakers, not really, but most everyone knows of their existence, and of their preferred location. Narnia for druggies, some kids call it. Accessible only to those who believe.

There are no rule breakers here tonight. There's one girl wrapped around another near the far end, but they just look like they're sobbing and needed a quiet place to let loose. I'm all alone on this side, save for the mumbling roar of the crowd above and their shifting shadows cast through the slats between the rows.

I shut my eyes and breathe in deep, trying to chase thoughts of Pixie and Violetta and rabbits and my years in the basement from my mind, and when I open them, Katharina is there. She's just standing there, her hands in her coat pockets, staring at me, and I get the sense that she's been there longer than a few seconds. I never heard her approach. *She's a ghost,* I think wildly. *She's a ghost, Pixie, and she's here for revenge.*

But if she were a ghost, the rational part of my brain chimes in, how could Connor and Cynthia and Rob and the others interact with her? And why would she be my age? She died when we were twelve.

And there's no way even the most irrational part of my brain would put her in the awful, awful Five Banners polo during the workday.

"Hey, Katharina," I say. "What's up?"

"I told them I'd come down to make sure you were okay and hadn't passed out and died under the bleachers or something." She's staring up, at the underside of the bleachers, at the wads of chewed gum dotting the metal like brand-new constellations.

I let out a nervous titter. "The way you say it makes it sound like you came down for something else," I say. She doesn't answer. "Did you?"

"You seem like a nice person," she says. "I wasn't expecting that."

I feel like I should make a joke here, lighten the mood somehow, steer this conversation in a different direction, but my mind is blank. And I want to know why she was expecting *anything*. "What were you expecting?"

We stare at each other, and I get the feeling we're sizing each other up, like we're about to step into a boxing ring. "Nothing," she says. "That slipped out. Pretend I didn't say anything."

"Okay," I say hesitantly.

"Sorry," she says. "You know what they say: better the foot slip than the tongue."

"What will you do when we escape?" Pixie asked me.

We were in the basement, exhausted and sweaty after a long day of work. We were cuddled close on the mattress, my front to her back, my face in her hair. She smelled like the girls' cigarette smoke. The smell didn't bother me anymore. "You shouldn't say that," I told her. "She might hear you, and she'll hurt you again."

"You're right," Pixie said. "Sorry. You know what they say: better the foot slip than the tongue."

"What did you just say?" I ask Katharina. My own tongue, not just the proverbial one, feels thick and heavy in my mouth.

"Nothing," she says. "Just a stupid thing my mom used to say. She had a whole host of them."

"Oh," I say. Because what else is there to say? "Okay. I should get back to Melody now."

Katharina sighs. "You're so lucky to have a sister," she says wistfully. "I always wanted a sister growing up. I had a friend—well, I don't know if I'd call her a friend so much as a neighbor—who was almost like a sister, but it wasn't quite the same."

"Oh?" I step back toward the light, back toward where Monica's brother or boyfriend is talking about what a vibrant force of life she is. How her house would never be the same without her, so please do give her back, thanks.

"Yeah, she had sisters," Katharina says. Her eyes narrow, or maybe it's just my imagination. "She always used to say, 'A sister is a little bit of childhood that can never be lost.'"

Pixie was a slow learner. Even though she didn't have anywhere to go back to, she tried to run almost every day. She always got beaten. I started to worry that Stepmother would kill her and that I would be alone again. She wouldn't dare to bring in someone else after taking such a big risk with Pixie, after doing me such a great kindness. So I tried not to indulge Pixie in her fantasies of escape, and whenever I could, I blocked her way out as if I didn't know what she was trying to do. I didn't want to lose her.

I didn't want to be alone again.

Sometimes the only way to keep her from trying to run was to distract her with talk of the outside. If I talked too much about what was happening around us, about which girl had the best hair or how Stepmother seemed to be in a particularly good mood because she'd had us scrub the bathrooms only once, she'd withdraw and get quiet.

"What do you miss most about out there?" she said once as we were stripping the sheets off the girls' beds. "I actually miss homework. I could do a whole pile of homework right now."

"You must be going crazy," I cracked. She didn't laugh.

"Scarlett, what about you? What's the first thing you would do if you got out?"

I didn't want to answer her, but I knew that if I didn't, she'd get quiet and her mind would turn back to escape, and then I'd spend another night sopping blood off her back. So I said, "I would buy as many baby rabbits as all the pet stores in town have, and then I would give them to you. There would be so many baby rabbits I wouldn't even be able to see you, just a big, furry pile."

She let out a weak laugh. "That's funny." Her eyes closed. "Do you think we'd even see each other?"

"Of course!" I said immediately, though I didn't know whether I was telling the truth. I'd never really thought about it. "We're basically sisters."

She let out another sound, a laugh so dry I could hear it scrape against the inside of her throat. "This isn't childhood, though. I don't know if we'd want to hold on to this."

"What are you talking about?"

"My foster mom had a lot of sisters," Pixie said. "She always said, 'A sister is a little bit of childhood that can never be lost.'"

Everything is fuzzy. The world is coated in gray velvet. "What did you say?" My tongue feels like stone.

"You heard me," Katharina says, though distantly, as if through a wind tunnel.

And then Melody is there, floating in the corner of my vision, her arms crossed and her chin jutting out. "What did you do to her?" And she's in front of me, waving her hand through my field of vision. "Scarlett? Scarlett? Katharina, what happened?"

I slump forward. Melody catches me and cradles me in her arms. My head hits her shoulder and bounces and then comes to a rest. "You're like a piece of childhood," I say, and then my knees are crumpling, and everything is black.

I hope they don't hold a vigil for me.

CHAPTER SIX

I wake up under the watchful eyes of a circle of people: Connor, Cady, Cynthia, and Rob. No Melody or Katharina, I note. The quartet stands above me, peering down; I feel like I'm a specimen they're preparing to study, or a meal they're about to eat.

The ground is cold under me, and I can feel the sharp metal of a soda can pushing into my back through my jacket. I wince. "Where's my sister?" I ask. She caught me. She didn't let me fall to the ground.

"She ran to call an ambulance," Cady says. I go to get up, but she kneels beside me and gently pushes me down. "Don't move, you could hurt yourself. Katharina says they're on their way."

Why did Melody have to run anywhere to call an ambulance? She has a cell phone. She could've called them right here, with one hand, while her other hand kept my head off the dirt. "Katharina ..." An electric jolt surges through my body; Cady must be made of rubber, because it doesn't rock her at all. "Katharina," I say again. My voice is high and thready. "What do you know about her? How long have you known her?"

Cady's brow creases in concern. "Are you okay? Do you know what day it is?"

"I know what day it is," I say, and I realize I'm shaking, and not just because of the chill. "What do you know about her? When did she start at Adventure World?"

Cady recoils a tiny bit, just enough for me to notice. "I don't really know," she says. "This year, I think. Her family moved here a few months ago. I don't know."

"Where is she?" I push myself up again, and this time Cady doesn't stop me. "Where did she go? Did she run?"

Cady glances over her shoulder. "I think she hit her head," she says. "When's the ambulance getting here?"

"Soon," Connor says. He's hovering overhead, just behind Cady, like he wants to kneel beside me, too, but doesn't want to intrude. He catches my eye and he cocks his head, asking through body language if I'm okay.

I sit all the way up and answer him with words. "I'm not crazy and I didn't hit my head," I say. "I just need to talk to ... to Katharina. Where did she go?"

"Maybe Katharina gave Scarlett drugs," Cady says.

"Katharina seems like someone who might do drugs, doesn't she?"

"I can hear you—I'm right here," I say hotly. "I didn't do drugs. Let me go." I stand, and the world wobbles around me for only a second. "I'm not going anywhere in an ambulance."

"You should really get checked out," Cady says. Her eyes are heavy with sympathy. I don't want sympathy from her, of all people.

"I'm not getting checked out," I say, and lurch forward, away from the hovering group. "Call 911 again and cancel the ambulance, if that's even what you do. I need to find Katharina."

I lurch forward again, and again, until I'm doing something resembling walking. Murmurs rustle behind me. "Should I go after her?" "Someone should go after her." "She might have a concussion." "I got it. I'll go. No, you stay here."

There's a gentle touch on my shoulder, and someone else's footsteps echo my own. "Scarlett?" It's Connor. "What happened under there?"

"I didn't hit my head." Well, I might have hit my head when I went down, but that's not important. What's important is that I find Katharina and shake her until her eyes pop out, and make her tell me what she's trying to do to me. If anyone's guilty of hurting my head, it's not me, it's her. "And I'm not doing drugs."

"I didn't think that," Connor says. His voice is quiet,

cautious. "But you can understand why everyone is worried. You're acting kind of strange."

Tears burn the corners of my eyes. "How do you even know what strange for me is? We haven't even known each other that long."

"You're a Skywoman fan," he says. "And that's all I need to know."

I snort and roll my eyes, more to disguise the oncoming rush of tears than anything else. "You don't know me."

"Fine. We'll go with that," he says. "But what I do know is that you seemed fine today, then fine in the bleachers, and then you step away for a few minutes with Katharina and you're a shaking, white-faced mess."

I want to talk to him. I can't talk to him. "It's really nothing," I say. "I swear, I'm okay."

He doesn't look convinced. "Let me take you home, at least."

"Then what would I do with my car?" I say. "Anyway, Melody can drive me if it gets too bad. But really. Look, I'm fine, I swear." I hold my palm out to demonstrate. It barely trembles. "I swear."

"But do you swear?" A smile shines through a crack in his face.

I return a tiny smile of my own, the most I can muster. "I swear on your grave."

"I'm not dead."

"You will be if you keep asking if I'm okay."

"Ouch." But he's no longer creased with concern. "Give me a hug."

He's on me before I can react, a pure force of warmth enveloping me whole. I close my eyes and breathe him in: deodorant, smoke, a faint sweetness that might come from dried baled hay. I pull my arms tight against his back, feeling the rangy muscles under his pilled flannel. I've never considered backs a particularly attractive body part, but he might change my mind. He surrounds me and his smell is inside me and now I'm not shaking anymore.

I pull back. I can't touch him, knowing Cady is standing there—probably within sight, though I can't bear to look—and knowing that he's hers. That she gets to touch him anytime she wants to. That I can't. "Thanks," I say thickly.

"Of course." His smile flickers. "If you ever need anyone to talk to, you can always come to me, okay?"

I want to say, *Apparently, you have a girlfriend.* I want to say, *That's weird, because what about Cady?* But there's no official rule that you can't talk to someone with a girlfriend. There's no official rule that says we can't be friends. Close friends. Just as long as we don't get close enough where he probes too deep. Or maybe that would be okay. Maybe he *wouldn't* go running. "Okay," I say.

"Are you absolutely sure you don't want me to drive you home? I don't know where Melody went."

Melody couldn't even wait around long enough for me to wake up, which hits me like a punch in the gut. I square my shoulders, trying to muster an appearance of strength, and hold up my hand. "Stop. Stop it. I'll find Melody. Go back to your friends."

He sucks on his bottom lip, like he wants to object, but he only nods. "You guys drive safe."

"We will." I watch as he lopes back to his friends and Cady's waiting arms. I bet she has noodle-arms. She looks like she has noodle-arms. I bet her hugs are limp.

Melody is still gone. I pull out my phone to call her, but my phone is already blinking with a text message. Nobody ever texts me, so I know before I open it that it's from Melody. *Going to stay and get a ride home with Kat. Feel better* ☺

Kat. Katharina. Melody is getting a ride home with Katharina? When did they get all buddy-buddy? How long was I out? *Kat?*

Whatever. I don't bother texting her back.

As I walk to my car, my feet start dragging. I look everywhere for Katharina and Melody, maybe braiding each other's hair or painting each other's nails, but they're nowhere. They're gone.

As I pull out, I pass the ambulance on its way in, sirens shrieking, lights flashing, looking for someone headed in an entirely different direction.

· · ·

My dad is nowhere to be seen when I get home; he goes to sleep at a ridiculously early hour, sometimes before the sun even sets, so he can wake up at a ridiculously early hour and enjoy the sunrise. Matthew is everywhere to be seen, though; I see him in the pajama shirt tossed on the hallway floor and the chocolate cookie crumbs on the kitchen table and then, finally, in the milky-smelling body of the little boy draped across the couch, head lolling against the armrest. The TV plays, but quietly—Matthew isn't a stupid kid.

I shake him gently by the shoulder. "Morning, sleepyhead."

He blinks up at me and winces at the overhead light. "It's morning?"

"No," I say. "It's nighttime. You should be in bed." I glance over at the TV. I'm expecting a cartoon or the Disney Channel, but it's some angry news show. An old fat guy is yelling at three young, pretty blond women who might well be triplets. "Why are you watching this?"

He shrugs. "I don't know."

I sigh. "Get up. Brush your teeth and go back to bed."

He smiles angelically at me. "I just wanted to wait for you and Melly to get home." I might have bought it if it weren't for the chocolate smeared across his front teeth.

"Yeah, okay."

"Are you okay?"

I'm about to ask him why he would ask when I notice

something wet sliding down my cheek. "I'm crying," I say, surprised.

"Yeah," Matthew says. "Did someone hurt you? Are you hurt?"

Matthew is seven. I can't tell him what happened. "I just like this boy," I say. "But he has a girlfriend. Kind of."

"Oh," Matthew says. He's staring at me, nodding, seeming entirely interested. I buy it for a second before I realize he'll do anything to avoid going back to bed. "Is she prettier than you?"

"She's a hideous beast," I say. My eyes hurt. These tears aren't even for Cady, and she's still ruining everything. "She has a hunchback and buckteeth and a clubfoot like the Jersey Devil. And an annoying voice. And she's stupid."

Matthew's eyes are huge and round. He's actually interested now. "Really? Can I see her?"

I sigh. What kind of lesson am I teaching my baby brother? "I was kidding," I say. "She's perfectly normal and probably a lovely person."

Matthew gives me the stink eye. He doesn't believe me. Or else he doesn't want to believe me. Given the choice between a hideous beast and a lovely girl, he'd take the hideous beast anytime.

When he starts going for the lovely girl, or the lovely boy, that's how I'll know he's growing up.

"Where's Melly?" he asks.

Good question. "She's out with one of her friends," I

say. "She'll be in later." Hopefully. "No, you cannot wait up for her."

He hops up. "I'm just going to stay awake in my room anyway."

Okay, Mr. I-Fell-Asleep-on-the-Couch. "As long as you're in your bed, under your covers, that's fine. Now come on."

I make him brush his teeth, then tuck him into bed and kiss him on the forehead. "Sweet dreams," he says drowsily.

Sweet dreams. Ha.

I actually wait up for Melody. I sit on the couch facing the hallway, my legs crossed, one foot jiggling. The news show is still playing in the background. I kind of find it soothing to see people upset about things that don't involve me.

I wait. And wait. And wait. Old Fat Guy's bluster starts to wear on me, so I switch him off. It has to be nearly midnight, and still no Melody. I might fall asleep on the couch myself.

Turns out, I do. My dad shakes me awake in the morning, the rich aroma of coffee drifting from the mug in his hand. "Scarlett, you okay?"

I touch my cheek. My hand comes away smeared with mascara, and I know without looking that my eyes dried red and swollen. "Fine," I say. "Just . . . the vigil, you know."

"Right. I understand." He moves away to give me privacy, or so I figure.

I fell asleep in a way that, naturally, cricked my neck, so I roll it back and forth, trying to make the pain stop. In all my rolling, my eyes land on the small, unassuming picture hanging almost behind the TV, peeking out as if it's apologizing for its existence.

I nearly forgot it was there. I get up and move closer.

There's my dad, hair slicked back, baring his teeth in an artificial smile. There's Melody, her smile so wide you can barely see her face. There's me, my hair in sleek black braids, cheeks so rosy you'd think I'm wearing blush. I look so innocent. I find it hard to believe I ever looked so innocent.

And there's my mom, standing in the middle, the sun around which our universe revolved. She stands proud and tall, her shoulders thrown back. She's the only one who doesn't smile, like she's spurning the traditional conventions of picture-taking and getting ready to show the world what's what.

I wonder what happened to her.

She didn't die, at least not that we know of. Soon after I returned, she just disappeared. At first I wondered if she'd joined the club—mother-daughter solidarity, right? But then the police told us she'd withdrawn a suspicious amount of cash in the weeks before she went missing, and she was spotted in a city far away with a different hair color, and my dad was forced to admit she'd left a note. "She was sorry," he said. "She said she loved you all."

I still wonder if that was true.

Melody looks like her.

Speaking of Melody, I head upstairs and crack open Melody's bedroom door. She lies on her back, sprawled across the bed like she has all the room in the world. I've never really thought about it before, but suddenly I wish I could sleep like that too. Even after all these years, I still sleep curled up like a comma, like there's another little girl beside me.

I hover in the doorway, wondering whether I should wake her up, when she lets out a great gasp of a snore and jolts into a sitting position. "You," she says. "What are you doing? Why are you watching me sleep? That's so creepy. You're so creepy."

"I've been here for, like, a second," I say. "I wasn't watching you sleep. I swear."

"Whatever," she says. "Go away, creeper."

I stand my ground. "I waited up for you last night." I realize how pathetic I sound and switch tacks. "What were you and Katharina doing at the vigil?"

"We were just hanging out. She's new to the area and wanted to talk to someone who was actually involved in her school. God, will you go away already?" She plops her pillow over her head.

I wish I could plop a pillow over my head too, so I'd never have to see her looking at me like that again. "Whatever," I say, and go, making sure to slam the door behind me as hard as I can.

• • •

For the next couple of weeks, Five Banners Adventure World cycles me through all five of its sections a few times over. My best days are in the south side under Connor and Rob; my worst are easily under Cady in the north side, where I work in another kids' store and have to deal with hordes of screaming kids and, worse, with Cady, whom I discover (to my absolute displeasure) to be a normal and totally lovely person. In central I become pals with Wonderman and Slugworth; underneath their costumes they stink of cigarette smoke and have raspy, rattling coughs. The east and west sides are largely unremarkable—I learn the ways of Games one day when they're shorthanded, and on another day fill in in Foods, a day that leaves me soaked in sweat, stinking of french-fry grease, and swearing never to step foot in a kitchen again.

Interestingly enough, I don't run into Katharina. After the first few days, I think there must be some sort of backroom juggling going on, and that Cynthia must be involved. I'm afraid to speak Katharina's name for several days, like saying her name will make her burst through the closest mirror, but I finally get up the courage to say something to Rob one slow morning in headquarters. "Hey," I say. "Does Katharina still work here?"

Rob looks at me, then at the floor, then at the door, then at the counter. He clears his throat. "Yeah," he says. "Why?"

"Just curious," I say as airily as I can manage. "Just haven't seen her in a while."

"Yeah," he says. It's more about what he doesn't say here: *That's weird. Huh. I'm sure you'll see her soon.*

Soon enough I'm seeing her everywhere—in the face of a guest with long, dark hair; in the shrieking smear of people riding a roller coaster over my head; in the strong chin of a Skywoman action figure, for God's sake. I think I might be going crazy.

Crazier.

A few weeks into my Katharinaless period, Connor's and my lunch schedules line up again. My heart skips a beat, but I sternly flash it with a mental picture of Cady— painfully normal, painfully lovely Cady—and it calms down. Stupid, stubborn thing; it just won't let up.

Connor and I walk together in companionable silence, our hands in our pockets, stopping every few minutes to answer someone's inane question. Just as we're passing the entrance to the secret passage he tried to lure me down on my first day, I stop. Melody would never be afraid of something so silly as a secret passage in the park.

"Let's do it," I say.

He looks over his shoulder and arches an eyebrow in a surprisingly elegant fashion; I expect him to shake a monocle out of his sleeve. "Excuse me?"

I roll my eyes. "Get your ginger head out of the gutter," I say. "I mean, let's do the secret passage."

"You sure?" he says, and the skeptical way he says it, like he doesn't think I can do it, makes me sure.

"Sure as sure can be," I say. My feet don't seem to want to move, but I grit my teeth and yank them from the cobblestones; I feel like I'm leaving bits of blood and skin behind. "Let's get this over with."

Connor pushes open the door, and I breathe in and step through. It clangs shut behind me, locking automatically, and there's a moment of scrabbling panic in my chest before I exhale it out and I'm okay again. *One breath at a time,* I tell myself. *You're with Connor; he won't let somebody grab you. You won't let somebody grab you. Not again.*

The secret passage is surprisingly underwhelming. We're not the only people taking it; it seems to stretch around this whole side of the park, encompassing multiple entrances that lead outside the fence, and so there are lots of other groups of Day-Glo workers chattering and laughing as they stroll along to the Canteen or to a staff smoking area, or to make quick stops at stores or stands or restaurants throughout the park. The ground is packed dirt, and the wooden fence separating us from the park rises up above on our right; to the left are series of long, low buildings interspersed with long alleyways and rusting trailers and piles of God knows what. I tense every time I pass an alleyway, but it helps that the sun is shining and birds are twittering overhead; I can see the other ends of the alleys sparkling like they're pathways straight to heaven, and soon my shoulders give up and relax.

"What's in there?" I ask, gesturing to the low buildings we keep passing.

Connor shrugs. "Lots of stuff," he says. He points toward one behind us. "That's full of all sorts of retail crap."

"Like stuff that's out of season?"

"Some of it," Connor says. "Mostly it's stuff we can't have in the stores anymore but we feel too bad throwing out. You can barely move in there."

I shudder. It sounds awful. "What about that one?"

"That one, Grasshopper, is the changing studio for the costumed characters on this side of the park," he says. "If you've ever wanted to see Wonderman's junk, we can stop by."

"No thanks," I say, and he laughs. "That one?"

"Where more merch goes to die. Rest in peace," he says. A roller coaster roars overhead; its wind rushes through my hair.

"That one?"

Somehow Connor knows what every single building and trailer holds. "It's amazing," I tell him.

"You're amazing," he says back. A smile spreads across my face, a flower poking its head out from the dirt, until I stomp on it hard with my mental picture of Cady and it shrivels back into the hole it came from.

We slow as we approach the Canteen. There are two cops posted outside, balding guys sweating in their navy garb; both have pit stains the size of the sun. "What's going on?" I say. Connor seems to know everything—maybe he'll know this, too.

He shakes his head, though, and bites his lower lip.

"I hope nobody else is . . ." He doesn't have to finish. *Missing.*

He doesn't even have to say he hopes they haven't found a body.

I trail behind him as we approach; both the cops eye us up and down as we climb the steps leading into the Canteen. "Afternoon, officers," Connor says affably. If there's one thing I wish I had, it's this: Connor's remarkable ability to talk to anyone, anywhere, exactly how that person would like to be talked to. I could have friends, then, maybe. Instead of worrying that I'd blurt out the truth at any moment, I could twist my words around, make people think I'd answered them when really I'd told them nothing at all.

Connor continues. "Mind if I ask what's going on?"

One of the officers clears his throat. "They found Monica Jackson's"—my stomach lurches into my throat—"shirt. They found a piece of her work shirt in the woods out behind the park."

I swallow air and heave. Connor's hand finds my elbow and squeezes firmly, but not too firmly. "But they didn't find her?" he confirms.

The officer looks back at him soberly. "No, they didn't find her."

The mood inside the Canteen is subdued; people are huddled together over tables, whispering, their arms wrapped around each other, the occasional shoulders shuddering with muffled sobs. Connor and I grab our grease-laden food and make our way to our—I think I can call it ours now—usual table. Cynthia is there, along with a few other green shirts I vaguely recognize, but they all shove over to make room for Connor and me.

"Did you hear?" Cynthia says. She isn't talking to me or Connor. She's talking to the table. "They found her shirt."

"It doesn't mean anything, Cyn," Connor says, but his voice is rough and even I can tell he doesn't mean what he says.

Cynthia throws her arms on the table, rattling all our trays. One of the girls across from me jumps and her eyes fill with tears, but Cynthia doesn't seem to notice. "It doesn't mean anything?" she says. "Tell me, then, oh wise one, how finding Monica's shirt after she's been missing over three weeks can possibly be anything but bad."

"She could have . . ." Connor's mouth hangs open. I can practically see the cogs in his head turning. "She could have . . ."

"She could have been running and had to slip out of her shirt to escape." I swoop in like the roller coaster overhead, which roars in agreement as it shakes the floor beneath our feet. "Someone grabbed her, but she broke free and ran. These shirts practically glow in the dark; she knew she'd never be able to outrun him or hide in it, so she ripped it off and ran."

Connor is looking down at me with something like awe. My cheeks burn, but I don't look away from Cynthia. "So finding her shirt doesn't mean anything," I finish. "She could still turn up. You can't lose hope." The words feel tacky and wrong in my mouth, but I let them go anyway.

"I just don't think you're being realistic," Cynthia grumbles, but her fingers curl out of their fists, and she shoves a fry into her mouth. She chews hard, like the french fry's done her some great personal affront.

"I just don't think you should assume things," I say. "You know what they say: it's better to be missing than dead."

"People keep telling me that," Cynthia says. That fills me with relief. "People" is more than one. "People" means others besides Katharina.

"Imagine what Monica will say when she turns up again and she hears what you've been saying." Connor reaches across the table and grabs one of Cynthia's fries, earning a swat. I don't know why he needs to steal hers; he has plenty of his own. "She'll be so insulted."

"I hope so," Cynthia says fervently. Her eyes are shiny.

She's able to sit with us for only a few more minutes before she's called back to work by a crackly "Code eight" over the radio clipped to her belt. She quickly excuses herself as Connor mutters in my ear. " 'Code eight' means attempted burglary," he says. "Probably some kid caught pocketing an action figure."

The other green shirts have to leave not long after, and soon enough it's just me and Connor at the table. Our table. "That was great, Scarlett," he says. "Way to go."

"What are you talking about?" I snatch one of his fries. He deserves it.

"That story you spun for Cynthia," he says. "I thought she was going to have a meltdown, but you pulled her back up and saved the day."

"Saved the day," I say. "You make me sound like Skywoman."

"Trust me, if the other kids on the south side knew what you just did, they'd be worshipping you like that weird cult of cheerleader boys who always seem to pop up when Skywoman does something heroic," he says. I know what he's talking about. Whenever Skywoman vanquishes the Blade or rescues an innocent civilian from a pit of sharks or encroaching spikes or a stampede of rampaging wildebeests (or, on one memorable occasion, all three), there's this crowd of devoted fans, all male, who pop up and swoon, hearts exploding from their anime eyes. I think it's supposed to be a play on girl groupies, but honestly, it creeps me out. I mean, they all look the same.

Connor continues, "An upset Cynthia makes everybody miserable."

It's kind of exciting, warming almost, to be the source of something helpful. Maybe this would happen more if I talked to people more often. "Well, I'm glad I could help her, I guess," I say.

"You didn't just help Cynthia," Connor says. He's staring intently at his fries, and I wonder if he's afraid I'm going to try to steal more. "You helped me, too. I've . . . I guess I've kind of been losing hope too."

"Did you know her well?" I ask.

He shrugs. "Pretty well, I guess," he says, and peeks at me through a coppery fringe. "We weren't friends, really, but we worked together for two years. And she and Cady were practically best friends. Besties?"

I don't want to talk about Cady. I want to talk about anything other than Cady, actually. I'd rather talk about Pixie.

No, self. Don't go that far. "I'm sorry," I say. "If she was best friends with your girlfriend, you must have known her pretty well anyway."

"Cady's not my girlfriend," he says immediately. "She . . . no, forget it."

"No, what?" I say, too quickly. I am failing at casualness. I am the opposite of casual. Fancy. No, I'm not that, either. But seriously, I saw them kissing. Katharina said they'd been together for two years. *Something* isn't right.

He sighs. "I loved Cady, and some part of me will always love her, but I fell out of *love* with her a while ago," he says. He's barely even moving his lips. "I knew we'd have to break up, but I put it off because I still care about her, a lot, and I'd really miss her."

"I get it," I say. My whole body thumps in tune with my heart. "Plus, you work together."

"Exactly," he says. "But I finally got up the courage to do it a few weeks ago, right before Monica went missing, and we went for a walk and I . . . broke up with her, and we both cried and it was as awful as I thought it would be, but I was still relieved." He pauses and licks his lips. "I knew it had to be done. And then we got back to Cady's house, and we found out about Monica. That she'd gone missing. And so I stayed there with Cady for a while and let her cry on me, and then I left, and she was texting me and calling me and everything like usual. And it doesn't feel like anything has changed. I'm not sure if it has, for her." He's squinting at the table like it's a treasure map.

"You're saying that she just . . . forgot you broke up with her?"

He shakes his head. "I don't think she forgot. I think that with everything going on with Monica, with all the grief coming from that, she just . . . decided to ignore it."

"But she can't ignore it," I say heatedly—probably too heatedly. I take a mental step back. *Casual. Stay casual.* "Can't you remind her?"

Connor sighs again, and I try not to imagine the way his breath would feel brushing against my ear. "I did, once, but it didn't change anything. Her best friend just went missing," he says. "We both know the relationship is over, but I don't want to be cruel to her. She needs me."

I need you. "You're a good person," I say. *Better than me.*

He looks me straight in the eye. "It's just that—" His radio crackles, and we both jerk in surprise. "Sorry. One second." It crackles again, someone—a robot, perhaps— saying something indistinguishable, but he frowns, and the crease between his eyebrows deepens. "They want me back," he says. "It's difficult, Scarlett. To be so beloved."

"I'm sure," I say drily. "What were you going to say?"

He shakes his head. "I forget," he says, and fiddles with a fry. I keep waiting for him to pop it into his mouth and put it out of its misery, but he only continues toying with it, picking it apart the way a cat plays with a mouse. "It's just about time for us to be heading back anyway."

We toss our food and leave the Canteen. The cops are still waiting outside; I feel suspicious eyes trained on my back, but when I turn around to check, I see the cops are looking in the opposite direction. When I turn back around and trot after Connor, though, my back still prickles.

Halfway through the secret passage, Connor's radio crackles again, and he swears. "They're saying they need me in the north right away."

"Why do they need you in the north?" I say. "You work in the south."

He doesn't answer. "Quick. We can run back to your store and then I'll run up to the north." He pretends to flick sweat off his brow. "It'll be good exercise."

His radio crackles again, and I raise an eyebrow. "Don't they need you right away?"

"I can walk you back," he says, and he smiles. There's nothing patronizing or impatient about his smile, but I can't help feeling silly that he thinks—no, he knows—that I can't walk the secret passage alone. Which is ridiculous.

Because there are plenty of people around and it's the middle of the day.

I don't want Connor to think I'm a coward.

"Go," I say, waving toward the north. "I'm fine. I can go the rest of the way by myself."

"You sure?" he asks.

I nod vigorously, like that's going to convince me. "It's stupid for you to have to go all the way to the south with me and then run all the way back. I'm okay. Anyway, it'll be nice to enjoy the fresh air without your stench getting in the way."

His mouth falls open in mock dismay. "If I didn't have to run, I'd so tell everybody about you, you Sky-fanatic."

"Blackmail doesn't become you, Mr. Wallace."

He's already moving backward; he's remarkably graceful, fluid like an ice-skater. He doesn't so much as look behind him. If I tried to walk backward without looking, I'd probably manage to walk off a cliff, and there isn't a real cliff around here for miles. "You just wait," he says, and then he's gone.

I take a deep breath. There isn't any other option but for me to walk the rest of the secret passage alone; if I go into the park, I won't make it back to my store on time. At Five Banners, if you're late, I'm pretty sure your supervisor is allowed to eat you, and Cynthia looked pretty hungry, even after lunch.

So I walk alone. *It's fine*, I keep telling myself. *Look,*

Scarlett, at all the people walking beside you. Listen, Scarlett, to all the tourists being cheerful on the other side of the fence. Bask, Scarlett, in the rays of the beaming sun. Bad things don't happen in sunlight.

I conveniently ignore that I joined the club under rays of beaming sun.

I was alone then, though, and now there are people streaming around me everywhere I can see. I let myself melt into the crowd, lose my identity. It's nice not to be Scarlett for a little while.

Until I hear "Scarlett?" that is. Then everything comes crashing back. I turn to the voice, which is coming from the open door of one of the metal buildings, and see Katharina.

I could run. I could. But I don't.

"Scarlett?" Katharina says again. "Can you come here for a second? I want to talk to you."

I take a step toward her but don't go any farther. Over her shoulder I can see the inside of the shiny metal building stuffed with boxes and shelves labeled with things like T-SHIRTS, 2013 or BROKEN SNOW GLOBES, 2015. (Why in the world would Five Banners need to keep around a full box of broken snow globes?) The corrugated metal walls practically bow out with the strain of keeping all this crap inside. Everything, from the vacant-eyed old action figures to stacks of Wonderman-emblazoned light-up sneakers, is covered with a thick, plush-looking layer of dust. My eyes itch just looking at it. What in the world is she doing in there? "What is it?"

Since I'm not moving toward her, she moves toward

me, closing the door behind her. "I just wanted to talk to you and apologize for what happened at the vigil," she says. "I don't know what I did, but I clearly did something to really freak you out."

I don't know what to say to that. If I say, *Yes, you did,* she'll ask me what, and I'll have to spill everything. Ask her if she's a dead girl.

So I go for no. "I just wasn't feeling well," I say. "It had nothing to do with you."

"Oh, good," she says, though she's still eyeing me like I'm a radio that could burst into the Wonderkidz sound track at any moment. "Melody thought I might have done something."

"She talked to you about me?" The words burst out before I can stop them.

She shrugs. "Your sister's a cool girl," she says. I want to ask her why she's so cool, what they were doing without me, when Katharina snaps her fingers. "That's what I wanted to ask you. We should do something sometime. Are you working the night shift tomorrow?"

I might have absolved Katharina of her guilt—as far as I know—but that doesn't mean I want to spend time with her. "I can't," I say. "I have a . . . thing."

She cocks her head. Waves of hair flow over her shoulders. I didn't realize a human head could grow so much hair. "Melody said you'd be free," Katharina says. "She's the one who suggested the three of us get together. Oh well. Another time, then."

I perk, feeling like a dog who's just heard the can opener click. "Melody wants to hang out?"

"Yeah," Katharina says. "It was her idea. She thought it would be fun."

My heart is racing. "I might be free," I say. "I have to . . . check my schedule."

"Good," she says. "Check it and let me know."

My heart races the whole walk back to my store, and not just because I have to run to make it there on time.

I slide into my store in the nick of time; the digital clock on my register screen tells me it's been exactly one hour since I left. Cynthia, who's there to take my replacement off the register and send her to cover someone else's lunch, doesn't even give me side-eye.

"I just ran into Katharina," I say, making conversation as she signs me on. Maybe trying to prove I'm a normal person. "We had a normal conversation." Way to go, ace.

Cynthia squints at the register. "That's weird," she says. "Katharina's not scheduled to work today."

My breath catches in my throat. I want to ask her if she's sure—absolutely, positively sure—but I'm not sure I want to hear the answer. So I say nothing.

CHAPTER SEVEN

Why would Katharina be hanging out in the park, in uniform, if she's not working?

I think it over, but it's difficult, considering the number
of distractions surrounding me.

I'm working alone in a south-side candy store today,
which is both the best and the worst. For one thing, there's
no sound track, and after Wonderkidz, I can't help but note
the music (or lack thereof) every time I step foot in a new
store. Also, it smells like heaven: my register is right next
to the fudge counter, where rolling acres of fudge stretch
toward walls lined with giant, swirly neon lollipops and
strips of button candy. The store has stations where guests

can fill superhero- or supervillain-shaped plastic bottles with candy sand all the shades of the rainbow.

The worst part? I'm surrounded by all this mouth-watering sugary goodness, all this fudgy, chocolatey perfume, and I'm not allowed to eat even a single tiny sliver. I'm not sure if I'd want to, honestly; flies tend to hang out on the fudge's surface. That doesn't stop it from smelling amazing, though.

There's a brief burst of after-lunch sugar buying, and then the store quiets down. I should wander the store and straighten items on shelves, make sure nobody's opened a package and left the wrapper crumpled on the ground. But I've done enough cleaning for a lifetime, so I don't think any god would penalize me for being lazy this one time. Instead, I find myself having a staring contest with the peanut butter–chocolate fudge.

"Do it." Connor strolls in the front door. "No one will know."

All thoughts of Katharina vanish. I gaze wistfully at the bricks of candy. "You will."

"I don't count," he says. "Go. Do it. Do it. Eat it. Eat it."

"The cameras will know too," I say. I don't even have to look up to know there's a camera lens aimed right at my register, ready to document any rule breaking or idle behavior.

"Most of the cameras don't work," Connor says. "It was a big deal when . . . you know. When Monica . . . because the cameras were supposed to be on, but all the cameras in her store and on the way out were broken."

"Oh," I say. "That sucks."

"Yeah. They're in the process of getting them fixed, but it takes time. This one's still on the list, since there are other cameras right outside. So go. Do it."

I sneak another glance at the fudge. It glistens with its sheer deliciousness. "It's stealing."

"Delicious stealing."

"True." I look again at the fudge, then at the camera. "A tiny sliver would probably be okay." I use the fudge tool to slice a tiny sliver from the end of a piece of fudge (the next guest to be rude will get the smaller piece), but Connor stops me with a touch to my elbow. Sparkles shoot up my arm to my shoulder.

"Scarlett," he says with utter seriousness. "Go all in. Do it."

I swallow hard. Before I can think about it, I grab the entire piece, shove it in my mouth, and chew. And choke. It's like paste, with a note of chemical and a burny after-taste. I scrabble for an abandoned strip of receipt paper and spit it out. "God, that's awful," I say. My face is squinched tight. "Are you sure that's fudge and not rat poison?"

"That's a good question," Connor says. "The answer is no."

I spit into the garbage can, but I can't get the taste out of my mouth. "Do any of the others taste better?"

"Afraid not," Connor says. "Here, have some sand." At some point while I was stumbling around in half-real agony, he filled a water glass with the sugary sand. "Cheers."

I tip it back and let the sugar dissolve in my mouth. It tastes like chemicals too, but at least it gets the taste of the fudge out. No, "fudge." I can't in good conscience refer to what I just ate as fudge. "Good God." I run my tongue over my teeth, feeling the grit dissolve. "How could you do that to me?"

"Do what to you?" Connor says innocently. "I just urged you to follow your heart."

"Oh really?"

He acknowledges me with a tip of his head. "Also, it was really funny."

"I'm sure it was," I say. I sigh. The door jingles open and I turn to greet the customer, but when I give the family my usual smile, they give me an odd look and retreat to the wall of fruit snacks. I realize too late it's probably because my teeth are stained blue from the sand. That's just wonderful. "You owe me."

Connor waits for me to help the family with their afternoon treats, then leans back against the counter, propping himself up on his elbows. "I owe you, do I? What is it that I owe you, exactly?"

My cheeks and forehead are on fire. If I were in a movie, I'd tell him he owes me a kiss, and he'd kiss me, and it would sweep me off my feet both literally and figuratively, and we'd depart the next day on a journey to ride the tallest, fastest roller coaster in each Five Banners park across the U.S.

But it's not a movie, and just the thought of asking him for a kiss makes my throat close in on itself and sweat prick cool on my forehead. "You owe me your hopes and dreams."

"All of them?" He raises an eyebrow.

I cross my arms. "Every last one."

His sigh gusts across the room. "In a fantasy world, in a few years I'll be leading the U.S. men's soccer team to a World Cup victory," he says. "In the real world, I'll be doing physical therapy. Exercise science."

"I wouldn't write off your soccer dream," I say seriously. "Given the number of people who care about soccer over here, you might have an actual chance."

A package of candy buttons bounces off my head. I rub the spot in mock pain. "Nice throw, but I'd be way more convinced of your ability to follow your dream if you'd kicked it."

"You should come see me play sometime," he says. "We have practice over the summer. At Riverside."

The fire spreads to my entire face. "I don't know anything about soccer."

"So I guess your dream isn't to head the U.S. women's soccer team in the World Cup," he says, sighing. "What is it, then? Don't tell me—president of the Sky-fanatics?"

My dream. I don't have a dream, not like that. I didn't have time to dream when I thought I'd die in that basement. "I just want to be happy," I say. "That's all I want."

"So profound." One of his elbows slips, but he catches himself before he hits the counter. "You put me to shame."

"Yeah?" I can't see how; he knows exactly what he wants to do with his life, and the only thing I know is that I want my life to make me happy. I have no idea how I'm going to do it.

"It's a good thing to want. I wish I could be more like that. Less about the planning."

"You think so?" I say. "It makes me nervous, not having any kind of plan. Or even an idea."

He squints at me and presses his lips together. "Well, what do you like to do? What kind of activities do you do?"

A laugh bubbles in my throat. This is a question for Melody. I like being free. Being free is my main activity. "I don't know," I say. "I'm still trying to figure that out." I chew on the inside of my cheek. "I like math."

"That's practical," he says. His eyes are almost golden in the light.

"Much more practical than soccer."

His elbow slips again as he laughs, which makes him stand up and adopt a mock frown. "What about the rest of your life? You know that my brother plays the bari sax in the jazz band, which is really all you need to know about me. It's your turn."

I laugh again, but this one is plastic. "What do you mean?"

"Siblings, parents, school, pets, innermost secrets."

He ticks his words off on his fingers. "I want it all. Ready, set, go."

I'm suddenly unable to swallow. This is where, in the past, I'd cut the friendship off.

But I can't imagine losing Connor, so change-the-subject time it is. "Speaking of secrets, I'm glad to see you survived the secret crisis on the north side."

Connor visibly shrinks; his shoulders fold in upon themselves, and he leans up against the counter, doubling over, so that his hands rest on his knees. "It was Cady," he says. "She had a meltdown."

"Oh," I say. "I'm sorry."

"She was working in one of the stores where she and Monica always worked together, and I guess she kind of lost it," he says. "They called me in to help calm her down."

"Is she okay?"

Connor shrugs. "She's functional," he says. "She's doing her job. I think that's all they can ask at this point."

"Yeah," I say. "It must be really hard."

"Yeah," he says. "But enough of that." I worry he's going to go back to the whole innermost-secrets thing, but he continues with, "What are you doing this weekend, Scarlett?"

I hope I make it to the weekend after going somewhere with Katharina tomorrow. "I don't know," I say. "Working."

"That sounds exciting," Connor says. "Just kidding, it doesn't. Are you free Saturday?"

"If I'm off," I say. "I haven't checked my schedule yet." This time I'm actually telling the truth.

Connor waggles his eyebrows. "We're all off," he says. "As in, all of Merch. The park is closed for a private event on Saturday night, and most of the stores will be closed. So we're having a special bonfire."

"Yeah? Special? What makes it so special? What are you burning?"

"You know, the usual," Connor says. "Effigies, animal sacrifices, the occasional young child."

"Sounds like my kind of bonfire," I say.

"We'll be burning some of the hay I suffered to bale," he says. "Don't worry if you hear the smoke screaming. That's just my spirit."

"So it's at your barn?" I say.

"At my house," he says. "Well, in the fields behind my house."

"I don't get it," I say. "I thought you lived in a barn."

He picks up a chunk of fudge and tosses it up and down a couple of times for effect. "You'd better watch it, you," he says. "Or I'll make you eat an entire brick."

"I feel like it would burn through my stomach and set my insides on fire," I say. "On the bright side, I'd be a great fire starter on Saturday."

"Very true," he says. He puts the piece of fudge back. "Don't worry. Just give it to the first person who's mean to you. No one will know."

. . .

A few months into our captivity, Pixie still hadn't learned. She didn't try to run three times a day anymore, but I could tell she was always looking for a way to escape.

I woke one night not to Pixie elbowing me in the stomach or kicking me in her sleep (that, I was used to), but to something rattling. I blinked, drowsy, and realized that my stomach was cold. Pixie wasn't there. I sat up, suddenly awake. "Pixie?"

"Shhhh!" Her voice was rushing water. I squinted into the dark to see her hands silhouetted against the tiny barred window; she'd pushed the table underneath and was standing on it, one of the legs teetering just off the ground. Even with this extra height, she could hardly reach. "Someone will hear!"

I pushed myself to my feet and padded over. The floor felt like ice under my bare soles, and I shifted from foot to foot, trying to keep warm. "What are you doing?"

My eyes had adjusted enough to see the look she shot me. She looked like she thought I was an idiot. "Trying to see if I can get through the window, duh."

"It's too high," I said. "I tried when I first got here." And then I clamped my mouth shut, because what if Stepmother heard me?

"If I stack a chair on top of the table and climb on that, I should be able to reach," she said.

"You'll fall," I said. "And anyway, there are *bars* on the window."

"But maybe I could get the bars off," Pixie said

heatedly. "And if you hold the chair so that it doesn't fall off . . ."

I blanched. Hold the chair? So Pixie could escape?

No one would be here to hold *my* chair.

Not that I could escape anyway. I had nowhere to go back to. My parents didn't want me anymore. Stepmother was the only one willing to take me in.

"I'll run and send someone back for you," Pixie was quick to add. "I swear."

"It won't work," I said. "And anyway, you—"

We hadn't realized how loud we were getting. The door at the top of the stairs banged open, and I jumped. Pixie jumped too, right off the table. She landed with a shriek, her ankle folding beneath her.

"What's going on down here?" Stepmother took a step down the stairs. She was all done up for bed, silver hair piled into a bun on top of her head, the skin under her eyes ghostly white with cold cream. Pixie whimpered. "What are you doing, girl?"

"Nothing." Pixie's voice was a gasp. "I was just . . . just trying to look out the window."

Stepmother trained her eyes on me. They were ice blue, so pale they almost glowed in the dark. "Jane, what was the other girl doing?"

Stepmother at least called me a name, even if it wasn't mine. Pixie didn't even get that.

My heart felt as cold as Stepmother's eyes.

"Jane," Stepmother prompted. I stared at her. "Jane,

tell me what she was doing, or you won't like what's going to happen."

I couldn't look back at Pixie. I couldn't look into Stepmother's eyes, either. I could only look at the floor. The cold, cold floor. "She was trying to escape, ma'am."

I could hear Pixie gasp. It was drowned out, though, by the palpable sense of satisfaction oozing from Stepmother. "As I suspected," she said. "Jane, would you like to sleep upstairs tonight?"

My mouth dropped open. I couldn't look back at Pixie, but I could look into Stepmother's eyes now. "Upstairs? Ma'am?"

"Candy is gone for the night," Stepmother said. "There's a spare bedroom upstairs. Would you like to sleep there tonight, Jane?"

I still couldn't look back at Pixie. "Yes, ma'am." It felt like a choice, but really, this wasn't a choice. It was all Stepmother.

I didn't look back at Pixie as I climbed the stairs, or as Stepmother ushered me through the door, or as Stepmother closed the door behind me. Stepmother stayed behind on the staircase, but I could hear her through the door. "You and Jane are close, girl, are you not?" she said. I would have nodded, but I pictured Pixie staring back defiantly, her chin thrust into the air. "If you try to escape, if you let her help you, I will kill her. I will kill her and it will be your fault."

Pixie said nothing, but I didn't think she would. A

141

splinter of resentment pushed its way into my heart. She had to stop trying to escape now, now that she knew my life was in her hands. Not that Stepmother would actually kill me; I didn't think she would, anyway. I was a good worker, a quiet worker, and I'd stopped trying to escape. She'd told me before how hard it was to find someone like me.

Once Stepmother came through the door, I let her lead me to Candy's room, at the end of the main hallway. The house felt big when we were cleaning it, but, looking back, it really wasn't a large house: a hall lined with rooms that were divided with false walls to make more rooms, but there were only two and a half baths for everybody. One floor and a basement. Maybe there was an attic, too, but we never saw it.

I waited for her to nod at the bed before I sat down. I cast my eyes down, looking at the floor and expecting her to leave, but she took a step inside and closed the door behind her. I blinked hard, focusing on the floor like it was the most fascinating thing in the world.

"Jane, look at me."

She didn't have to tell me twice. She was staring down at me, her lips ruby red, her cheekbones slicing the air. Her eyes narrowed as she studied my face. As she studied *me*. My skin prickled, and I had to fight the urge to look away.

She did a strange sort of shimmy with her shoulders. Back then I assumed that she'd been bitten by a bug or something—really, I didn't give it too much thought. But it has stuck with me all these years, and now the leading hypothesis? She was fighting an urge herself.

Of course, it's only a hypothesis. It's entirely possible that she was cruel all the way through, her heart a shriveled black fist.

"You remind me of someone, Jane," she said finally. "She had the same black hair, that same olive skin, those big, dark eyes." Her throat worked. "Of course, you are eight now, are you not? Or nine? She was never eight. Or nine."

I knew better than to respond; that had earned me the back of her hand striking across my cheeks enough times now. So I sat there primly, hands folded in my lap and back as straight as I could make it, until she nodded crisply at me and walked away.

I slept in a real bed that night, a real bed that still smelled a little bit like passion fruit, Candy's favorite perfume. It was the most comfortable bed I'd ever slept in.

I didn't dream of Pixie. I dreamed of another girl, a girl with black hair, olive skin, big, dark eyes.

Soon after our fudge-eating adventure, Connor has to leave and go do actual work, so I spend most of the afternoon planning my interrogation of Melody. Also wondering if the amaretto fudge is as lethal as the peanut butter fudge, but you know what they say: once bitten, twice burned. Or something like that.

Mostly I occupy myself with the Melody thing. I'm not at all surprised or suspicious that she and Katharina are such fast friends; Melody makes friends the way most people order hamburgers, and Katharina is beautiful and popular enough to be a worthy addition to her harem. No, what I'm most surprised and suspicious about is that they want to spend time with *me*.

I started seeing Dr. Martinez mere hours after I was found. She'd spoken with my parents, and Melody, too. I only found out years later what they'd talked about. Apparently, my rescue was just the beginning: a happy beginning, sure, but just the beginning of a very long and difficult road. I'd been in that basement for a span of time approaching four years: nearly a third of my entire life, more if you don't count the baby years, which really you shouldn't. They shouldn't be surprised, she cautioned, if I didn't remember basic things, like how to use a real toilet or interact with old friends, or if I woke screaming every night from one nightmare or another.

I never woke screaming. There had been enough nights where I'd woken whimpering or crying only to have my half-asleep bedmate kick me in the stomach to make me stop.

I did, however, forget basic things. My parents had kept my bedroom exactly the way I'd left it, dirty clothes in the hamper and hidden stash of (now rotten and crumbling) candy in the back of my sock drawer, but I didn't remember which door off the upstairs hallway led into it. I remembered my best friends, Maddy and Nicole, and could point to their grinning, gap-toothed faces in my old pictures, but I'd totally forgotten the face of my cousin Ella, who lived way out in California. I could put together my favorite sandwich, peanut butter and honey and banana, with one hand, but I'd forgotten where the toaster was.

And so on.

At first I tried to ask Melody for help. Ask her how to manipulate the shower handle so that the water wasn't scorching hot *or* freezing cold, or where the apples were stored in the garage. Sometimes she'd answer, pointing wordlessly to a spot or showing me which dial to turn, but she never spared one more word than necessary, and those words she did spare were always accompanied by a stone-cold stare. One of those stares that looked right through me, like I wasn't there at all.

I remember one Sunday morning, not long after I came home. I woke up early and determined that today would be the day I'd get my sister back. I knew Melody's favorite breakfast was almond french toast (at the time—now, of course, she'd never touch it), so I gathered all the ingredients together and set to cooking. It took me a while, but I'd figured out most of the pantry and how the stove worked, so I was feeling very pleased with myself when Melody came plodding down the stairs, rubbing her eyes, and I was just taking the first delicious slice out of the pan.

"Breakfast is served," I announced. She stood in the doorway staring, as usual, and then our dad came up behind her and stared too. I licked my lips and held the plate before me. "It's not poisoned, I swear."

Out of nowhere, Melody let out a laugh. This startled

me more than a hug would have; I hadn't heard her laugh at all since I came home. Not at our dad or the TV. Certainly not at me. "Do you remember," she said, looking back at our dad, "for my sixth birthday, Scarlett woke up at, like, four in the morning and came downstairs to make me breakfast? She came in to get me and I screamed so loud I woke you and Mom up."

A smile twitched at the corners of our dad's lips too. "She was covered in so much flour and sugar you thought she was a ghost."

Neither of them looked at me, and the pain cut me in a flash through my core. "Yeah, I remember that," I said, way too loudly. "That was so funny."

They both hushed midlaugh and exchanged another glance, one I couldn't quite read. "I miss . . . ," Melody started, then stopped.

"What?" I said. My heart was beating fast.

"Nothing," she said, and looked away. Our dad had already turned and was beating it to the living room. "Thanks for breakfast, but I'm not actually hungry. I think I'm going to go back to bed."

I cooked every single piece of french toast and piled them, glistening with syrup and snowy with powdered sugar, on a plate, then tipped them all, one by one, into the garbage can.

That wasn't the last time I tried to win Melody over, but it was the most emotion I ever got out of her. She made it very clear she wanted nothing to do with me. Which is why I'm so confused about why she wants to spend time with me tomorrow night. Voluntarily. Without any ulterior motive I can gather.

I don't figure it out by the end of the workday, and I'm no closer to figuring out a way to confront her without the possibility of her canceling tomorrow. Whatever happens, I don't want that.

On my way home, I stop at my favorite place. I used to call it my thinking spot. Is it entirely wise for me, a teenage girl, to be wandering around alone in the woods when a teenage girl is missing in the area? Probably not. But I can't bring myself to be afraid of the woods. The dark? Sure. Basements? Obviously. Dark, lonely secret passages? Uh-huh. But the woods are wide and open. Nobody can sneak up on me over the carpet of crunchy leaves and pine needles, and there's endless space for me to run. And the air is clean. Every breath purifies me.

Soon after I came home, I spent a lot of time in the woods. I'd ride my bike down the road, get off, and walk for miles, wandering, sometimes hoping, I think, somewhere deep down, that I'd get lost and wander forever. It was the only place I found peace; I certainly didn't have it at home, where my mom was gone and toddler Matthew was always crying and Melody's cold stare followed me around like a pet I didn't want.

During one of my wanderings I found the cabin. It was located way deep in the woods, off any sort of track, and the smells of rot and mildew made it clear that nobody had been inside in years. My best guess was that it had once been located off a hunting trail, maybe twenty years ago, built and maintained by a pair of hunters, and then one of the hunters accidentally shot the other one and then went insane from guilt and spent the rest of his days wandering the woods, cackling madly. Just like me, except for the cackling thing.

I made the cabin my own, cleared out the rot and mildew, fixed the windows, lugged in a few old cushions to sit on, and used it to think. It was easier to think there, to think over what I'd done, than it was anywhere else. I haven't been there in a while, months probably, but I can't imagine anyone else has found it.

I'm right. Well, mostly right—one of the windows is broken, and a squirrel or raccoon seems to have made a nest out of one of my cushions. Still, I sit down and close my eyes and let myself think. Melody. Melody. How to talk to Melody.

An hour later, I've come up with a big fat nothing.

She's not home when I get there anyway; she's out, presumably at a bake sale or helping orphaned children cross the street. I tickle Matthew and make him dinner, rice with broccoli and edamame, which he moans about but then downs when I promise him a cookie for dessert. Okay, two cookies, but only if I get a bite.

Work the next day passes in the most boring way possible. The only Connor I get is a glimpse as I'm leaving for the day and he's coming back from lunch; the grin he gives me from fifty feet away is enough to make me glow inside.

Certainly, my day spent working under Randall, a prematurely balding teenager with a kind smile and a head for sports (if not hair), hadn't done much to put it there.

And so evening rolls around. I shower, perfuming myself with some of Melody's bath oils I pilfer in hopes that unconsciously associating my scent with hers will make her warm to me, and then change clothes a good seven times. Eventually I decide on jeans, a flowered top with a low neck, and some chunky necklaces: an outfit not too nice (so Melody won't think I'm trying too hard) but not too underdone, either (so Melody won't think I'm dressing like a slob in order to intentionally embarrass her).

At seven, I knock on Melody's door. She opens it—actually opens it, doesn't grunt at me or yell that she's busy. I'm enveloped in a cloud of perfume, negating any effects left over from her bath oils. Maybe it's for the best. Come to think of it, Melody probably wouldn't look upon my pilfering all that kindly, no matter the motivation. "What?" she says in her usual monotone.

Maybe I've gotten the date wrong. Maybe I've gotten this all wrong. Maybe Katharina didn't talk to Melody at all. "Nothing," I say, backing away.

"Wait," she says, her voice softening. "Are you still coming out tonight? We're meeting Katharina at nine."

A glow fills me, one not entirely unlike the one infused by Connor's smile. "Of course I'm still coming," I say. "If you want me to."

I immediately regret that, because even if, by some

crazy chance, Melody does want me there, there's no way in all the hells in the world, from the coldest of the cold to the hottest of the hot, that she'd ever admit it to my face.

I'm right. But she doesn't deny it either. She just smiles enigmatically. "You look nice," she says, and closes the door.

Matthew looks up to me with round eyes. "You're going somewhere with Melly?"

"Yes," I say. It's 8:47. I'm waiting by the door. Lurking, really, more than waiting; I'm hovering just out of sight in the kitchen so that I can casually sidle out into the hall when I hear Melody coming downstairs. "Don't look so surprised."

"I can't help it," Matthew says. "It's just so weird."

"It's not so weird," I say. "When we were little, you know, we used to be good friends."

His eyes don't flatten out. "What if she takes you somewhere and kills you?"

"Matthew!" I reprimand him, though I can't deny that the same thought has crossed my mind. "Don't say things like that."

His mouth is open again, probably to defend himself with all the murderous thoughts he thinks he's seen (or, hell, has actually seen) in Melody's eyes, when I hear her feet tapping their way down the stairs. "Be nice to Jerica, okay?" I say. The babysitter is already parked in the living room, TV on. She doesn't bother to fake that she cares, unless my dad is here.

"I'm always nice."

"Dude, last week you put a dead spider in her ice cream."

"She should've let me have some," Matthew says reasonably.

I sigh. I don't have time to argue with him; I'm already moving toward the door. "Fine. But no spiders."

"What about beetles?"

"No beetles."

"What about caterpillars?"

"No caterpillars."

"What about . . ."

The door closes behind me. Godspeed, Jerica.

I can count on my fingers the number of times I've been allowed in the passenger seat of Melody's car; I half expect her to point me to the backseat. But she doesn't. She even unlocks the door for me. I slide in, my butt pressing reverently against the warm leather. I am on hallowed ground; I can practically hear the angels singing *Hallelujah*.

Melody revs the engine, breaking the spell. "Oh yeah," she says. "You have your Five Banners ID, right?"

"In my wallet," I say. "Why?"

She twists her neck to look behind her, bending it into such an awkward angle it looks almost like it's broken. "Because that's where we're going."

"We're going to the park?"

"Yes," she says. "That's what I just said."

A sick feeling spreads through the pit of my stomach, working its way into every nook and cranny and fold of my intestines. This could all be some awful practical joke. Melody and Katharina could be planning to do something humiliating to me in front of the first people I've gotten to know and like in years and years. In front of Connor.

"What are we doing there?" I ask.

"Whatever you do in an amusement park," she says. "You work there. You should know."

A night riding roller coasters and eating greasy food and shoving through crowds of tired moms and sweaty children to go to the bathroom? That doesn't sound like Melody's idea of fun. "Okay," I say. I can always run. I'm not that little girl on the sidewalk anymore.

Not that I think Melody would actually dare to harm me in any (physical) way.

It's just that I never thought I'd join the club, either, and look at me now.

I bet Monica never thought she'd join the club. Nobody ever thinks she'll join the club. I bet Monica was fully confident she would graduate from high school and move on to TCNJ and earn that degree in special education. She'd down fruity mixed drinks from red Solo cups and go, hungover, to her morning classes and fall in love with a frat guy or a kid in her kinetics class or a girl down the hall in her dorm. Eventually she'd pocket enough credits to graduate in four or five or six years, and she'd move on and make kids' lives better.

Melody pulls into the employee entrance and commands me to flash my ID at the gate. "I don't want to pay for parking if I don't have to," she says as we pull into the parking lot, and I let myself relax a little, let the muscles in my shoulders unwind. Maybe it is really that simple: she wanted to get free parking, and that was worth bringing me along for.

Walking beside Melody through the gates, I see the park with new eyes, with what I imagine to be hers. The plastic garlands of superhero cutouts aren't cute, but tacky. All the workers look washed out and pissed off, like they'd rather be doing anything but scooping ice cream or selling hats, which, really, is probably true. The music blaring from the speakers all around clashes with the hawkers at the game stations and the rushing of the roller coasters and the chatter of guests and workers. I'm used to it after working here for the last few weeks, but I suddenly find myself with a headache.

"We're meeting Katharina at the Canteen," Melody says. She's wincing; the headache must be contagious. "Do you know where that is?"

My nose wrinkles in response to both Melody's words and the smell of cotton candy in the air. Ever since I spent that day in Foods and learned that the Foods guys occupied themselves on slow days by peeling dead flies off their stores' flytraps and flicking them into the cotton candy machines, where they vaporized into the stuff, I, for some reason, haven't been able to stomach it. "That's, like, the employee cafeteria," I say. "It's way back behind the scenes. And the food is disgusting. Why does she want to meet there?"

"I don't know," Melody says, but that means nothing. "So you do know where it is?"

"Yeah," I say. My heart skips a beat at the thought of walking through the now-dark, still-twisty secret passage with Melody by my side. We'll take the long way around. "This way."

Melody doesn't move. "Kat said we have to go through a secret-passage kind of thing to get there, but that you wouldn't want to go that way because you're afraid of it," she says. There's no hint of snark or nastiness to her tone. She just speaks like she's stating a fact, and somehow that makes me feel worse.

"I'm not afraid," I say. "I was going to take the secret passage. It's way faster."

She knows I'm lying; I can see the skepticism on her face. To her credit, she doesn't say anything. She just follows as I turn around, pretending I just realized I was walking in the wrong direction, and doesn't say anything when I pause in the secret passage's entrance, feeling for a moment like I'm about to step into the great black maw of some enormous beast. I half hope for Connor to turn up, to lope beside me with his easy smile and tease me about being a Sky-fanatic and offer me the pleasure of his company during my trip through the passage. He would have eyes only for me, of course, and wouldn't so much as look at Melody, even after she cleared her throat two or three times. She would fall for him immediately, of course—who wouldn't?—but he wouldn't turn that dazzling smile on her, wouldn't let her take that freckled elbow, and so for once in her life she'd be jealous of me.

I don't realize I'm smiling until Melody asks me what's so funny. "Nothing," I say, and step into the void.

CHAPTER EIGHT

Connor doesn't find me. He might not even be working tonight, I tell myself. He might be at home, curled up on the couch, watching a movie. With Cady. Naked. She might be solving the maze of his freckles right now.

I want to throw up.

Katharina finds me instead. Right around that merch storage facility where she accosted me before, she appears. And by *appears*, I mean I don't see her approach, or hear her footsteps, or smell the floral scent that clings to her hair. She materializes before us like she's a shadow come to life. "Hey, Melly, Scarlett," she says. "Glad you could make it."

Though it's not at all cold, Melody rubs her arms like

she's pushing down goose bumps. "It's creepy back here," she says.

"It's creepier where we're going," Katharina replies.

"The Canteen isn't really that creepy," I say. I feel wise, giving information Melody doesn't have. "Kind of gross, sure, but not creepy."

"We're not going to the Canteen," Katharina says.

Of course we're not going to the Canteen. I tense, my eyes darting, mentally calculating all the different ways I could run. It would be harder now that there's two of them. I should never have come.

"We're pregaming in one of the storage buildings," Katharina says, like she senses my spike in stress. "Relax, girl." She trills a silvery laugh. It floats above us, sparkling like a bubble, wavering and threatening to burst at any moment. "Come on. This one's my favorite."

Despite my best instincts, I follow. Melody already thinks I'm a coward. I need to prove her wrong, because Melody would never be friends with a coward.

The storage building is dark and dust fills my lungs and I will probably be crushed beneath a tower of boxes before anyone has the chance to hurt me, but then Katharina pulls a string and a light flickers on and I see that the piles of boxes are steady and I blow the dust out of my lungs and I can breathe again.

"There aren't any cameras in these buildings, or at least none that work," Katharina says, her voice echoing from somewhere in the back. She's pushed her way through the boxes and piles of old clothes, opening a narrow, mazelike path to the back of the long room. I'm not sure if I'm supposed to follow her, but I sneak a glance at Melody and she's leaning up against the wall, the thin sheet metal warping behind her, her arms crossed over her chest. Good. If Melody's not following, I don't have to either. I, too, lean up against the wall and cross my arms. Not because that's what Melody's doing. I just feel like crossing my arms.

Katharina continues, "So it's the perfect place to hide out for a while." Her voice grows louder as she moves back toward the front, back toward us. "And it's not like anyone's going to be looking for anything in here." She jerks her head at the box of broken snow globes. "I mean, why?"

"What's that?" I say, declining to answer. She's carrying something behind her back. A gun. A knife. A garrote. But she swoops her arms around front with a flourish to reveal three red Solo cups, liquid sloshing at the top.

"Drink up, ladies," she says, handing Melody and me each a cup. Melody uncrosses her arms to take it. I do too. She doesn't drink. I don't either.

Katharina shows no such hesitation. She tosses her head back and takes a big gulp, two, three, then brings her cup down with a wince and a sigh. "Good stuff," she says. "Well? What are you waiting for?"

"What is it?" Melody asks, peering deep into the cup like there's treasure buried at the bottom.

"A mix," Katharina says. "Everything I could take without getting caught. It's good, though. Strong."

That seems to be all Melody needs. She takes a sip, then grimaces. "Strong is right," she says, then takes another sip. I half expect her to stick her pinky out.

I'm not going to wait for Katharina to interrogate me. I raise the cup before me, as if I'm toasting them, and drink.

I haven't drunk much alcohol in the past. I've had a few glasses of wine at family events, Christmas dinners and graduations and one memorable evening at six years old when the soon-to-be-fired family babysitter passed out and left her half-empty bottle next to her on the floor. I tried a sip of vodka once, just out of curiosity, from my dad's rarely used liquor cabinet. But drinking is something that happens mostly in social settings, and to have social settings you have to have friends. A seventeen-year-old drinking alone is possibly the most depressing thing in the world.

All this to explain that I'm not expecting the trail of fire that flows down my throat, or the smoke my burning flesh pushes out through my nose, or the heat that flares up in the pit of my belly. I choke, but most of that first sip is already down; only a trickle of clear liquid dribbles back into my cup. Everything burns for a moment and then zips shut, like a cauterized wound, and I'm left with a scorched aftertaste and a faint sense of being stunned.

"You don't drink much, do you?" Katharina sounds

faintly amused. "Go slow. Or else go fast and just chug. Either way works."

I need to catch my breath first. "It's good," I say, but even I can hear the woodenness of my words.

"Kat's right," Melody says. She's still sipping away, like there's nothing in her cup but water. "You have to get used to it. You probably shouldn't drink it all either. You have to build a tolerance."

There's no judgment in her voice. That encourages me to take another sip. It still burns going down, but I confine my reaction to a grimace. "I'll be okay," I say. It's true. I'm already feeling okay. Very okay, actually. There's a lightness tingling in my brain I've never felt before, and I somehow don't feel as conscious of Katharina's and Melody's eyes on me as I did earlier. Melody crosses her arms again and leans back against the wall, but I stay standing free, loose, floating.

A few more big sips and I feel like I actually *am* floating. My feet are on the concrete, but my head is hovering several feet above the ground, tethered to my body by ropes of artery and tendon and bone. "So what now?" I ask. I have a feeling it's the alcohol, but I'm suddenly feeling very daring. I want to rush to Connor's side and confess my love.

No. Stop it, alcohol. That's a terrible idea. I lean over and set the cup on the floor and pray that we won't run into Connor tonight, because I'm not sure I can rein my new friend alcohol in. "So what now?" I ask again, more subdued this time.

Katharina downs the last of her cup and checks her phone at the same time. Such multitasking. So multi-talented. "The park closes in about a half hour," she says. "It takes an hour or so to get everybody out and close the park. Then the security sweep." She gestures to my cup, cold and forlorn all by itself on the ground. "Drink up, babe."

It looks so *sad* all by itself. I lean back over and pick it up. "Liar," I tell it. It's not cold and forlorn. It's lukewarm.

"So we're going to be in the park after closing?" Melody says. Again, no emotion in her voice—I can't tell if she's excited or cautious or repelled. "To do what?"

Katharina shrugs. "It's exciting to be here when everybody else is gone." She points at my cup again. "Drink it, or I'm going to dump it on you."

I obediently take another sip. My head spins. "But what are we going to do?" I echo Melody. "Won't all the rides be shut down? All the stores and everything will be shut. And ... and ..." I can't think of the words. "The attractions," I finally force out through numbing lips. "The dolphins will be sleeping."

And then the colors start swirling. The colors take me back to one of my favorite story lines from the Skywoman cartoon.

So many issues and episodes and fan sites have spent hours and hours and hours talking about the similarities between Skywoman and the Blade. They're both women, of course, which sets them apart from most of the denizens of superhero-land. They both inexplicably tend to choose outfits that maximize cleavage and fit tightly around their butts (thanks to their male artists). They're both stubborn, and brash, and fully dedicated to their ideals.

There's one episode where Skywoman and the Blade meet up and talk. In fact, it's the only canon instance where they're together and not fighting in that season. Soon after the murder of Skywoman's first husband at the Blade's hands, Skywoman corners the Blade against the railing atop the roof of a skyscraper. The Blade's arms are pinned to her sides by Skywoman's lasso, and Skywoman's other hand holds the sword granted to her by Wonderman. The sword's tip hovers against the Blade's throat. The Blade's face is blank, as always, but one of the superb animators made her lips tremble every so often; if you aren't looking for it, you might miss it.

The viewer naturally expects Skywoman to try to kill the Blade, and for the Blade to escape just in the nick of time. But Skywoman just stares. "How could you do such a thing to me?" Skywoman asks. "Alex was the love of my life. Your fight wasn't with him. He had nothing to do with this."

The Blade stares back, her eyes cool and hard. "Because he made you happy," she says in her typically monotone fashion. "And as long as you're happy, I can never be happy."

Just as Skywoman was once Augusta Leigh Sorensen, the Blade was once Emma Leigh Jacobs. They shared more things than their middle name. They grew up on the same street, played together as little kids. They went up through the school system together, were both on the cheerleading squad, fought neck and neck for the title of valedictorian before settling into a tie. They were frenemies, the type who would nod sorrowfully as you spilled your darkest secrets and then turn around and spread them to the world.

That last part isn't canon. Every flashback—of which there are few—shows them getting along beautifully; Emma even carried a limping Augusta to the finish line of a race in gym class once. Frenemies is just canon in my head and the fan fiction I may or may not have written at the beginning of high school.

But back to the skyscraper roof. Skywoman—once Augusta—pockets her sword and pulls out a poison dart. "This'll put you out for a while," she says, and tosses it. It sticks in the Blade's—Emma's—throat, where it vibrates from the impact. Skywoman lets her lasso relax as the Blade sags against the railing, her mouth dropping open, a trail of drool sliming her chin. I think the drool was animated for comic effect, but it was always so profound to me—even this great supervillain, the only one to best Skywoman, drools in her sleep.

The cartoon then jumps to the Blade's point of view for thirty seconds or so, showing what's going on in her drugged-up head. Blackness, mostly. Swirls of color. Voices murmuring in the background: first Skywoman, telling her that she'd wait to kill her, that it would be more satisfying (plotwise, I can only assume) to kill her later, when she had more to lose; then Augusta, cheering her on during her first back handspring and comforting her after a failed chemistry test and telling her that the scar on her forehead wasn't so bad, really, it was kind of dashing.

And then more blackness, and more swirls of color, and the camera moves back to reveal a single tear sliding its way down the Blade's stony cheek.

Unlike the Blade, I don't cry the moment I realize what's happening to me; I think the single-tear thing is a myth, anyway. But colors swirl around me in gauzy ribbons, and I sink to the floor, and the blackness envelops me. It all happens too quickly for me to feel anything but shock. The last thing I hear—or that I think I hear—is the whispering of the wolves hovering above me, deciding who will get to devour the thighs, who will feast upon the succulent throat, who wins the head. They won't eat the head; there's not enough meat. The head is for the wall, a trophy.

I wake embedded inside a piece of popcorn. White, soft haze fills my vision, but I'm lying against something hard and cold. Everything smells like butter, and my skin is coated with a thin slick of oil.

I move an arm. It flops a bit against the cobblestones, a dying fish.

That's when I realize I'm on the ground.

Cobblestones. Cobblestones are from, like, the 1800s. I did not travel back in time.

Besides, they didn't have popcorn in the 1800s. At least not movie theater popcorn, the kind I smell around me, the kind drenched in rivers of butter that tastes like chemicals and salt.

I wince and try to lift my cheek from where it lies pressed against the stone. I can tell before it rips away that there are now grooves in my skin that might never smooth out. "Hello?" I say, or try to say. My throat is dry and raspy. A chilly wind tries to cut off my hair.

Cobblestones. Popcorn. I'm in the park, on the main street, on the ground.

My cheek falls back against the stone. Lifting my head is too much work. "Hello?" I try to say again, but this time the stone snatches my voice and doesn't give it back.

I fall.

Somewhere behind me, so faintly I might be imagining it, someone is laughing.

"Hello?"

I blink and cough. That didn't sound like my voice.

"Hello?"

Ah. I'm not the one speaking. I'm sitting up now, somehow, though I don't remember doing it, and someone is speaking to me. Someone who ate an entire head of garlic for breakfast, it smells like. "Hello," I say back, wrinkling my nose.

My wrist drops.

Apparently, someone was holding my wrist.

"She lives," Garlic Breath says. "You okay, kid? Do you need an ambulance?"

Light cracks around my eyelids. I open them and let it in.

I'm in the park still, but not on the main drag. Above me rise the electric-red loops of the Dragon King, the tallest, fastest roller coaster in the world. Cars rush around the tracks, but there aren't any shrieks or screams or idiots who didn't lock their safety belts tumbling from the sky and smashing on the ground. Warm-up loops, then.

I'm not cold, but I shiver. "How did I get here?"

"You tell me." Garlic Breath stands, bathing me in a neon-green glow. He's just a regular peon, like me, I realize, nobody important. Surrounding me are a few other green shirts. "Guys, we should call a supervisor."

A pit yawns in my stomach. "Don't call a supervisor," I say. I don't remember how I got here, or what's going on exactly, but I know I don't want a supervisor involved. I'll get in trouble once they check the security tapes to see precisely how I ended up here and discover I've been here overnight. I'd lose my job for sure. Maybe even get arrested for trespassing.

As Melody would say, that's not good for my college applications.

Melody. The pit yawns wider, aching, like it's the pit where a missing tooth should be. "Where's Melody?" She was here last night. She caught me when I fell under the bleachers. She wouldn't leave me now.

"What's going on here?"

The pit turns into a stone and falls. The questioner wears the casual suit and tie of a supervisor. (Not having to wear the green polo is kind of a big deal around here.) "Do you work here?" the supervisor demands. I can't stop staring at the light gleaming off his bald head, at the shadows that sweep it every time the Dragon King rushes overhead. "Do I smell alcohol?"

"Scott, hey." I breathe in the smell of sweet hay and Axe and sweat and smoke. Connor. "You found Scarlett. Scarlett, you okay? You must have fallen. Here, let me help you up." His hand finds mine and pulls, so hard I feel my shoulder strain in its socket. He probably expected me to help him a bit, but now that I'm standing, it's all I can do not to fall back down. I sway like a scarecrow, nodding at the calm understanding that any strong breeze or loud noise might send me tumbling into a pile of rags and hay.

"What happened to your uniform? Did you leave it at the office before you could change?" He exhales loudly and claps me on the shoulder, enveloping me neatly with one arm before I can fall. "Crazy girl. So dedicated to her job, this one. Well, come on, Scarlett, let's find your uniform before the park opens so we can get you on register." He steers me away. From the corner of my eye, I can see Scott's brow creased in suspicion, but it relaxes as he, like everybody else, falls under the spell of Connor.

"Nice to meet you, Scarlett," he says. There's a heavy sort of skepticism to his tone that says he believes nothing Connor just said, but there's something about the way Connor says things and the way his face glows when he smiles that makes people trust in him. Like I said: the spell of Connor.

Once we're a safe distance away, far enough that the roar of the Dragon King has faded into the roar of the wind, Connor drops his arm. I sway, but I stay standing. "Okay, so you better tell me what you were doing there," he says. His voice is warm, as usual, but measured. "Because I know you're not scheduled to work today."

"What, do you have my schedule memorized?" I feel like I might throw up on his shoes. I know I can turn, but whatever direction I go, it's going to be his shoes.

"Don't change the subject." He lowers his voice. "Were you in the park overnight? Katharina said something about that, but I didn't think—"

"Katharina?" The world around me crystallizes, sharpens, and the feeling like I'm going to throw up disappears. I see everything through a sheen of blue. "What did she say?"

"That she and a few others were going to party after hours in the park. We didn't think she was serious. It's a crazy idea. But were you . . . ?"

Anger shoots through me. Party? That was no party. She poisoned me, sure as Skywoman poisoned the Blade.

But I can see the worry on Connor's face, even through all the blue and the bright. He's worried. About *me*.

Worry means that he cares, but I can't have him worrying too much, especially after the heart-to-heart we shared. Worrying means that he'll want to get close. Worrying means that he'll want to know what's going on. He'll want to know my secrets, and nobody can get that close. "I have to go," I say, and turn to shuffle away. My mind is racing. I feel terrible and furious and like I want to push someone off the top of the Dragon King, but at the same time, I want to cry. Because Connor cares. About *me*.

"Wait, Scarlett!" Connor calls after me. I pause, but I don't turn around. I don't know what my face looks like at the moment. It's possible I've transformed into a black swirling vortex of emotion. "Are you okay?"

A hysterical laugh bubbles up in my throat. *Okay*. Who even knows what that is anymore? "Yeah," I say. I hear him approaching and lurch forward before he can place a comforting hand on my shoulder. A comforting hand from him might break me. "I just need to be alone right now. Please."

I hear him hesitate, then back away. "Okay," he says. "But are you still coming tonight?"

"Tonight?" I can't think. Black swirling vortexes of emotion don't have brains.

"The bonfire," he says. "You know? At my place."

The bonfire. Of course, the bonfire. "Of course, the bonfire," I echo. "Of course I'll be there. Wouldn't miss it for the world."

I can hear the smile in his voice. "Awesome," he says. "See you there."

I slept soundly in Candy's bed that night, and then, when I woke up, I got to have a real shower and eat breakfast in the kitchen with two of the other girls. We had sugary cereal, that kind that crunches with sweetness. I hadn't had anything like it in months. It made my teeth hurt.

Of course, I still had to clean. Stepmother brought Pixie up and left her there with me in the room, closing the door behind her with a mild "Behave," almost as if she hoped we'd fight it out.

We didn't. Pixie wouldn't even look at me; she focused on her cleaning, her eyes following the movement of her rag as if it were the most fascinating thing in the world. I watched her clean as if she were the most fascinating thing in the world, which she was. "Are you mad at me?" I asked after years of silence.

Scrub, scrub. Scrub, scrub. She didn't reply.

"Because she didn't really give me a choice. I had to tell her. I was in a really bad position."

Scrub, scrub. Scrub, scrub.

"You were doing something that might have gotten us hurt. And you didn't even tell me about it. It was like the time I caught Melody trying to light a fire in her room to toast a marshmallow. Even though she got in trouble, I had to tell, because she could've burned our house down."

Pixie peeked up, then back down. Was it the story of my family? Maybe with all her foster-family issues, she liked hearing stories about my family. Well, I could do that. "My family was really happy, at least until they left me and didn't want me anymore," I said. It was getting easier to accept, but it still stabbed me in the stomach and left me breathless. Pixie must have seen the pain; her eyebrows made wrinkles on her forehead. "I had a mom and a dad and a little sister. We lived in Merry Park, outside Chicago. My sister is eight now. Her name is Melody."

Pixie peeked up again. "I always wanted a mom."

My mom? I could talk about my mom. "She's pretty," I said dutifully. "She has short black hair and is part Cuban and part Italian and has very white teeth. She buys too many clothes and too many shoes, my dad says, but she says she doesn't like to wear the same thing more than once so he just has to suck it up, even though he's the one working and making the money, he says. Sometimes she cries a lot."

"But she has a family," Pixie said. "Why does she cry?"

I shrugged, my insides singing. Pixie was speaking to me. She was forgiving me. "I don't know," I said. "I've asked her before, but she said I wouldn't understand." I paused. "She sleeps a lot too."

"I would sleep a lot too, if I could," Pixie said. I wondered what she meant. Maybe she'd had to keep watch over her rabbits. "Tell me more about your family."

I told her more: I cherry-picked our happiest family memories, our vacations, our various deceased pets, the time we visited my dad's cousins in Mexico and got sick from the water, the time I decided Melody needed a haircut and chopped off one of her braids. That anecdote even made Pixie laugh. Lifted by her laughter, I told her about the time my dad tried to make us his mother's tostadas and set the kitchen on fire, about the time my mom passed out in the middle of the grocery store and I got to ride in an ambulance with its sirens wailing, about the time I tried to pierce Melody's ears with paper clips. "Poor Melly," I said fondly, and then realized that, compared with us, Melody was unquestionably the lucky one.

I told Pixie about the time Melody and I jumped off our roof after eating chicken wings, convinced we could fly (unaware that chickens were terrible fliers). I told Pixie about how, whenever I got sick, my mother would wipe my forehead with a cool, damp cloth and bring me toast and flat ginger ale. I told Pixie about the canopy bed I loved with the fire of a thousand suns, and the plastic glowing stick-on stars I'd plastered all over my ceiling, and the new pink sneakers I'd just gotten for gym class.

She was perking up a bit. I had to bring it home. "Wanna see my scar?" I asked.

Her eyes brightened. Good. "Scars are so cool."

I leaned over and lifted my shirt above my belly button. "I had to get my appendix taken out," I said. I watched her eyes trace my scar, a thick, wormy ridge that stretched across my right hip. It bowed up and out, like a pair of smiling lips. "I didn't clean it good enough. My mom was supposed to help me, but she didn't, so the cut got infected. It was so gross."

Pixie's eyes were bright, still, and round. "Can I touch it?"

I nodded, and she leaned over and traced it, up and down, up and down. "It's like a smile," she said. "On your belly." And she smiled herself.

"I'm really sorry that I had to tell on you," I said.

"Tell me more about your sister," she said.

It was only later that I realized she didn't accept my apology.

CHAPTER NINE

I'm out in the employee parking lot before I realize I have no way to get home. Melody drove me here, and, clearly, Melody isn't here anymore. I survey the lot just to be sure, but her car is gone. She left me.

She *left* me. Again.

I feel bad, but I feel worse that I'm actually surprised.

My phone chooses this moment to buzz against my hip. I pull it out to see the indicator light blinking, and swipe across the screen to see that I have eight new voice mails and fourteen new texts. I scroll through. *Melody. Melody. Melody.* I read a few: *Where are you? S this isnt funny come back. S we are getting worried come back.* I listen to a voice mail, the most recent one, in which Melody babbles that I need to come back or they're going to have to call the cops and we're all going to get in major trouble so please just come back.

I wonder where I went.

It's still buzzing, *Melody* flashing on the screen, so I pick up. "Morning," I say, and Melody unleashes a gust of wind in my ear.

"Oh my God, Scarlett, you're alive," she says. "Where *were* you? Where are you now?"

"What are you talking about?" I say. The bad feelings are still simmering inside my stomach, bubbles of bad traveling up my throat and popping in my mouth. "You left me here."

Another gust of wind. "You were so drunk," she says. "You probably don't remember."

I'm about to tell her everything I do remember, the drinking in the storage room and the passing out and the swirls of colors like in Skywoman and waking up in the park, but I stop myself. I want to hear what she has to say first, in case she's going to lie. "What?"

"I shouldn't have let you drink so much," Melody says. "Kat just kept egging you on. I feel bad."

"What happened?"

She is a sack of sighs. "The stuff Kat had was super, super strong," Melody says. "Like, ridiculous strong. I have a pretty good tolerance, and even I was feeling it after half a cup. You have no tolerance. You had no chance."

No. I was drugged. I had to have been drugged. It felt

just like it looked in the cartoon. "I drank too much and passed out?"

"You downed, like, that whole cup," Melody says. "And you were already out of it, but you had some more. Finally we went out into the park, and you fell over on the cobblestones and blacked out for a little. I thought I was going to have to call the cops and we were all going to get in so much trouble and I was going to get arrested, and that wouldn't have—"

"I know, your college applications," I say impatiently. The pit in my stomach is back. "What happened then?"

"We were trying to lift you to carry you out, but you popped up on your own," Melody says. "And took off. We tried to chase you, but we lost you. Seriously, Scarlett, we looked for you all freaking night. I'm so tired right now and I have to go to practice."

It sounds plausible. So plausible it might be true. "But I don't remember drinking that much," I say. "Why didn't you call someone? I could've been dead somewhere."

Melody hesitates, and in that hesitation I can hear *college applications*. "Never mind," I go on. I don't want to hear whatever lie she's formulating. "What about Katharina?"

"We ran around looking for you together," she says. "Eventually we had to get out because the park was going to open. Where were you?"

"It doesn't matter," I say. "Can you come get me?"

"I have to go to practice. Can't you walk?"

"Are you kidding me?"

She's silent for a moment, then blows a long breath into my ear. This one isn't a sigh. "Fine," she says. "I'll be there in a few minutes. Be ready to go." She hangs up without saying goodbye.

My mind swirls the whole ride home, which is fortunate, as Melody doesn't speak to me and I need something to do besides look out the window at the nauseatingly fast-moving trees and mailboxes flashing by. Why was I so convinced I'd been drugged? Was I really that eager to think the worst about my sister, about Katharina?

I don't know what I think about Katharina.

Melody drops me off and I crawl straight into sheets that smell too much like me and sleep.

I don't dream.

I wake up a few hours later feeling at least somewhat refreshed, and set about planning for the bonfire. Yes, I'm still going. I need something, anything, to distract myself from everything else going on right now.

I pick out my clothes (long white maxidress, about as far as I can get from the Five Banners uniform, and it covers my right hip and the scars on my back, which is the most important thing) and take a shower, then settle in to wait for dusk. I cocoon myself on the couch and grab a book from my childhood and turn on Food Network in the background and plug my ears with my iPod. Basically, I do all I can to keep myself from thinking, and Matthew and my dad are kind enough to let me. My dad takes Matthew to a friend's house and then shuts himself in his office to work or whatever.

Finally evening rolls around, and I unplug my ears and toss the book onto the table and flip off the TV to find I'm still in the same world as I was this morning. I shoulder the disappointment well and go off to change. I select cute sandals and even put on makeup, a shimmery layer of lip gloss and a swoop of eyeliner, though I know chances are good I'll sweat it off later.

The drive to Connor's takes me down a series of increasingly dark and winding roads that reach deep into the woods, then open up into a wash of pastoral farms. I pass fields of what I think is corn, of hay swaying in the breeze and waiting to be baled (whatever that means), fields ambling with horses. Fences are nothing more than markers of wood. Houses are squat and cheerful and all have chimneys, and bright red barns dot the landscape. I would quite like to live here, I think. Maybe I can convince my dad to move and take up farming. Maybe baling hay would make Melody's college applications glow.

Connor's house fits right in. I pull into a winding dirt driveway and park my car at the end of a long row; I'm evidently not the first one here. There's still a ways to walk to get to the top of the driveway. When I get out of my car, I'm greeted by the sound of faraway laughter and the crisp, summery smell of burning leaves and what might be the whinny of a horse.

Connor's house, a small brown ranch, sits dark and

alone in the middle of an expanse of fields that ends in woods several hundred feet away. Near the edge is what I'm guessing is a barn, though it's rough and unpainted and doesn't fit in with its cheery red compatriots. The ground is scoured down to the dirt and scattered with bits of hay, though one part of the fields is lush and green—that must be the pasture for the horses. Everybody is gathered near the woods, where they're silhouetted black against the glow of the bonfire; words and laughter float above the crackling of the blaze, and movements are hazy, spooky, through the billowing smoke.

"Hey, Scarlett," a familiar voice calls. Cynthia.

Hay bales are scattered about for seating; on one bale sit Cynthia and a few other girls I vaguely recognize from the park, all clutching red Solo cups that glisten with condensation. Cynthia grins at me. "Glad you could make it," she says, and lets out a laugh that sounds very much like a cackle. "Connor will be glad to see you."

I blame the heat that climbs my throat and cheeks on the nearby fire. "Hey, Cynthia. How are you?"

"Go get a drink." Cynthia points behind her, nearly toppling off the bale of hay with the effort; she cackles again as her friends lift her back up. "Don't drink too much, though," she shouts, and her friends laugh. "It's bad for you!"

You don't need to tell me twice. Yet somehow I find myself wanting a drink anyway. Tonight can be a test—I can see if the colors come back to visit.

There are a lot of people here, but somehow, maybe because we're outside, it doesn't feel claustrophobic. I weave my way through the crowd, saying hello to people who may or may not be fellow Five Banners peons. It's hard to tell without the shirts, and near impossible to remember any names without the name tags.

Several kids are clustered around a fold-up table loaded down with drinks and stacks of red cups. They part as I approach, revealing a kid I don't recognize, shaking and stirring and pouring. The "bartender" looks up and grins, and I realize it's Rob.

Though I've seen his gauges and tattoos before, somehow it's hard to reconcile uniformed Rob with the Rob in front of me now. This Rob, while still short and thick and hobbitlike, is decked out in black from head to toe, with silver spikes jutting out from unexpected places, like his left shoulder. Piercings glitter in his eyebrow and his lip, and the gauges stretch out his ears, so large I can see two nickel-size slices of the woods through them. Gel slicks his hair to his head, and the tattoos crawling over his shoulders, leering faces and skulls and flowers and initials in Gothic font, are in full, glaring display. I haven't had anything to drink yet, but I already feel a little dizzy. "Evening, Scarlett," he says. "What's your poison of choice?"

"Um." I survey the options. The table is loaded with a staggering array of drinks; if this is Connor's parents' raided liquor cabinet, he must come from a family of alcoholics. "Just make me something sweet. Please."

He tips an imaginary hat. "Sweet it is." He shakes and stirs and pours from a glittering glass bottle, topping it off with something purple and syrupy. He presents it to me with a flourish, like he's handing over a crystal goblet rather than a plastic cup. "It's pomegranate."

I smell it, and it smells enough like juice that it doesn't make my stomach lurch. "Thanks."

"Enjoy." He turns to the next person, a girl I've worked with a few times at headquarters. "Denise. You look like you're in the mood for tequila."

I don't hear Denise's reply; I've already melted back into the crowd. The taste of pomegranate and sugar makes my back teeth tingle, and warmth floods my belly. I need to get close to the fire, I decide. I take another sip of my drink, and it's like the fire is inside me. No colors though, I note.

Somebody claps me on the shoulder. "Scarlett!" It's Cady. Her cheeks and forehead are shiny with sweat; streaks of mascara decorate her cheeks like war paint. "Scarlett, I'm so, so happy to see you."

Her words are slurred. I try to wiggle away, but she drapes an arm, slick and damp and fuzzy as sealskin, around me and pulls me in close. Her breath stinks of beer. "It's so, so, so good to see you. I'm so happy you came. You're a good friend."

"Um, okay." I wiggle again, trying to extricate myself, but her grip is a vise. I take a gulp from my cup. If I were drunk, this wouldn't be nearly as painful. At least, I hope not. Only one way to know for sure!

"Monica was a good friend too," Cady says. I recoil from her breath; it smells the way being hit feels. "But I think Monica is probably dead. I want you to be my friend now, okay?"

"Okay," I say. "Maybe you should sit down."

She laughs and leans in closer. Her forehead rubs against mine. "Let's sit down," she says. "Let's sit down on the hay. There's so much hay everywhere. I hate hay. There's so much hay."

"Okay." I duck under her arm and spin away before she can latch on again, all without spilling even a drop of my drink. Then I sigh. The fire shines before me like a beacon, but I can't leave Cady here, crying by herself. "Come on." I move back into her orbit and let her grab my arm again. She leaves enough space for me to snag the drink from her hand and inconspicuously spill it into the nearest bale of hay; some splashes onto Cady's shorts, but she doesn't seem to notice. "Let's go sit."

By some miracle, we manage to push our way through the crowd and find an empty bale without Cady accosting anyone else or falling over. I sit her down and look around. I'm certainly not going to shove her and Connor together more than necessary, but I don't know who else she's friends with. "Do you have any good friends here?" I ask.

Her eyes fill with tears and overflow. "Monica was my good friend." The tears make rivers down her cheeks. "And Connor was my boyfriend, but he dumped me. He doesn't love me anymore. Scarlett, why doesn't he love me?

I still love *him*." She shakes her head, and when she speaks again, her voice is low and determined. "It's just a break, right? We're still best friends. He'll come around. That's what M-Monica would say. We'll get back together."

And I'm certainly not getting into *that* with her. "Okay, okay." It's either sit here with her myself and listen to her talk about Connor or find someone to take care of her. Cynthia, maybe? Except Cynthia didn't look much more sober than Cady does. I sit down with a sigh that echoes the rush of the hay settling beneath me. "Let's just sit and take deep breaths."

Cady sniffles. "I miss Monica," she says. "I met her on my first day at Adventure World. We worked in headquarters together. Nobody had taught us how to use the cash register, but we didn't tell them, and somehow everything came out right at the end of the day." She lets out a laugh that sounds more like a sob. It might be a sob. "We called ourselves the Register Mafia."

"I'm sorry."

"We got promoted on the same day. She didn't have a boyfriend, but she would come hang out with me and C-Connor anyway. She called herself the third wheel, and I always told her, 'You're never a third wheel. Connor is the third wheel.' And she would laugh, but Connor wouldn't laugh. He didn't think it was funny." She rests her head on my shoulder. My arm twitches as her tears soak into my dress. "I miss Monica. I miss my boyfriend."

"I know. You already said that." There's a tender spot,

somewhere deep inside me under all the caked-on annoyance and frustration, that twinges when her tears touch my skin.

"Cade?" Someone pulls Cady off my shoulder. It's warm outside, verging on sticky hot, but the air feels chill where she was. "What's going on? Is she okay?"

I turn. I recognize the speaker vaguely as a girl from Adventure World, but her name escapes me without the aid of her name tag. Mina, maybe, or Nina. Tina? Yeah, Tina. "I think she just had too much to drink," I say. "She'll live."

Tina heaves a sigh. "Oh, Cade," she says. "What to do with you." She looks over at me. "Thanks for taking care of her. I got it now."

She doesn't need to tell me twice. The sweat and tears are beginning to dry on my skin. "Okay," I say, but hesitate. "I hope you feel better, Cady."

Cady's face is already buried in Tina's shoulder. I'm clearly not needed anymore, but I still can't help hesitating again before plunging back into the crowd.

By now my drink is lukewarm, and the buzz in my head is amplified by the buzz of the crowd. I wave hello to a few people I may or may not know, neatly duck under outstretched arms and around groups of girls taking selfies, and set my eyes on an empty bale of hay on the other side of the fire. It's not as crowded over there, perhaps because of the area's proximity to the dark woods. But here people would hear me if I screamed. I fight my way through and collapse onto the empty bale with a huff; there's finally space for me to breathe.

The fire crackles so loudly, spitting sparks like fireflies into the air, that I can hardly hear the other people whooping and laughing and talking. I stare deep into the flames, looking for the molten blue center. I can't see it, but I know it has to be there. This fire can't be missing a center.

A log crashes into the fire, spitting up more sparks and making me gasp a lungful of smoke. I'm so busy coughing I barely notice when somebody crunches onto the hay bale next to me. The smoke irritates my eyes, but I don't want to rub them and smear the makeup that I so painstakingly applied. By the time I'm done blinking the smoke away, my chin tilted up at the stars so that tears won't overflow and smear that stupid eyeliner, Connor's already been there for a few minutes, so close I could fall over and land in his lap.

"Hello to you too," I say.

"I was wondering how long it would take you to notice me," he says. His smile is crooked, like one of his front teeth, and the sheen of sweat on his face makes his freckles look like glitter. "What are you thinking?"

"That your freckles look like glitter," I say without thinking, and glare down at my drink. Stupid alcohol. "I can't believe I just said that. This is so embarrassing." And I can't believe I just said *that*. They should really raise the drinking age. To, like, eighty. Not that that would've stopped us tonight.

"They're not freckles," Connor says seriously, but his eyes are dancing, or maybe that's just the reflection of the flames. "They're angel kisses."

"Angel kisses?" As if of their own accord, my fingers drift over and trace the constellations of pigment on his right cheek. I feel his breath catch in his throat. "You're telling me this many angels were willing to put their lips on your face?" I say to lighten the mood.

"That's what my mom says." He doesn't move. He doesn't breathe. I realize I'm not breathing either.

My shoulder, where Cady rested earlier, suddenly begins to itch like it's caught fire. I jerk my hand away and draw in a great gulp of air. "Did you see Cady?" I say, swinging back toward the fire. Through the flames and the billowing clouds of smoke, the other partygoers are nothing more than shadows. "She had too much to drink and she was crying. She thinks you're going to get back together."

"We're not getting back together. I told you, it's over." Still, he looks around for her; when his eyes land on her and Tina, he says, "And Tina's taking care of her, anyway. She doesn't need me. She's fine." He shifts closer; his drink sloshes over the rim of his cup, and a few drops splatter my bare foot. My muscles clench, but I don't move. "Are you fine?"

"So fine." I'm suddenly very aware of all the ways my body is working to keep me fine: the thud of my heart, the rush of blood through arteries and veins, the sloshing of acid in my stomach and intestines. "So where are the famous horses? I was promised horses."

"I don't remember promising you horses."

I raise an eyebrow. "I promised myself horses."

He raises an eyebrow right back. "I can show you the horses. If you want?"

His words trail off into the smoke. I know what he's saying. If I go with him to see the horses, there's no coming back.

Cady. Cady. Cady. I try to drum up my mental image. *Cady is there crying her heart out over this guy.* It should be easy, considering she was just crying on my shoulder. *This is wrong. Cady will hate you, and so will everyone else. Think of Cady.*

But Cady is far away, and the pleasant buzz of the fire in my brain is blocking all pictures other than the one of Connor sitting a few inches away. Heat floods me, heat that is decidedly not from the bonfire. "I would very much like to see the horses," I say, lowering my voice, hoping it sounds sexy.

His face doesn't change. "Really?"

"Yes," I say. I don't think about it. I don't need to think. "Let's go. Right now."

We go.

This is the fourth choice. And it's the choices we make that make us who we are. By making this choice, I know I'm removing the possibility that Cady and Connor will stumble back into a relationship. I'm not a girl who could be a bridesmaid at their potential future wedding. I am the girl who pulls Connor into the barn in hopes that any thought of that potential future wedding will poof into a cloud of smoke.

The barn is at the far end of the field, far away from the crowd of people. Connor and I race to the barn at the edge of the woods, tossing off laughs as we run, using the darkness as cover.

We burst into the barn gasping, still laughing, and Connor shuts the door behind us. Panic swells for a moment in the dark, but my eyes soon adjust, thanks to the stripes of light filtering through the uneven boards of the wall; there's also a dim glow coming from the other end, where the snorts and creaks signify the presence of the horses. I inhale deeply and smell the sweetness of the hay and the warmth of the horses and the smoke clinging to Connor's shirt. "The horses are over there," Connor says. "Ernesto and Bessie." He points, but his eyes don't move from my face. He's staring unabashedly, as if memorizing my eyes, my nose, my lips. I flex my fingers. Somewhere on the run I lost my drink.

"I don't care about the horses," I say, and somehow he's got me in his arms, and somehow we're up against the wall, nails digging into my back and probably giving me tetanus. He gazes into my eyes, hesitating, so I swoop in, and then my mouth is on his and it's hot and tastes like sugar. A little noise, almost like a growl, escapes his throat and reverberates through all my bones. I press myself against him and feel him shudder. A breeze dances over my skin, standing all my little hairs on end.

He draws back for a moment, and I resist, pressing my face into his throat. His pulse throbs like there's a moth fluttering under his skin. I kiss it, gently, to feel it flutter against my lips.

"You're so beautiful," he whispers, his voice rough.

"Well, duh," I say, putting on my best imitation of Connor's braggadocio, and we can't help but laugh. One of his hands rests on my hip, pressing me into the wall; the other traces the line of my jaw, drawing a trail of fire so intense I have to close my eyes or I'll burst into flame.

"You really are," Connor says, and he kisses me again. This time his tongue eases its way into my mouth and touches all the little hidden crevices where food sometimes gets stuck. Fortunately, I flossed before I came. I've never felt so thankful for the dentist who terrified me into daily flossing with his slides of decaying gums.

No, Scarlett. Don't think of decaying gums now. There is a time and a place for decaying gums, and this time and place is so far from that place it might as well be on Jupiter. "You are too," I murmur, and lick at his lips just as he pulls away. He laughs as he catches me with the tip of my tongue poking through.

"Sometimes the barn cat does that," he says. "She'll be licking herself and get distracted in the middle and just walk around with her tongue sticking out."

I jab him in the ribs—on the side, obviously, because

we're still pressed together so tightly there isn't space for so much as a nudge. His belt buckle is carving a permanent mark in my belly. "Are you calling me a barn cat?"

"Hey," Connor says. "It's about the cutest thing in the world."

I breathe out through my nose, then tilt my head back for another kiss. When Connor doesn't bite—literally or figuratively—I bury my face back in his neck and nibble, feeling almost like a vampire. He sighs, and I pull back. "I shouldn't be doing this right now," he says. "It would break Cady's heart all over again."

My heart, previously so light, fills with dread and drops to my feet with a thunk. "She's not your girlfriend anymore. Not your responsibility."

The dim glow from the horses' corner illuminates flyaway strands of his hair, turning them into molten copper. It flows into the darkness as he shakes his head. "That's not true, though," he says. "I still care about her a lot. She's still one of my best friends. I don't want to hurt her any more than she's already hurting."

His words are making my stomach hurt, but my not-so-sober state makes it easy enough to ignore them, and it. I stand on my tiptoes and press against him, and he leans back down, and I drink him in, his smell and his taste and his heat.

It's somewhere in the middle of our sixth kiss, his hand beginning to trace circles of gold and glitter over my waist, when we realize something is different. I put it down to a shift in brain chemistry, or the amount of smoke and vodka I've inhaled. But it gets to the point where I can't deny it anymore; the horses are stomping and snorting, and the wave of chatter outside has reached a fever pitch, and someone is screaming.

I pull away. "Do you hear that?"

He purses his lips, which have swelled and turned red with the force of my own. "What's going on out there?"

There's definitely screaming now, and crying. Someone is shrieking loud enough for us to hear it clear across the field and through the wooden walls of the barn.

He eases back reluctantly. His hands don't slip from my waist. "We should see what's going—"

The door slams against the wall. Connor leaps back like my skin's turned into a hot stove, and I gasp a mouthful of hay pollen. Somewhere in the middle of all the coughing and choking, I realize the small, squat figure standing silhouetted in the doorway is Rob. He spares a cursory look at me, one that fills my belly with shame because I know I've done wrong by Cady and now he knows too, but he focuses on Connor and his words melt everything else away.

"It's Monica," he says. "They found her."

Outside someone wails, a high, desolate sound that tears apart the sky.

CHAPTER TEN

After my night in Candy's bedroom, I expected everything to go back to normal: I'd clean everything up, eat a quick lunch under Stepmother's watchful eye, help the girls at night, eat a quick dinner under Stepmother's watchful eye, and then get shooed into the basement to curl around Pixie and fall into an exhausted sleep.

That's not what happened. I cleaned everything up. Ate a quick lunch under Stepmother's watchful eye. Helped the girls at night. But when Pixie and I were excused to the kitchen to shovel down our usual tuna fish sandwiches, Stepmother was waiting. "I would like to thank you again for your loyalty, Jane," she said. "You were such a good girl, you deserve a nice dinner."

I glanced over at Pixie, who was determinedly staring at the floor. Maybe she was looking for an escape tunnel. I'd just regained her goodwill. If I lost it again so quickly, I might have a much harder time getting it back. "I love tuna fish, ma'am," I said earnestly. "It's exactly what I'm in the mood for."

Stepmother laid a hand on my hair. My head bowed forward under its weight, and my hair prickled. I had to fight the urge to shake it off. She'd never touched me like this before, and she didn't move her hand now, just let it sit. "I want you to have a roast beef sandwich. I won't take no for an answer, Jane."

From the corner of my eye I could see Pixie's lips thin. Roast beef was one of Pixie's favorite foods. "It's really okay, ma'am."

"Nonsense," Stepmother said, and she removed her hand. I suddenly felt so light I might float away. "I've already made it. Eat it."

I glanced again at Pixie. She was looking at me, but as soon as my eyes met hers, she looked down at the floor. "Okay," I said helplessly.

Stepmother sat us down at the table and placed our food in front of us. Pixie's was the usual: chunky tuna fish on white bread, cut in half. On my plate was what looked like half a crusty baguette, stuffed full to bursting with roast beef and pickles and dripping with sauce. There was even a mountain of chips on the side. Despite myself, my mouth watered.

If I'd had the choice, I would have shared half of it with Pixie. But I didn't have the choice.

Stepmother sat there the whole time, watching me. So I ate the sandwich with my eyes on my plate. It was the most delicious sandwich I'd ever eaten.

That night, Stepmother sent me down into the basement, the feeling of her hand still imprinted in my hair. I knew this wasn't it, though. More nights in beds and more roast beef sandwiches waited for me if I ratted Pixie out again.

I could tell Pixie was upset; she crawled to our mattress and curled up, facing the wall. I followed and sat down beside her. "My scar hurts," I said.

She didn't say anything, but she reached her hand backward in what looked like an incredibly uncomfortable position. I took it and squeezed. "Tell me about your school," she said. "I bet you had a nice school."

I'd never thought of my school as nice, but now I couldn't think of any place nicer in all the world. "I wonder what happened to my desk," I said. "If they just left it open waiting for me, or if someone else is sitting there now. And all my stuff. I wonder what they did with all my stuff."

"Tell me about your school," Pixie said. "Tell me about your friends."

I told her about my school. I told her about my friends. I told her about my old life until my voice literally stopped working and I sagged against her shoulder with sleep. She patted my head, stroking, really, like I was some kind of pet, or a wild animal she was trying to tame.

• • •

In the dizzying moments after Rob leads Connor and me
from the barn and into the fray of screams and cries around
the bonfire, I think that "They found her" means "They
found Monica, here, at the party." Maybe while Connor and
I were kissing, Monica was so incensed by this betrayal of
her best friend that she willed herself away from wherever
she was and burst from the fire, showering the partygoers
with sparks and starting a hundred little fires in the fields,
and tore around the party shrieking like a devil before col-
lapsing into a heap of ash.

But no—as I learn on our walk, Monica hasn't been
found here (obviously). Her body has been found several
miles away, half buried under a drift of leaves, somewhere
deep in the woods, by police who showed up at the area in
pursuit of a drug bust.

Rob doesn't tell me, of course. He tells Connor, their
heads leaning close together, as I trail behind, no longer
a part of the group. It's probably better this way, I think,
or I try to think. This way, nobody will see us walking
together. Nobody will know what happened in the barn.
This isn't the time for everyone to know what happened in
the barn.

As if he's reading my mind, Connor stops and looks over
his shoulder, face apologetic. "Oh no," he says. "Look. . . ."

The wail I heard in the barn came from Cady, I immediately understand. She's still wailing, her mouth a pit
you could drown in; if there were birds flying overhead,

her cries would drop them. She's draped over one of the bales, curled into a knot like she has a stomachache, one of her hands dangling uselessly over the side. A couple of her friends, Tina included, hover around her, but most of the people here are clustered in knots of their own, foreheads touching, their murmurs forming a roar. Some are leaving; the sounds of slamming car doors echo from the driveway.

"I need to go to Cady," Connor says. He rubs his forehead. The creases are back. "I just . . . I have to." He looks at me, eyes doleful, like he's a kid asking his teacher for permission to go to the bathroom. "She's still my friend, and I'm the only one who's going to be able to make her feel better."

And it's just that, the fact that he seems to feel he needs my permission, that makes me sigh and nod. "You should go to her," I say. "I'll see you later."

"Later," Connor says. He makes an awkward little bob, like he's going to hug me, but Rob clears his throat and Connor jolts away. He nods his head instead and takes off, running in Cady's direction.

Rob clears his throat again, and I realize he's directing it at me. "He broke up with her," I say defensively.

"They've broken up before," Rob says. For someone with piercings in his face and tattoos peeking over the collar of his shirt, he manages to look an awful lot like a disapproving old woman. "He's a good guy. He won't do this to her when her best friend just died."

I feel like he's kicked me in the gut. When I realize I'm upset over being inconvenienced by a dead girl, I feel like I've kicked *myself* in the gut. "Not to be a bitch, but it's really none of your business." I take a deep breath and am embarrassed to feel it shudder in my throat. "I should probably go."

"Scarlett, wait." I stop, but I don't turn around. "I know he likes you," Rob continues. "I know you like him. You're probably good for each other. But sometimes the timing just doesn't work, you know?"

I take another deep breath. This one doesn't shudder. "Like I said, I don't want to be a bitch, but it's really none of your business." I hear him clear his throat again, but I flee before he can say anything else.

The whole party is trying to leave at once, and so I have to wait in a line to turn off onto the road. As I'm waiting, I wonder about Monica—where exactly she was found, what exactly had happened to her, how long she'd been lying there, alone and unfound, in the dark—and I realize one thing.

I saw what seemed like every person I've ever worked with at Adventure World at that party.

Except Katharina.

I feel like I've spent years of my life at the bonfire, like I've gone from seventeen to eighteen to nineteen and am now an unfathomably ancient twenty, just one year away from being a real legal person. But the bonfire lasted only two hours. Somehow I drove there, got my drink, let Cady cry all over me, made out with Connor, and fled under Rob's judgy eyes in 120 minutes. I want to laugh at the thought.

As I pull into the driveway, the living room lights glow through our front windows—not surprising, since it's only ten o'clock. Seriously, only two hours?

It's past his bedtime, so Matthew is sleeping, or pretending to sleep. My dad is the one the lamps light up, and he waves at me from the couch as I walk by. "Good party?" he asks, the glow of the TV flickering over his cheeks. Flashing lights chase a phantom car.

"Okay," I say, ready to walk past, and then stop. "They found the missing girl. Monica."

"Found her?" My dad shifts in his seat and his mouth twitches, like he's not sure if he should smile or frown, whether he should clap or jump up to hug me.

He stays seated.

"Dead," I say flatly.

"I'm so sorry. Do you want to talk about it?" he asks, but he still doesn't stand.

"No," I say. I'm already moving toward the stairs. "I just want to go to sleep."

That is a lie. I tiptoe past my bedroom door and nudge Matthew's open. As I suspected, he's sprawled out beside the door, under his night-light, his face buried in the pages of a book. Little snores escape his throat. I crouch at his side. "Hey, kid," I say, nudging his shoulder. "Get in bed."

He lifts his head. A crease indents his cheek from forehead to chin where it had rested against the edge of the pages. "I'm not tired," he says.

"Yeah, okay," I say. "Get in bed and I'll tuck you in."

He lets me lift him up and cart him, heavy and warm and smelling like baby, to his bed. I lower him gently to his sheets, leaning over one extra second to breathe him in. There's something about the smell of freshly washed little kid. It's the smell of everything good in the world, and for a moment it makes me forget the way Monica's body must have smelled lying out there, broken, under sticks and leaves.

"Can you read some of my book?" Matthew asks. His eyelashes flutter sleepily.

I practice my stern face, but it melts in two seconds. "Looks like you read plenty," I say. I draw the covers over him and tuck them under his chin. "It's way past your bedtime."

"Did they find that girl?" Matthew asks. He blinks at me slowly, drowsily. "The one who was missing?"

My throat closes up. I can't lie to him. "Yes, they found her," I say, and pray he doesn't ask me anything more.

His blink lasts a shade longer than the last. "You were missing too," he says.

"Yes," I say. "I was."

"But they found you, too," Matthew says, and this time his eyes don't open again.

I let the words ring in the room for a moment, hang in

the air and paint the walls black with streaks of shadow. *Too.* My heart beats hollow in my chest. It's amazing what one word can do.

"Scarlett?"

I jerk and immediately glance down to make sure I didn't wake my brother. He's still slumbering peacefully. I wish I were seven years old.

"Yeah?" I ease my way up—Matthew snorts and his lips twitch—and make my way to the door. I've shut it behind me before I realize I'm face to face with Melody. I don't know who else I thought it would be. "Oh," I say. "Hey."

She leans against the wall, still dressed in her going-out clothes—a thigh-skimming skirt and lacy top. Black eyeliner smudges shadows around her eyes. "I heard they found the missing girl," she says breathlessly. Her cheeks are flushed—I can't tell if it's from makeup or blood.

"Her name was Monica," I say.

"I heard they found her in the woods," she says. "I heard she'd been there for a few days already."

My legs are weak; someone's sucked out all my muscle and blood and pumped them full of air, and now they're deflating like twin balloons. "I need to go to bed."

"That's all I heard," Melody continues, like I haven't even spoken. "Do you know anything? I know you were with Five Banners people tonight, right? Did they know anything? Like, do the police think they know who did it?"

I try to squeeze past her, but she extends an arm and

blocks my way. I'm just glad she doesn't touch me. I'd pop. "I really need to go to bed."

"You don't look so good," Melody says, and this time she does touch me, links her elbow in mine. The touch doesn't pop me. It invigorates me instead, shoots me with an extra blast of air. "This whole deal must be bringing back all your trauma and stuff. Do you feel weird that they found you alive and not her?"

"Yeah," I say. "That's it." It's not.

"You know what would be just splendid right now?" she says. She doesn't wait for me to answer. "Tea. I'll make us some tea, and we can talk more. You can spill your soul."

I'm too weak to protest, so I let her lead me downstairs and sit me at the kitchen table. I lower my forehead to the surface, letting the grain of the wood blur and unblur as she clinks about with her teapot and tea leaves and spoons and perfectly square cubes of sugar.

She didn't even ask if I wanted tea.

I hate tea.

"So are you feeling okay?" she asks. She nods at my teacup. "Drink the tea. It'll make you feel better."

I obediently take a sip. It scorches all the taste buds from the surface of my tongue, which is actually kind of great because now I can't taste it. "I'm feeling okay," I say. I'm not, but there's no way I'm confiding in Melody, of all people. "Sad, obviously, about Monica. She seemed really nice."

"Really nice," Melody echoes. "Yeah. I felt kind of bad tonight, actually. I was at Alexa's and we heard the news and they didn't even seem upset or anything. I had this epiphany, like, you know, she was a real person, like us, you know? And now she's dead and it could've been any one of us. So I left."

Her look is so earnest, maybe even apologetic, that it bolsters me enough to take another gulp of tea. "The tea is really good," I say, trying not to let the ruin of my tongue touch the roof of my mouth.

She looks quite pleased with herself. "Thanks," she says. "I've been practicing. They're loose tea leaves, you know. Not tea bags. Tea bags are cheating, basically."

I take another sip. "I always wished I could cook stuff like you," I tell her. My tongue feels thick, but that's probably just the burn complaining. "You're so good at the . . . at the . . ."

I squint. Yellow light swirls in the corner of my eye; it floats across my field of vision, followed by green, blue, violet.

No. Oh no, oh no.

I shouldn't have drunk the tea. I don't even like tea.

Why did I drink the tea?

I slump over, but Melody catches me before I hit my head on the floor. She cradles me in her arms, and it feels almost like someone loves me. A cool hand slips under my dress, cradles my hip. "Hey!" she shouts over my head. "Dad! Dad!"

And I fade.

• • •

I wake the next morning cocooned in blankets, the plastic stars of my bedroom ceiling giving off a faint glow above me. My breath tastes like the air trapped inside a dirty Tupperware container.

Then I remember how I got here. I jolt out of bed, realizing as I find my footing that I'm dressed in my clothes from the night before, still cloaked in smoke. I avoid the mirror on my way out; I'm sure makeup streaks my cheeks. I hope Matthew's already out, because if he sees me, he'll probably run away screaming. Actually, I might be okay with that right now. I'm in the mood to make people run away screaming.

I bang open Melody's door. She's awake, but just barely; she sits at the edge of her bed, yawning, scratching her arm. Her eyes are puffy. "Morning," she says. The exertion of that one word is enough to make her topple back over.

She's not getting away that easily. "You drugged me again," I say abruptly. "I know you did. You put something in my tea. Why? Why do you keep doing this?"

Over the course of my speech, her eyes have slowly expanded into portholes; it would be comical if I weren't so angry. "Are you on something right now? Because if you're on something, I'm going to call Dad."

"Don't turn this around on me," I say. "Besides, I'm not on anything except for whatever you put in me. You drugged me at the park with Katharina, and you drugged the tea. I know you did. Don't lie to me."

The portholes grow into manholes. She slowly sits, stands, so we're looking each other in the face. I could fit through one of her eyes. I wish I could for real; I'd dive right in and dig around in her brain until I uncovered whatever it is she's planning. "I literally don't know what you're talking about," Melody says. She's breathing like she's going to pass out. "You fainted at the table last night. You were drinking at the party, weren't you?"

"Yeah, but not enough to pass out," I say defiantly, but I wilt all the same. "And I saw the colors swirling and the—"

"Are you taking that from the Skywoman cartoon? That's why you think I drugged you?" She doesn't wait for me to answer. She doesn't need to. "Oh my God, Scarlett, seriously? Are you serious right now?"

"That's not the only reason—"

"Yeah?" Melody raises her chin. Her eyes have narrowed; I couldn't get into them now if I wanted to. "Go tell Dad, then. See what he says."

We both know that's the end. I'm not going to go running to our dad and tell him that Melody drugged me, twice. He'd look at me like I was crazy. He'd keep an extra eye on me. He wouldn't let me be alone with Matthew, because I'd be the crazy one in the family. Every family has one, and ours would be me.

"Don't you have to go to work now anyway?" Melody continues. She sits back on her bed with a thump. "You're going to be late."

I'm going to be late if I leave right now, to say nothing

of taking time to brush my teeth and shower, which I really have to do. So now I'm going to be *really* late. "Shoot," I say, and whirl from the room. I don't thank her. I can't go that far.

More details come out in the next few days, which I spend working under Randall on the east side. From what I hear, Cady doesn't come to work. I see Connor once, hurrying away from the Canteen, but he doesn't have time to give me much more than a quick hello before Cynthia bears down and he has to run off. It's a somber few days; nobody's really in the mood to chat. Even the guests seem muted, like they've unearthed a bit of common decency and decided to avoid pitching a fit over the lack of Pepsi products in the park.

According to the police examiner, Monica had been lying in the woods for weeks, since the time she went missing. She was found naked and covered in leaves, and the bottoms of her feet were bloody, like she'd been running barefoot. Her eyes were closed and her mother was devastated and all the money that had been donated to the family was going to be put into a trust for Monica's sisters and brother called the Monica Rose Jackson College Fund. Her funeral will be at the end of the week, with a private viewing and burial for family and close friends only, and then a memorial service open to the public later that night. I wonder if I should go. Cady will be there, and I think even a look from Cady would wither me right now.

But Monica was a part of the society. Like me. And she didn't get lucky. Like I did. I'm not sure whether I want to go and pay my respects to a comrade or if I want to avoid ever thinking about her again, just so I don't have to think about what might have happened to me. What might still happen to me. There's no time limit on going missing. Sometimes lightning strikes the same tree twice.

Finally, four days after Monica was found, I'm sent back to the south side, and I hurry to headquarters with worms squirming in my stomach. Lizzy of the most serious lack of eyebrows is at the registers; she stares at me dully as I walk in, but doesn't say hi. It's okay; I don't say hi to her, either.

Rob is in the back filling the whiteboard schedule with swoops and squiggles. Connor isn't there, unless he heard me coming and dove behind the stack of boxes filled with new Skywoman T-shirts and Wonderman-shaped baby bottles. "Good morning, Rob," I say formally, adjusting an imaginary cravat.

He turns. "Hi, Scarlett," he says. "Connor's not here yet. He'll be in later."

My cheeks heat. "I didn't ask. But okay. Where am I going today?"

Rob turns back to the board. Now that I've seen the real Rob, piercings and tattoos and spikes galore, this Rob feels inauthentic, sanitized almost, like the versions of the Skywoman comic that take out her conflicted (lesbian) feelings for the Blade, and the Blade's feelings back. I know somehow that this Rob isn't going to have the guts to say anything about me and Connor and Cady.

"I was going to send you to Wonderkidz, but that's already full," he says. "So I'm going to send you to Iceworks."

"Iceworks," I repeat. I've never been there before, but Rob must not hate me that much, because it can't be worse than Wonderkidz. Nothing can be worse than Wonderkidz.

Except Iceworks. Iceworks is a tiny, one-register discount store full of outdated celebration T-shirts and three-eyed teddy bears, located directly under the coils of the Blade's Revenge, which whooshes overhead only a few feet from the roof every ninety-five seconds and gives the store a bone-rattling shake you can barely feel over the roar of the track. I have plenty of time to count, as it turns out, because it also turns out that nobody wants outdated celebration T-shirts or three-eyed teddy bears. "The name is awfully ironic," I say weakly as Rob sets up my register, though I don't know if he hears me, as just then the Blade's Revenge roars overhead.

"It is," he agrees, wiping beads of sweat off his brow.

It's called Iceworks, and it's the only store on the south side without air-conditioning.

Rob hurries out—who can blame him?—leaving behind a rattling fan, flurries of dust, and a trace of a smirk. Well played, Rob, well played.

I settle in for a morning of swampy heat and monotony.

The best way to break it up, I find, is to scrub the store clean. Evidently, generations of cashiers and managers have seen the sad merch and shrugged off the fuzzy layers of dust coating the shelves, the grime caked on the floor, but not I. I set upon cleaning with a vengeance, improvising with ancient T-shirts when I run out of rags, improvising with spit and tears when I run out of cleaner. Each swipe makes me hate myself more—the fact that cleaning like this soothes me, brings back the feeling I'm doing something that will help me survive, maybe get me a reward. At Stepmother's house, cleaning was the only thing that kept me alive, and now it's the only thing that keeps me sane. I hate Stepmother for doing this to me.

Fortunately, no customers come in during this time. It's entirely possible that people peeked in the door as they exited the Blade's Revenge, super psyched to buy one of last year's collectable snow globes or commemorative anniversary T-shirts from three years ago, and recoiled upon the sight of the panting, red-faced monster clawing maniacally at the floor. I don't blame them. I would run from me too.

So I'm more than a little surprised when I hear footsteps click through the entrance just as the Blade's Revenge whizzes by overhead. I turn, the wince on my face instinctive, and see Connor. He's not smiling.

"Hi," I say. "I'm cleaning the store."

"Good job," Connor says, almost robotically. His eyes are rimmed in red, but they're not puffy. Tired, not crying. "I'll give you a positive write-up."

I stand. "I'll give you a positive write-up" isn't something you say to someone you made out with. "How are you?" I ask, my insides writhing.

He sighs and rubs his forehead. "Not so great," he says. "How are you?"

"Okay," I say. All the moisture vanishes from my mouth and throat. Swallowing is painful.

"Look, I wanted to talk to you." Connor shuffles his feet. I haven't gotten to that part of the floor yet, so he shuffles around chunks of dirt and clouds of dust. "I really like you. Obviously. That goes without saying."

If it goes without saying, then you wouldn't need to say it, I think. "I really like you, too," I say. The words hurt my throat.

"But with Monica . . . with Cady. I . . . I don't think I can give you what you want."

I can't breathe. I can't breathe. "But you're single, and I'm single, and we really like each other." I know I sound shrill, but I can't help it. "I don't see what the problem is."

He takes a deep breath. *He* can breathe, apparently. It's not fair. It's so not fair. "If I started going out with you right now, or even hooking up with you right now, it would crush Cady. She's grieving her best friend. I can't do that to her right now, Scarlett. I just can't."

"You're not being fair to her," I say, even shriller. "She's just going to keep thinking you're going to get back together."

"But with Monica, and . . ." The Blade's Revenge rushes

overhead right on schedule, shaking the world around me and the floor beneath my feet.

Once the dust clears, he starts speaking again. "I'm really, really sorry, Scarlett. And I know this doesn't mean anything right now, but I do want to be with you. I do. I just can't . . . right now."

He's sorry. Well, that fixes everything. "You're right. That doesn't mean anything."

He takes another deep breath and turns his eyes up toward the ceiling. Is it my imagination, or are they especially shiny right now? "I know. I know. In a few months . . ."

I'm squeezing my T-shirt rag so hard my nails are biting into my palms. "What, do you think I'm just going to sit around and wait for you? That I don't have anything better to do?"

"Of course not," he says. His eyes are definitely shiny. "Please, Scarlett. I want—"

It doesn't matter what he wants. I throw the T-shirt rag at him; it splats against his chest, leaving a dark splotch on his polo. Good. I hope the stain doesn't come out and he has to pay Five Banners for a new one. "I'm going to lunch," I say. I'm not sure if it's my lunchtime yet, but I don't even care. I'm not going to let him see me cry. "Get someone to cover my register. You'd better not be here when I come back."

I don't stick around to hear his response.

. . .

I spent almost four years with Pixie in the house, sleeping curled around her on the mattress and waking to the weak strains of light trickling through the window.

Four.

Years.

Four years of shivering in the basement. Four years of listening to the girls cry in the bathroom. Four years of scrubbing mysterious stains off the floor.

It wasn't all bad. It made me laugh, the first time I thought that: it wasn't all bad. Sometimes if I was especially good, or if I had to tell on Pixie for doing something bad, I got to sleep upstairs in one of the girls' vacated beds and eat something that wasn't tuna fish.

Pixie didn't feel the same way. To Pixie, it *was* all bad. She never gave up the thought of escape. She stopped darting away at every opportunity, but the idea was always there, a film shimmering just out of her reach, and her plots grew more daring, more convoluted. But she always got caught, and the beatings got bloodier, more painful. Angry welts painted her back like the stripes on the American flag.

I don't know what I would have done if she had actually gotten away in those four years. I'd say she was my rock, but rocks are cold, unfeeling, just *there*. Pixie was *there* too, but she was anything but cold and unfeeling. When she was upset, I'd soothe her with stories about my family and my school and my home. When I was upset—when one of the girls made a nasty remark to me, or when Stepmother

slapped me after I spilled bleach on her hardwood floor—
she'd coax the stories out of me and calm me with the
thought of happier times. Sometimes I even let her touch
my scar. Her touch felt like home almost, or what I thought
home was like. I had a hard time remembering sometimes.
I could barely remember my mother's face or the color of
Melody's eyes.

But I was okay. We were okay.

CHAPTER ELEVEN

When I stand in line at the employment office the next morning, waiting for the receipt that will tell me where I'm to work today, I can't blame the other people in line for side-eyeing me and edging away. I know I look like a crazy person, but I can't help the chanting under my breath. I feel like if I don't chant, if I don't want it hard enough, the universe won't listen to me. "Don't send me to the south side. Don't send me to the south side. Don't send me to the south side."

The machine beeps and spits out its slip of paper. I snatch it from the girl behind the desk. "No," I say.

She looks at me through cakes of mascara. "Next."

I trudge to headquarters wishing I would just fall

through the ground and disappear. Maybe I'd drop so far I'd eventually carbonize and become a diamond, and in thousands of years they'd dig me up and I'd get to be the diamond in some loving couple's engagement ring. That would be kind of a happy ending, I guess.

I enter the back room of headquarters to find Connor, alone.

Naturally.

I clear my throat. Connor, working on the schedule, jumps, and a trail of ink flies off the edge of the whiteboard. "They sent me here," I say. *Sink through the floor,* I will myself. I even jiggle my knees to try to help the process along, but no luck. Damn concrete. "I didn't want to come here."

"Good morning." Connor looks at me in what I think is a hopeful way. "How are you?"

I don't answer. His face falls. "We need someone in Sweet Treats. I think I'm going to put you there."

"Okay," I say. "That's fine."

"Okay, good," he says.

The walk to the store is painful, and the wait for him to set my register up, when we're all alone in the dark store, even more so. It's amazing how he can spend upward of fifteen minutes not more than three feet away from my body, and yet I can manage not to look at him at all. It's almost like he doesn't exist. I almost wish he didn't exist right now.

He leaves with a "Let me know if you need anything," and I settle in for a long morning. Even the fudge doesn't smell appealing anymore, partially because I know it tastes like lighter fluid, but mostly because it's associated with Connor's laugh and the sparkle of his eyes.

He visits once, but I turn my head whenever he tries to speak to me. Eventually he gives up and leaves.

It's a long morning.

When Rob finally comes to release me for lunch, bringing, to his credit, small talk and sympathetic looks, I book it for the employment office, racing through the secret passage. I've very sneakily snuck in two granola bars for lunch, which I eat on the way. Energized by my nongreasy meal, I approach Mascara Girl, who's still waiting behind the front desk. "Hi," I say, and then continue all in one breath, "I'm Scarlett Contreras. I've been working in Merch, but I wanted to ask about transferring to another department."

She looks at me from beneath heavy lids. She does not seem impressed. "You'll have to fill out a departmental transfer form," she says. "It probably won't be accepted. Most of the departments are already full for the year, but you might get lucky."

I wilt. It doesn't sound like she thinks I'll get lucky. "Okay. Thanks."

The form she gives me is in triplicate and is at least ten pages long, and when I try to fill it out, it leaves dusty carbon smudges all over my fingers. I give up halfway through. It's not worth it. No matter where I end up, I'll still be in this park, with Connor, knowing he could be around any corner. Maybe making out with Cady.

A lump forms in my throat halfway through my walk back. I still have twenty minutes left of my "lunch," so at least I have time for emergency maneuvers. Like a crashing airplane, I veer into the closest metal building and hope against hope it's not a changing room for the costumed characters.

Fortunately, I've chosen wisely, and the building I duck into is one of the many storehouses for old merch. As long as nobody has an urgent need for extra Slugworth coffee mugs in the next few minutes, I should be safe. I shut the dead bolt (because you never know), sag against the inside of the door, and cry.

I've never been a loud crier. I did so much crying at Stepmother's those first few months—in the basement, the bathroom, the girls' bedrooms—that I learned how to suppress it. The secret is in managing the inhale—if you don't take in much air, there isn't much to wheeze or shriek out—and in looking up at the ceiling, which keeps your eyes from puffing up too much or getting too red.

So it's easy to hear something fall at the other end of the room.

I stiffen. I may be a quiet crier, but I'm not silent. If someone is there, they've definitely heard me. I reach over my shoulder, trying to unlock the door without exposing my back.

"Scarlett? Is that you?"

My fingers freeze. "Katharina?"

I take a step forward. Katharina may be crazy, and she may do crazy things, and she may be making me crazy, but I don't think she'll hurt me. Not during the workday, when anyone could hear me scream. I weave through the maze of shelves and dust and boxes. My fingers are tense on the can of pepper spray I keep in the pocket of my work pants. I don't *think* Katharina will hurt me, but you can't be too careful.

Katharina is in a nest—that's the only way to describe it. She's gathered old T-shirts and costume pieces and uniform parts, the way birds gather bits of string and leaves, and piled them high in the corner of the warehouse. She's curled up in the middle, only her head and hair visible. "Scarlett?" She sits up, and pieces of cloth tumble to the floor.

"What are you doing here?" I have my answer before the words all leave my mouth. There's a sink in the corner too, with a toothbrush and toothpaste poking from a commemorative Wonderman mug. Next to the sink is a pile of food wrappers, beside other piles: folded clothes, boxes of granola bars and bottled water and tampons. A miniature refrigerator hums. "You're living here."

"No, I'm not."

"I think you are," I say.

Her eyes are opaque. Her jaw tightens. "Are you going to tell?"

Am I? I probably should. The chance that the park

management knows about this is approximately zero percent. Living here can't be safe or healthy for Katharina.

I put off the question. "Why?"

"I had to come to this town and I had nowhere to live," she says. "Now. Are you going to tell?"

I feel like I should be horrified at the thought of a girl my age living all alone, with no family, but I find myself feeling calculating. If I tell, Katharina will probably be arrested, or at least taken away by Social Services. She'll be a subject of gossip throughout the park, an urban legend, like the alleged ghost that floats through the walls of the old haunted mansion, supposedly the sixteen-year-old ride operator who died when the attraction burned to the ground in 1971.

If I don't tell, Katharina will owe me.

"I won't tell," I say.

"Good," Katharina says. "Thank you."

"No problem." I start feeling my way backward. I don't want to be around Katharina anymore. There's no possible good reason for her to be living here. "I have to go or I'll be late. See you."

"Wait," she says. She rises, shedding pieces of cloth. "I'm glad you're here, because I really need to talk to you."

"I really need to go." I turn my back and flee. I don't have to be afraid of her anymore; I have the upper hand now. If I ever feel threatened by her again, all I have to do is tell, and she'll poof and be gone. Like magic.

Rob is waiting for me at the candy store when I get

back, chatting with the cashier who covered my break. "I'm not late," I say immediately, and sneak a look at the register clock. I'm not late. I'm early, actually, by three minutes.

"I know." Rob looks over at the other peon. "Marley, want to get a head start over to headquarters?"

The other kid nods and hustles, as though sensing that an awkward conversation is coming. I almost want to yell after Marley, "Take me with you!"

My head is still spinning with the Katharina revelation, and I don't think I can take any more revelations today. "What is it?" I say. Maybe he'll fire me. I'd actually be okay with that, I think. It would not be cool with my dad if I quit the job that lets me pay for my car insurance and gas, but he couldn't blame me if I got fired for reasons beyond my control.

"Are you going to go to Monica's memorial service?"

That isn't what I was expecting. I'm vaguely disappointed. "I don't know," I say. "It's tomorrow, isn't it? Tomorrow night? At Riverside?"

"Yeah," he says. "Don't go."

I blink. "Excuse me?"

"Cady and Connor are going to be there. It's their night." Rob shuffles papers around on the counter. They're inventory reports, I think. There's no reason for them to be shuffled. "You've done enough. Let them grieve without worrying about you."

"I didn't think Cady knew about me and Connor," I say cautiously.

"She doesn't," Rob says. "I wasn't about to do that to her. Not now. And Connor is my best friend."

"So what's the issue?" I ask. Icicles, cold and sharp and glitteringly dangerous, protrude from my words. "They're not together anymore. If she doesn't know, and she isn't going to know, then what's—"

"The only people who know what happened between you and Connor are you, me, and Connor," Rob says. "And that's how it's going to stay. Cady's been hurt enough. You break Cady's heart again, I'll break you."

I stare at him. The look on his face is so stone-cold serious that it's ludicrous, and I can't help but laugh. That's the wrong thing to do, I can immediately tell; Rob's jaw clamps down, and his eyes narrow. "You can't hit a girl," I tell him.

"I don't need to hit you to break you," Rob says through his teeth. "I'm telling you, stay away from the memorial service. If you're there, all Connor will be able to focus on is you, and he needs to be able to focus on Cady."

With a lack of anything else to do, I toss my hair. "I don't think you have anything to worry about," I say. "I didn't even talk to him today." I wonder, fleetingly, if Rob's had this talk with Connor, too. The absolute last thing I want to do with that look on Rob's face is test it. "Let Cady have him."

"Good answer," Rob says, and his face relaxes. "Give me a ring if you need anything. I'll be at headquarters." He strides away, whistling. I want to cram squares of caustic fudge down his throat until it burns through his insides and lights him on fire.

The rest of the day passes slowly; I can't stop jumping at every noise and every greeting, certain Katharina is going to pop out from behind the candy-sand station or Connor is going to drop through a trapdoor in the ceiling to confess that he actually does want to be with me right now. But nobody shows up except customers (ugh), and so it's almost a relief when Rob comes to take me off register at the end of my shift, his small talk extra small. I don't leave through the secret passage. The last thing I need today is more Katharina weirdness.

The last thing I need any day, ever, is more Katharina weirdness. I'd be perfectly happy never to see Katharina again.

So, naturally, when I get home, her car is in my driveway and she's sitting on my stoop. "Nobody would answer the door" is what she greets me with as she rises. If she has no house, nowhere to live, how in the world does she have a car? "I texted Melly, but she didn't answer. I wanted to surprise her."

"It's Thursday," I say, unfailingly polite. "Thursday is field hockey night."

"Ah. I see," Katharina says, unfailingly jovial. "I don't get how she does all those things. Crazy, right?"

Crazy. She's going to drive me crazy. I can't keep doing this. "Please leave me alone," I say, still unfailingly polite. I will be unfailingly polite until the end. The end of the world, if need be. "I really don't want to talk to you any-more. If you keep talking to me, I'll tell everybody your secret."

Katharina squints at me. A curtain of hair falls across her face. "My secret?"

"I don't want to," I say. "But I will." *And I still think you drugged me*, I don't say, because that would get back to Melody, and Melody already thinks I'm crazy.

"My secret," she repeats. "Sorry, but I don't know what you're talking about."

The icicles from before are back, but this time they're in my arms and legs, stiffening my elbows and knees until I can't move. "From earlier today," I say, and my voice sounds tinny to my ears. Probably because of the way sound waves refract through ice, which is now spreading into my torso. "When I found you in the storage building where you're living."

Katharina squints at me the way I'd squint at a mouse chasing a cat. "What are you talking about? I didn't even work today."

The ice freezes solid, and somehow it's like it's making me stronger, protecting me against the rays of her wither-ing glare. Because Melody may think I'm crazy, but I'm *not*. I know what I saw, and I saw Katharina and her little nest in the storage facility in the secret passage. "I saw you," I say defensively. "I know it happened."

The look she's giving me now is the mouse's once the cat turns around. "I have a house," she says slowly, carefully. "I live with my parents on the other side of town. Ask Melly. She's been there."

And then all at once I melt. I sink to my knees and a sound escapes my throat, a sound so odd I don't think I've ever heard it before. I don't know if it's even me.

"Are you okay?" Katharina kneels beside me. "Are you dizzy or something? Is that it? It was hot today. Maybe you have heatstroke?"

She's handing this excuse to me on purpose, I know, a rope to help drag me out of this lake of crazy. "Maybe," I say. I can't take the rope. Taking it is akin to admitting I've fallen in in the first place.

"Yeah, I was dizzy before," she says. She flips her hair over her shoulder, lifting the curtain for the second act. "Sad about Monica, right? I was really upset."

"Yeah," I say. "Well, I should be——"

"Are you going to the memorial service?" Katharina talks right over me. "It's tomorrow night, at Riverside."

"I don't know," I say. Rob's stare flashes through my mind. "I didn't really know her all that well."

Katharina bares her teeth in what I think is supposed to be a smile. "Melody and I are going to go, and Melly didn't know her at all. It's all about paying our respects. Don't you want to pay your respects?"

What I want? What I want is to rewind time, spooling the hours and minutes back upon each other like the film in an old cassette tape, and plop myself back in Connor's barn, my back up against the rough wood, and then, as

Connor leaned to kiss me, I'd push him away, and then I wouldn't be in this mess at all. Connor and I would still flirt all the time, and we'd be friends, and that awkwardness wouldn't be there between us, hitting us in the stomach every time we moved.

But I've already made that choice, and if I made a different one, I'd be a different person.

Rob's glare flashes back into my mind's eye and ignites a flare of shame deep in my belly. It keeps burning, though, and the shame heats into anger. Why should I be the one hiding? Connor was the one who broke *my* heart. I should really be out there proving to him that I'm okay. "Okay," I say. "I think I will go to the memorial service."

"Cool," Katharina says. She's tapping away on her phone, her fingers practically a blur. "Well, if Melly's not going to be home soon, I guess I'll go." She looks up, and her eyes are bright and hard. "Nice talking to you, Scarlett."

I watch her get back into her car, and I watch her pull out of the driveway, and I watch her pull away, and I watch her drive down the street. I watch her until her car is nothing more than a speck in the distance, and then I keep watching, just to make sure she's really and truly gone.

I call in sick to work the next day. It's kind of true. I am sick. Sick in the head. Sick over Connor. Sick over Melody. Sick of worrying. It gets me a black mark on my record, but I don't much care.

Monica's memorial service is taking place at Riverside,

on the football field, the same place where they held the vigil. The mood is very different—whereas electricity zipped through the air last time, animating candle flames and making hairs dance, now the mood is somber, the colors muted, voices low. People pack the bleachers, murmuring and crying; Melody and I have to hold hands not to be separated as we push through the crowd, which unironically thrills me. We meet up with Katharina in the bleachers, where she's saved us seats; she greets Melody with a quick hug and whisper in her ear, then smiles big at me. It feels obscene to smile at such an event, and I don't know whether it's more awkward to smile or not to smile back.

"Hey, Scarlett," Katharina says. "Feeling better?"

"I feel fine," I say. I pretend to stretch, craning my neck for Connor and Rob and company. Turns out I don't have to crane far, because they're right behind us.

Immediately I feel guilty. Not because of Rob's glare, which could etch curse words into marble. Not because of Connor, whom I don't even let myself look at. Not because of Cynthia and Randall and the others, who say hello soberly, solemnly, with all the gravity expected in this situation.

No, it's because of Cady. Cady, whose shoulders are shaking and whose forehead is in her hands. She's squeaking and snorting and making all sorts of unattractive noises, and it's because she's *sad*, it's because she's *devastated*, it's because her friend is dead, and I'm using her friend's death to make some kind of personal point or jab or whatever. I don't even know anymore. All I know is that I'm terrible. I am officially, now, a terrible person.

I go to stand. "I should go," I say. "I'll wait out by the car."

Melody puts her hand on my arm. "It's starting," she hisses. "What are you doing?"

To go now, I would have to actively push her away, so I sit back down. The memorial service is endless and torturous, and I feel worse every time I think of it that way. Every time somebody gets up and talks about how Monica tutored him in bio and saved his grade, or how Monica sold the most Girl Scout cookies in the state through sheer charm and will in elementary school and won her troop a trip to Disney World, or how Monica read Harry Potter to sick children at the local hospital. Because all I can think about through all the speeches is me, me, me.

After a hundred years the memorial service ends, and Cady is still crying. I hate myself for feeling relieved that it's over, because of course, for people like Cady and Monica's family, who are standing only tens of feet away, it will never be over. For them it's only beginning.

"We should go," I say to Melody. "Get out of the parking lot before it becomes a madhouse."

Melody isn't listening. Well, she's not listening to me—she's listening intently, instead, to Katharina talking to the group behind us. "Monica would have hated this," Katharina is saying, tossing her hair. Hair is everywhere. I am choking on hair. "So schmaltzy and corny. Making her out to be some kind of saint."

Cynthia lets out a dry laugh at that. "She certainly wasn't a saint," she says. "You know I caught her making out with Scott one night in the back of headquarters?"

Scott, the bald supervisor. He has to be near forty. "Isn't he married?" Randall says. Poor, prematurely balding Randall. Perhaps in Scott he sees his future, chained forever to his first place of work, making out with teenage girls in sweaty concrete storage rooms.

Cady barks. I realize it's supposed to be a laugh. "Monica was the opposite of a saint," she says. "Sometimes she brought vodka and orange juice to work in her water bottle and drank it in the morning. Like, before noon." She shakes her head. "And she really liked Scott. She really thought he was going to leave his wife and his kid for her. She thought they were going to run away together to Tahiti or Jamaica or freaking wherever. Sometimes she would laugh at the thought of the wife and kid crying and left behind." She lets out a strangled-sounding sniff. "She was the exact opposite of a saint, and that's why I loved her so much."

"We all loved Monica," Rob says. He sounds subdued, and I let myself relax a little bit. Subdued people don't suddenly rear up and head-butt girls nearby.

Even if they kind of deserve it.

"Hey," Katharina says. Her cheeks are flushed, and her eyes are dancing with something a little bit insane. "Crazy idea. Monica was a rule breaker, right? So, second memorial service for Monica, for the *real* Monica. Tonight, Adventure World, after hours. Who's with me? Am I crazy?"

"Yes, you're crazy," Cynthia says. "But I'm in."

Cady snuffles, wiping at her nose. "I'm in too."

Rob spreads his arms like he's about to take flight. "Let's do it."

They're echoed by Randall, by Tina from the bonfire.

Connor.

Even Melody volunteers to go. Even though she wasn't invited.

If everybody else is in, how can I be out?

CHAPTER TWELVE

It was a miracle Pixie found the knife at all. It was a miracle *I* wasn't the one to find it. I usually stripped down the girls' beds and beat the sheets, while Pixie would wipe down the floor. In our four years together, we'd created almost a dance out of our routine, where I'd swirl by with the sheets as she swept her way across the room. But on this day, this one day, I'd slammed my wrist in the door and had asked her to take over beating the sheets.

So this wasn't a choice either. It just kind of happened that way.

If it had been me stripping Violetta's bed, and I'd been the one to see the knife's handle poking from underneath the mattress, I would probably have pretended I didn't see it. I didn't even want to think about what Stepmother would do if she found me in possession of a weapon. She'd probably use it on me, or she'd use it on Pixie and make me watch. I would have pushed it farther beneath the mattress and prayed that Violetta, who had always been nice to me, who smelled so good, didn't get caught.

But again, I didn't get the chance.

Instead, it was Pixie who pulled it reverently from its hiding spot and dangled it between two of her fingers by its wooden handle. "Check it out," she said. She snuck a peek behind her to make sure the door was closed, then held it out to me. "Look."

It was a big knife, but not too big. Bigger than a steak knife, not quite a cleaver. But sharp, very sharp. I leapt back as if she were holding a poisonous snake, its fangs bared and ready to strike. "Put it back!"

"No way." I could see it reflected over and over in her eyes. "I'm keeping it. It's not like Violetta can say anything."

I felt cold all over, then hot, then cold again. Sweat froze on my forehead. "Stepmother will know. She always knows."

Pixie looked at me levelly, then stuck the knife into her pants, securing it through the band of her underwear so that it fit snug against the inside of her leg. Or so I figured—the pants Stepmother gave us were the girls' old ones, so they were always pretty loose. "She won't know. Not if you don't tell her."

The cold traveled to my belly. My tongue was suddenly

thick in my mouth. Absurdly, my lips broke into a tiny, hysterical smile.

"You won't, will you?"

I couldn't speak. I couldn't say anything.

By the time we all get to the park and scatter our cars inconspicuously throughout the employee parking lot, the park is already almost closed. "You know we close in a half hour, right?" the woman at the front gate warns us, each and every one of us.

"We're just running in," we tell her, one after the other, each and every one of us. We are running in, of course. That's the truth. We just won't be running out. Not tonight. Tonight is for mourning the saint who wasn't.

We're with Cynthia, a supervisor with keys, so we have a better place to wait out closing time than the storage facility. That's good; I worry that seeing the place where I saw—or thought I saw?—Katharina living might break my mind. My mind is close enough to breaking, thanks to my close proximity to Connor and his close proximity to Cady. Her legs don't seem to be working; she clings to him with every step, and with every step I hate myself for hating her.

"We'll go to Iceworks," Cynthia says. Iceworks closed at eight, and it's beneath the Blade's Revenge, Monica's favorite coaster (she dressed as the Blade for five successive Halloweens, apparently, spandex and plastic sword and all), so it's a fitting place to wait.

We crowd in, all nine of us: me, Katharina, Melody,

Cynthia, Connor, Cady, Rob, Randall, and Tina. Cynthia clacks the lock shut behind us, and my heart jumps in panic before settling down. It's so hot the air is thick, and it's dark enough that I can't see anyone's face; we're all just shapes in the gloom.

"What should we do for the next hour?" someone whispers. Melody, it's Melody. I know my own sister's voice. "Play Never Have I Ever?"

I wince. How inappropriate of her, my sister, to suggest a stupid party game at a memorial for a dead girl.

But somehow, maybe because it's Melody and the world just opens up before her wherever she goes, thornbushes jumping out of the way and handsome boys lying down on puddles so she can cross over their backs, Tina bites. "Let's play Monica-themed Never Have I Ever," she says breathlessly. I can relate; I feel like the darkness is trying to suck the air right out of my lungs. "Things that Monica did."

"But we don't have anything to drink," Randall says.

Rob answers, "So?"

"I'll start," Cady says. Her voice is as thick as the air. "Never have I ever stolen from Five Banners."

Katharina laughs, then abruptly stops, like she's realized how inappropriate laughter sounds in this room. "Wait, what?" she says. "I can't picture Monica stealing."

"She totally did!" Cady says. Her voice has lightened, and I can picture the look on her face: wistful, dreamy. I wonder if eating Sweet Treats fudge counts as stealing. If so, the taste was a fitting punishment. "Not like money from the cash register or anything. When our first year was up, she stole a Blade figurine from headquarters, one of the nice ones with the rhinestone eyes, to have as a memento of our first year, she said. I asked her why she didn't just buy it with her employee discount, and she said it wasn't the same. It wouldn't be as exciting."

Everybody laughs, as if on cue. "Me next," Cynthia jumps in. "Never have I ever hooked up with a fellow employee."

I wish I could see Connor's face.

"I should be drinking right now," Cady says.

So should I, and I want to say it, but I don't.

"Okay, me," Rob says. He's the only one I can really make out, thanks to the piercings that glitter in the thin shafts of light filtering in through the covered windows. My heart skips a beat as I think of another room, another darkness pierced only by weak beams of light filtering through bars. But I take a deep breath and I don't pass out. "Never have I ever dared to eat the cotton candy."

It goes on like this for an hour and a half. It's a stretch of time that feels like forever, and yet I'm not angry at it, because by the end I feel like I know Monica, feel like I share a kinship with her besides the fact that we're both members of the club. She wasn't the girl they made her out to be, the sweet, innocent angel who never did anyone or anything wrong. She was a girl who did some good things and some bad things and sometimes did things that were wrong because they seemed exciting and sometimes did things that were right even when they were hard. She was a girl I'm glad I knew, even if it was only for a little while.

Someone's phone finally lights up the room, and Katharina speaks. "It's time," she says. "We can go. We should be safe now."

Her words meet silence. We can go. Go where? We haven't talked about it. We haven't thought about it, or at least I haven't. "There's a bunch of us," Randall says. The light from Katharina's phone gleams off his bare, shiny forehead. "We won't be able to evade capture for too long." *Evade capture*. Who says things like that?

"The Blade's Revenge," Cady says. Someone's added cornstarch to her voice and stirred. "It's right above us. We can make it to the top."

Cady's words meet silence too, but this silence is electric, racing with currents of thought and possibility. "We could climb the safety staircase," Cynthia says slowly. "I have the keys for the gates."

"Even if somebody comes after us, they'll have to climb all the way to the top," Tina says. "They can't fire all of us."

Yes, they can, I want to say, but again I don't say anything. I've been swept away in the energy, caught up in the rush, and I want nothing more than to say goodbye to this girl I wish so much I had known. We could have been friends. She could have shown me the Five Banners ropes, pointed the way around with her long red nails, introduced me to Cady. Cady and I would have become friends and I would never have noticed Connor that way then, because

I'm a good person, and I would never have hooked up with a friend's ex when she was still in love with him. I'm not a bad person. I'm not. I've done bad things, but I am not a bad person.

After the stuffy room, the air outside feels crisp and cool against my skin; I revel in the way it brushes sweat from my forehead and pulls the hairs sticking to the back of my neck free. The nine of us walk in a solemn procession out of the store and through the gates toward the Blade's Revenge, silent and focused on our task. Cynthia leads the way, unlocking the gates and letting us through. I'm in the middle, sandwiched between Katharina in front of me, where I can keep an eye on her, and Cady behind me, who threw herself there, insisting I'd proven myself the best shoulder to cry on, literally. I hope she doesn't touch me again. I can still feel her tears, or ghosts of them, anyway, soaking the air between us.

The safety staircase winds its way from the ground to the top of the tallest hill of the coaster, ensuring there's a way down besides the air for anyone trapped at the top, and providing a way for engineers and technicians to assess its safety (hence the name) and fix anything that needs fixing. So it's steep and narrow—meant for emergencies, not for the casual climber. I'm somewhere beneath a casual climber. I am not a climber at all.

So my calves are burning and I'm breathing hard less than halfway up, but I can't slow down because then Cady might bump into my back. Katharina doesn't seem to be feeling the stress at all: she's silent as she moves, her steps graceful and steady, and her hair, tied into one long braid, swings rhythmically across her back as if it's trying to hypnotize me. I won't let it. I look away and over the railing; the empty park stretches before us, strange in its stillness. I wonder if anyone's spotted us yet. Maybe not. The park is still lit up by streetlights and backlights, but none exist this high up—there's a blinking red light at the coaster's summit, perhaps to warn any particularly low-flying airplanes, but it doesn't do much to illuminate the group of vagrants scaling the coaster's side.

The staircase ends in a small platform, maybe the size of the average bathroom; the nine of us, crowded together, just barely fit. My face is in Randall's armpit, and my arm is rubbing up against Tina in a way that could probably get me sued, but the wind is whipping my hair and the park below looks like a fairyland now, like a theme park built for dolls. I want to experience this fairyland. I wonder if this is what I was thinking that other night, that night I was or was not drugged.

Somebody behind me shifts—the last person in line fitting in, most likely—and I'm pushed farther to the front, so that my stomach butts against the railing. The metal chills me through my shirt, sending waves of cold down my legs and into my toes. My eyes are drawn forward, down, and I'm seized by the sudden and wild urge to jump. I know I won't fall and go splat. I have faith that the park will save me, that the magic of the night will lift me up with its currents and bear me somewhere high, somewhere bright, somewhere basements don't exist.

A hush hovers over the group. "We should say something," Cynthia says. "Before they find us."

The hush uncrosses its legs, pulls out a newspaper, settles in. A breeze sweeps through, sends Katharina's braid bouncing onto my arm.

"I'll start," Cady says, shooing the hush away. If she'd actually made the motions, she would have hit me; somehow we ended up right next to each other, both of us pressed against the safety railing. For a safety railing, it could be a lot safer; it comes up only to our waists. A good shove could send one of us right over.

And just as I'm thinking that, there's a grunt, and someone jostles me, and then Cady screams, the scream that someone about to dive headfirst from the top of a roller coaster would scream.

The world turns into a blur. Someone elbows me hard in the side, and I shriek in response. What feels like a rope hits me on the cheek—Katharina's braid? I'm stumbling back, but there is no back, there is only a warm mass of bodies, and someone else is sobbing, but I can't see who it is because my eyes are closed. I don't want to see who it is. I don't want to see the thing that used to be Cady splattered over the cobblestones below.

"Oh my God, oh my God, are you okay?" someone is

saying, and I nod before I realize they're not speaking to me. Someone is shaking me hard by the shoulders, and my head is shaking like it might fly off.

"I'm okay, I'm okay," someone is saying, and her voice is shaking, and my knees start to shake as I realize that it's Cady, that she hasn't fallen after all.

"Scarlett, what the hell?" A fine spray of spittle coats my face, but at least my shoulders stop shaking. I don't know who spoke.

I'm so confused. I don't know what's happening to me right now, but I don't like it. Not at all.

"Did Scarlett just . . . ?" Rob is speaking now, in that slow, measured tone of voice he used when he told me not to come to the memorial in the first place.

Maybe I should have listened to him.

"Ask her," someone urges.

Rob clears his throat. "Scarlett, did you just try and push Cady off the platform?"

I recoil, sending my back into the safety rail and nearly sending *myself* over the edge. When did I turn around? "No!"

Cady is in a heap in Connor's arms, her shoulders shaking, but her words are distinct and clear. "I felt hands on my shoulders, somebody tried to push me, somebody tried . . ." She trails off, like she's unable to comprehend the depravity of that somebody's soul.

Somebody. Because that somebody wasn't me. "I didn't

do it," I say hotly, and beads of sweat spring up in a string of pearls around my throat. "I swear to God. I would never."

Rob is giving me that stare again, the stare that might mean he's about to press a button and fry me. "Did anyone see anything?"

"This is crazy," I say before I realize I'm talking over Cady, and that she's saying much the same thing.

"This *is* crazy," she echoes. "Scarlett would have no reason to hurt me. Scarlett's my friend."

Connor, Rob, and I share the same flinch, passed from one of us to the other like a particularly noxious brand of flu. Or mono, as the case may be. "Yeah," I say anyway. "I would never—"

"I saw it." Katharina's words stop us all in our places. She's commanding, regal; her hair, unraveling from its braid, flaps in a cape behind her. "Scarlett . . . how could you?"

I'm going to throw up my beating heart, and it's going to burst and spill my blood all over everybody's feet. They'll never be able to get their shoes clean. "I swear I didn't—"

"I saw it," Katharina thunders. I wait for anybody, for Melody, to defend me, but everybody else is silent. "They were both looking over the side, and all of a sudden Scarlett turned and shoved." Katharina clearly sees me blanch, and she shakes her head. "I'm sorry, Scarlett, but I saw it."

"I didn't." My forehead is getting very hot and there

are spots dancing in the corners of my vision. "I *didn't do it.*"

Cady—of all people—leaps to my defense again, but she sounds considerably less sure this time. "Guys, let's be real. Scarlett would never—"

"Scarlett hooked up with Connor," Katharina announces. Cady stops talking midsentence, and Connor's face goes so white his freckles stand out like stars. A hush clamps down on all of us. All of us except Katharina. How does she even know? "At the bonfire, in the barn."

I don't hear whatever she says next; the rushing in my ears is too loud. "I didn't do it," I say again, as loudly as I can, trying to speak over the noise.

Now Katharina's got her phone out. Her screen flashes as she turns it on. "Guys, should I call the police? Or Cady's parents? Anyone?" And then she glances up at me and gives me this little smile, the same smile I saw the time we found the knife.

It's her. She's back somehow. I don't know how, but she's back, and she's trying to ruin my life.

The dots cluster and swarm and then everything is black.

CHAPTER THIRTEEN

I didn't do it.

That's the refrain that runs through my mind the rest of the night. During the stiff, steep march down the safety stairs into the arms of two park security guards, one of whom is, conveniently, Tina's boyfriend and who therefore lets us stroll out the employee exit. During the walk back to the parking lot I am an island off to the side, plodding along, numb, whispering my refrain under my breath to drive it into my brain as the others whisper among themselves. During the scatter in the parking lot: Cynthia, Tina, and Randall race off, tossing excuses into the wind; and Rob and Connor walk off, Cady held up between them, staring at the ground, mute, like she can't believe everything that's happened, like her legs have just decided not to work anymore.

Katharina disappears. I look for her, a swell of fury rising in my chest, so ready to yell, and she's nowhere to be seen. I don't know where she went. The swell of fury rises in my throat as a hysterical laugh.

"Scarlett," Melody whispers, her eyebrows knitted together. "Scarlett, you sound crazy."

"I am crazy," I say drily. "Didn't you hear?"

"They're not going to call the police or anything," she continues, like I haven't spoken at all, like she hasn't heard me, or like she doesn't care. "They can't prove anything. But, Scarlett, did you really try to push Cady off the ledge?"

My shoulders slump and I shake my head, slowly at first, then more vigorously. I cannot speak. I've run dry of words.

"Okay," Melody says, but she doesn't sound convinced, and somehow that's the worst part of all.

All I want is for Melody to like me.

"Let's go home," she says.

The next day passes in a blur. I spend most of my time in bed. Matthew comes and prods me on the shoulder a few times, but I'm about as responsive as a dead frog and not nearly as interesting, so eventually he leaves me be. My dad does about the same thing, just more subtly, with calls through the door and concerned-sounding inquiries of "Are you okay?"

Connor tries to call once, twice, but I send him straight to voice mail, which I proceed not to check. Katharina doesn't show her face either, which does surprise me. I expected her to pop through my window or burrow up through my carpet, to do something so completely crazy I'd just completely crack.

On Sunday, I finally drag myself out of bed to go to work. I'm not going to let them scare me into missing work and getting fired and stopping me from being Skywoman. Because I didn't do it. I didn't do anything wrong.

I dress mechanically, eat cereal that tastes like shreds of paper, and head out the door. My stomach roils the whole time I'm waiting in line at the employment office; I don't know whether it would be worse to get sent to the south side with Connor and Rob, or the north side with Cady. Randall works on the east side, Tina on the west. There is no escape.

So I'm pleasantly surprised when they send me to central. Central is the park's Main Street area, with squat brick stores selling practical necessities like sunscreen and key chains and disposable cameras for the only people left on the planet who don't have a camera in their phone. I get installed on a cart just outside the entrance, which means I don't see any other team members but the manager assigned to ring me out and cover for me on bathroom breaks. Usually I hate being on a cart, because it's hot and lonely and you don't have a park phone, so if you need to go to the bathroom, you have to try to flag somebody down to tell your manager, but today I'm thrilled. If I were a super-hero, I'd be Luckwoman.

My new superpower holds until the end of the day, in the parking lot. Until I'm about to climb into my car, flush with luck and feeling like I've gotten away with something, which is stupid because I didn't actually do anything.

"Scarlett." Katharina sings rather than calls my name. I stiffen. "Showing your face at the park?"

I can feel her eyes raking the back of my neck. I can't turn around. If I turn around, she wins. "I'm not afraid to show my face. I didn't do anything wrong," I say evenly. One hand unlocks my door, the other wraps around my can of pepper spray. "Have a good night."

"Scarlett, wait." She's talking, but I've caught a flash of copper hair at the other end of the parking lot: Connor. I duck into my car and peel out before anyone can see me. Katharina tosses words after me, but they must land on the pavement, because I don't hear them.

My heart rate starts to calm as I turn out of the employee entrance and onto the road, but then I glance in my rear-view mirror and see it. Her. Katharina. She's in her car, and she's following me. *She's probably just going somewhere. She was going to her car at the same time,* I tell myself, but I make a left and she follows, and then I make another left and she follows, and I make a right for no reason but to see if she turns too, because nothing is that way but woods and my thinking cabin, and she *follows*. And I'm actually happy, because it's time to end this.

Still, my heart jumps into my throat. Recklessly, I toss my car to the side of the road, shift it into park, and lunge out before it shudders to a complete halt. I can see the surprise on her face as she jams to a halt too. Which is good. If she wanted me dead, she could have just plowed me over. "What do you want?" I scream at her. My shoulders are quaking, and my hand around the pepper spray is trembling too.

She's shaking her head as she gets out of the car. "I just wanted to talk to you, Scarlett," she says. "I really think you should quit your job. You're clearly not stable enough to be around people."

Maybe she's right goes through my head in a flash, but I push the thought away. "Why did you try to push Cady off the platform?" I don't know I'm going to say it until it comes out, and then it all comes rushing out. I didn't see anything on the platform, but this is the only explanation that makes sense. Katharina gaslighting me, trying to ruin my life. She was the only one who "saw" me do it, after all. "Did you do it specifically so you could blame me, or do you have something against Cady? Would you actually have pushed her over the side? Was she lucky she managed to catch herself, or did you grab her before she went over?"

Katharina smiles patronizingly at me. It's not even really a smile; it's just the corners of her lips turning up. "I don't know what you're talking about. *Scarlett.*"

It's the way she emphasizes my name. It's that that makes me certain, absolutely certain, it's *her.* "Get back in your car and drive away," I say, swallowing hard, trying to ingest some courage.

She "smiles" again, and this time it's twisted at the edges. "No, it's time we talk. It's about time. Don't you think?" And she takes a step toward me.

I've got my pepper spray out before I can blink, and it arcs in a long, shimmering line straight into her face. She shrieks in pain and doubles over, coughing so hard I think she might throw up. Her eyelids are already red and swelling. A little bit of pepper spray floats back toward me, a cloud, and I cough too.

I have to get out of here. Her car is blocking mine, so there's only one way to go: into the woods. To my thinking cabin. I can hide out there until she gives up. I go to run, take a step, and then stop.

If I leave her here, she could press charges against me. Even if I toss my can of pepper spray into the woods and claim ignorance, she can snap a picture of my car with her phone, drag me into a mess. I have a personal interest in avoiding the police, for reasons Katharina fully understands. If she's really her, alive somehow.

I just need time to think things through. I just need time.

I'm still not sure how I get Katharina to my thinking cabin; it's all a blur of leaves and pine-needle crunches underfoot. She shrieks as I pull her, but when I let her go, she can't do much but blindly stumble into trees, and nobody's around to hear her scream. My heart is pounding by the time I've gotten her secured in the cabin, my padlock locked. I brought it out one year to keep out kids or vandals or the ghost of the mad hunter who may or may not have built the cabin, and never took the key off my key ring.

Her screams echo in my ears all the way back to our cars, long after I've left her in the distance. Katharina's keys are still in her car. I don a baseball cap I find scrunched in the backseat and return her car to the employee parking lot, careful to keep my head low so all that the cameras will be able to see is the hat. We're similar enough in height and build and skin color that the black-and-white cameras won't be able to tell the difference, I hope. I walk back to my own car through the woods and toss the hat into a creek once I get far enough away.

I'm not a bad person. All I need is some time. Things aren't always black and white. Skywoman and the Blade could tell you that.

Skywoman, a.k.a. Augusta Leigh Sorensen, and the Blade, a.k.a. Emma Leigh Jacobs, were friends for most of their childhood and young adulthood. Their enmity began at age nineteen, when Emma Leigh Jacobs killed Augusta Leigh Sorensen's parents and then absconded with papers from their secret library. Augusta Leigh was shocked and horrified and racked with grief, from both the death of her parents and the betrayal by her friend. Augusta

Leigh's parents had always treated Emma Leigh with nothing but care and respect, and here Emma Leigh had slaughtered them, had bashed them over the head and cut their throats like animals, with no motive at all. Emma Leigh certainly didn't give one then, and every time she came face to face with Augusta Leigh–turned–Skywoman, she wouldn't give one either. She copped to killing Skywoman's first husband and many others, but she wouldn't give a reason for the murders that launched her into her status as one of the comic-book world's most notorious villains.

Until one of the later issues. Readership was flagging, and Prodigy Comics had to do something to boost it, so they started teasing the series' most dramatic revelation to date almost a year before the comic book was actually released. It worked. Everybody wanted to know, and everybody bought the comic book. Even the cartoon got on board, teasing the revelation with fades to black and dramatic voice-overs.

Setting: the roof of a skyscraper, headquarters of the Silver Corporation (where Augusta Leigh's parents worked for many years) in Silver City. Skywoman has been called to the scene of a dramatic break-in, only to discover scientists scattered dead over the floor and the Blade patiently waiting. Well, not so much patiently waiting as frantically searching, rifling through files and tossing papers over her shoulder. She stops as Skywoman bursts in through a window. "I thought you'd come," the Blade says.

Skywoman spares scarcely a glance at the five dead scientists. "You didn't think I'd come—you knew I'd come," she says. "We need to end this." Though the shattered window is at the other end of the room, somehow wind still causes her unmussed hair to float in the air.

The Blade stands, clutching a file to her chest. "Did you ever wonder why I killed your parents?"

Skywoman flinches at the Blade's bluntness. At this point readers were (or at least I was) screaming at the page, "Of course she wondered! She asks you every time you two see each other! She thinks it every night before she goes to sleep! She angsts about it to Wonderman every chance she gets!"

Skywoman is much politer than the readers (a.k.a. me). "It doesn't matter," she lies through her (perfect, shiny, straight, white) teeth. "This needs to end."

The Blade paces circles around the room, stepping carefully over the bodies. Skywoman follows, stepping over the dead just as carefully. "Your parents worked for the Silver Corporation, in this very building," the Blade says. Obviously, this was on the page and not on the screen, but I liked to imagine her voice as neutral, carefully measured, the same monotone as her voice actor. "For years. Did they ever tell you what they did?"

The next panel is a close-up of Skywoman's face, her eyes narrowed, her lips clearly trembling with the effort not to burst out and yell. All she says, though, is, "This needs to end."

"I'm sure you knew they were scientists," the Blade continues as if Skywoman hasn't spoken. The way she is stepping over the bodies over and over, backward and gracefully, is beginning to look like a dance. "But did they ever tell you what they *did*? What they were doing, here, in this building?"

At this point you'd expect Skywoman just to go ahead and end it already, but she stills. You can see the conflict in her eyes: she wants to end this, as she keeps saying, but she also wants to hear what the Blade has to say. "What does it matter?" she says unconvincingly. "You're just going to lie anyway."

The Blade slips the folder into her waistband and holds her hands in front of her, presumably to show that she doesn't have any of her fingers crossed. "I would not lie about this," she says, and something in her monotone must convince Skywoman, because Skywoman stops talking.

"Your parents were trying to destroy the world."

The next panel shows Skywoman in shock: gaping mouth, wide eyes, eyebrows shooting up nearly to her hairline.

"The Silver Corporation tasked them with the creation of a weapon greater than the nuclear bomb," the Blade says. "And they were almost there. I tried to convince them to stop. Talked to them about what the Silver Corporation wanted to do with the weapon." No indication is given about how the Blade found out about the Silver Corporation's supersecret plans, but I didn't care (though critics did). "They still wouldn't stop." The Blade pauses and looks at the ground. If Skywoman really wanted to, she could dive forward and snap the Blade's neck while she isn't looking. She doesn't, though. "I had to think of the world."

"You're lying," Skywoman says, but her eyebrows are knotted in a way that says she isn't convinced.

"Of course, the Silver Corporation didn't stop just because the project's two lead scientists had been assassinated," the Blade continues. "I couldn't let them complete the weapon." She hesitates again, probably for dramatic effect. "They even put the police on the case. To guard the weapon. I tried to convince them to take my side, but . . ."

"My husband," Skywoman says. "You killed him because the Silver Corporation employed him to protect the weapon."

"He was in on it," the Blade says. "Do you know what the Silver Corporation wants to use the weapon for?"

Skywoman shakes her head. Her mouth hangs open. She looks like a guppy. A beautiful guppy.

"First they're going to set it off in a city nearby. Not Silver City. A different city." The Blade's eyes are flat. "Kill everybody within a ten-mile radius. Gruesomely. The weapon isn't just about death; it's about suffering. A million people or more will bleed through their pores and feel their bones crumble and eventually choke on their own bodily fluids."

"My parents would never have taken part in something

like that," Skywoman says, but the shivery way her dialogue is written makes it clear her voice is shaking.

"Once they've slaughtered all those people, the Silver Corporation will come forward and claim responsibility. Tell the government it was only a demonstration of their power, and they'll do it again. They'll have the whole world at their knees. They'll be able to do anything they want to." The Blade shakes her head. "I couldn't let that happen, even if it meant I had to sacrifice people I cared about." She looks up and off into the distance. "Even if it meant I had to sacrifice everything I'd ever hoped and dreamed of, and even though it meant everybody I cared about would hate me. Even you, Augusta."

Skywoman jolts at the sound of her name. "It's been a long time since I heard that name," she says. She doesn't ask why the Blade didn't just come clean years and years ago, which would have saved everyone a whole lot of pain and heartache. Critics did, though.

"I'm sorry that I had to hurt you, but I'm not sorry for what I did," the Blade says. She holds out her hand. "Augusta. Will you join me? Will you help me take the Silver Corporation down?"

Skywoman stares at the Blade's hand, the hand that slit her parents' throats and shot her first husband to death. "Can you prove what you're telling me?"

"I can." The Blade doesn't waver. "I can't do it alone anymore, Augusta."

Skywoman stares at the Blade's hand for another moment, another very long moment . . . and then takes it.

This issue was a game changer. It turned readers' assumptions on their heads and caused months of outcry and speculation as to the future of the series, now that the Blade had brought Skywoman over to the "dark" side.

It was my favorite issue. Skywoman wasn't all good, and the Blade wasn't all bad. Until that issue, Skywoman had saved lives and protected Silver City, but she'd also unknowingly enabled evil. The Blade had killed innocent people and terrorized an entire city, but she'd also saved millions of lives and kept the country from being pressed under the thumbs of people who wanted to do it terrible harm.

You can be a good person and do bad things. And sometimes it may look like someone is doing something bad, or evil, but when you look more closely at the situation, you realize your assumptions were wrong, and that whatever's happening may not be so bad or evil after all. It may be warranted. Maybe even good.

As I head home, with Katharina in the cabin, tied to the windowsill and spitting mad, a gallon jug of water and some granola bars I stored there long ago at her feet, I feel like I might sprout a cape and fly away.

CHAPTER FOURTEEN

I don't get out of bed all the next morning. I'm supposed to work, but I don't remember until after my shift's supposed to have started. I may get fired, but I can't stop picturing Katharina's face as I left her behind.

I can't leave her in the cabin forever. Eventually she'll need more food and water. But I also can't let her out. I can't let her back into my life, not after what she did to me. After what I did to her.

The person who gets me out of bed, finally, is Melody, whom I haven't spoken with since the incident on the Blade's Revenge. After I've spent the morning hiding under my covers, she marches through my door and throws open my curtains. I squint at the sudden influx of light.

"You missed work today," she says abruptly, crossing her arms over her chest. She's in workout attire, T-shirt and yoga pants and hair off her face, so it must be the afternoon. There's a clock just behind me, but I can't be bothered to roll over to check.

"How do you even know that?"

She uncrosses her arms and lunges forward, stripping my covers off and tossing them on the floor. "My God, Scarlett, you're disgusting," she says. "What is that? Crumbs?"

I can't be bothered to roll over to check that, either. "Go away." I lean over the side of my bed to pull the covers back—the real world is cold!—but she neatly jerks them away with her foot.

"Five Banners has called the house, like, eight times," she says. "You didn't show up this morning. If you don't show up, you're going to get fired, and then Dad is going to murder you."

Maybe I can shame her into silence. "That's awfully bad taste to joke like that, considering what just happened to Monica."

"Oh, you shut up," Melody says. "That's so not what you're moping about. I told them that you had car trouble and your phone had died, but that I'd let you use my car, and they said they won't penalize you this once if you go in now. Get up and go to work."

"Let them fire me."

"You can't let them win," Melody says. "Get out of bed and go to work."

"No." I can't get out of bed because I can't see the people who might be panicking over Katharina's disappearance. I can't look into their eyes and know that I'm the one who caused their panic and their fear. That I'm the one who inducted a new member into the society.

"Just leave me alone," I say, and roll over. I still have a pillow to bury my face in.

"No." Melody yanks my pillow out from under me, sending my head thudding to the mattress below. It doesn't hurt, but I wince anyway. "I laid out your uniform. All you have to do is put it on. And maybe shower. You kind of smell."

Without my pillow, I am exposed. Naked. I sit up. "Why aren't you siding with Katharina? Don't you think I'm crazy? That I tried to push Cady?"

"No." Melody doesn't hesitate, or flinch, and her eyes don't dart away. "I think Katharina was wrong. Now get out of bed."

"You think she was wrong? Like, she made a mistake?" Melody's belief in me bolsters my spirits enough for me to slide to the edge of the bed and put my feet on the floor. The floor is cold.

"No," Melody says. "I think she lied. Now get up. You definitely need a shower."

I get up. I'm not used to standing after so many hours in bed, and I sway a bit on my feet. "Why would she lie?"

"I don't know." This time her eyes do dart away. She's lying. She knows. But I can't bring myself to press harder, to cut deeper, not when she's saying she believes in me. "Am I going to have to drag you out by your hair?"

"I'm coming," I say, and I am. I totter to the door, where she's so helpfully stacked my uniform pieces. I take a sniff of my armpit under the pretext of cracking my neck. God, I'm rank. "Why do you even care?"

I didn't expect her to come in and wrest me out of bed in the first place. I didn't expect her to tell me she believes me over Katharina.

Most of all, I don't expect her to burst into tears when I ask her such a small question. She sobs so hard her shoulders shudder and her ponytail comes undone; I feel awkward standing there, like I should be gathering her into my arms and telling her everything is going to be okay. Finally she lifts her head and wipes her eyes. "Because you're my sister," she says. "That's why I care." And somehow that sets her off again; she sinks down onto the edge of my bed and places her face in her hands.

I don't know what just happened, but I know I'm so overwhelmed I can't even begin to process right now. "Okay," I say. "Thanks for . . . this."

By the time I get out of the shower, smelling like soap and something artificially floral, Melody is gone.

I spent the rest of the day Pixie found the knife convinced that Stepmother would decide to give us a random pat-down, or that the knife would slice down Pixie's pant leg and clatter to the floor, flinging drops of blood into the air, but nothing happened. We finished our work, ate our dinner, and were ushered into the basement as usual.

Pixie sat down at one of our chairs and pulled out the knife with a flourish. "What should I do with it?" she said. She set it on the table and stared at it. I stared at it too. It stared back.

This was dangerous. "If she knows you have that, she could really kill us," I said. "This isn't a joke. Or a game."

"I know that," Pixie said, sounding insulted. "You could kill someone with this." She stood and backed away from it, as if she wanted to consider it from a different viewpoint, see if it looked any less threatening from another angle.

I said nothing to that, because what was there to say?

Soon after that Pixie retrieved the knife, and we went to sleep. She tucked it carefully under her side of the mattress and lay on top of it. "Night, Scarlett," she said.

"Good night, Pixie."

When she woke a few hours later to pee, her fingers scrabbled instinctively for her prize. It was gone.

I was awake, my eyes scrunched firmly shut. My breathing was fast and shallow. I didn't fool Pixie. "Scarlett, I can see you're awake," I could hear her say through her teeth. "Give it back."

I gave up all pretense and sat up. "I don't have it," I said, blinking at her.

Pixie dove forward and grabbed me by the shoulders,

shaking me so hard I thought my head would pop off. "Give it back!"

"It's too dangerous," I said. "It's for the best."

She shook me harder. Everything blurred, and something in my neck cracked. Her shaking slowed. "Give it *back*!"

I stared at her. She could shake me until my neck broke if she had to. I wasn't going to let her get us both killed. "No," I said.

She stared back at me. I stared back at her. And then the entirely unexpected happened.

Pixie buried her face in my shoulder and began to cry.

"Hey . . . hey." I patted her gingerly on the head. It had been a while since she'd washed her hair, and it was almost sticky to the touch. "It's okay. It'll be okay."

"No," she whispered. "I can't do it anymore. I can't." It turned into a chant. "I can't, I can't, I can't, I can't, I can't."

I petted her hair again. "Yes, you can. It's going to be okay."

She shook her head, and slime smeared over my arm. "I can't, I can't, I can't. I can't do it anymore."

"Hey, hey." She was making me uncomfortable, and I tried to edge away, only to have her scoot along with me. "Everything's just going to be like normal."

"I can't, I can't, I can't." She seemed to have gotten stuck. I shook her a little, trying to jar her, but it didn't stop the chanting.

I was going to hit her. I couldn't hit her. I *could* distract her. "Hey," I said. "Want to hear about my family?"

"I can't, I can't, I can't, I can't, I can't."

I wasn't sure what to do. An offer to hear about my life had never failed before. "I never told you about my sister's fourth birthday party," I said. "I thought she was cutting her cake too slowly, so I smashed her face in it."

"I can't, I can't, I can't, I can't, I can't."

"What about the time my grandma died?" That was a sad story, but maybe Pixie needed to hear something sad. "She was in hospice and had Alzheimer's, so she didn't know who I was at the end and she thought my dad was her husband, which was kind of gross and weird. She kept saying, '*Quiero hacerte el amor*,' and Melody and me knew it was wrong but we kept laughing anyway and we felt really bad."

"I can't, I can't, I can't, I can't, I can't."

I sat back, defeated. I had nothing left. Nothing left I could tell her. Nothing left I could give her. "I wish you were different." The words burst out before I could stop them, and they kept on falling. "When I asked Stepmother for a friend, I wish she had picked someone else."

This stopped her. She stopped chanting midword and spun to stare at me, her head making a full revolution like an owl's. She was already so close I could see the tears shimmering over her golden irises. "You what?"

Maybe I shouldn't have said that. "Nothing."

She stood, looming over me. "You *asked* her for me?" Her voice broke. "You're the reason I'm here?"

I wasn't sure what to say to that, so I said nothing.

"You did this to me." Her voice was stronger now. "You *did* this to me. This is *your* fault." Her eyes were beginning to shimmer again, this time with anger, and her fingers had balled into fists. "This is *your fault.*"

Forget Stepmother. *Pixie* was going to kill me. Without breaking eye contact, I backed away and rummaged around in the dresser drawer where I'd hidden the knife, then walked back and handed it over.

Pixie took the knife back. She didn't say anything. She didn't have to.

I grab one of Melody's homemade raisin bran muffins as I run out the door. It goes down in lumps and settles like a rock in my stomach. That's probably why I feel so heavy; it's not dread at all. I'm totally light and cheerful. The atmosphere inside my car is so warm and bright I might burst out of my chair and rise like one of Melody's muffins in the oven.

I swallow hard. This campaign to psych myself up? Not working. I feel like every person is staring at me. That every one of them knows about me and Katharina.

I trudge through the employee parking lot and toward headquarters, where I've been sent today. I'm so wrapped up in my internal mantra—*everything will be okay, everything will be okay, everything will be okay*—that it takes me a while to notice the buzzing around me, the whispers that cloud the air like fog.

It makes me think, with an unpleasant jolt, of my first morning. The morning Monica joined the club.

By now everybody must know Katharina is gone. That was fast.

My mouth dries out more and more the closer and closer I get to headquarters, and the bits of muffin in my stomach get heavier and heavier; I feel like the bottom of my stomach might burst and my intestines will just drop right out of my body and crush my feet. I hope I hope I hope Connor isn't working today. Of course, if Connor isn't there, then Rob will be there instead, and I hope I hope I hope Rob isn't there either. Maybe I'll get spectacularly lucky and learn they both decided, on the spur of the moment, to quit and jet off to Tibet to shave their heads and become monks.

No such luck: they're both there, in the back room, conferring before the whiteboard schedule.

Monks probably can't have tattoos, anyway. Or freckles.

I wait for them to notice me. I can't speak first. My tongue has swollen up and filled my mouth, roof to teeth.

When they finally do realize I'm there, neither of them will look at me. Their eyes are cockroaches and I'm a light; they skitter away whenever they get too close to me. Rob finally clears his throat. "You're going to be in Wonderkidz today."

I nod. I didn't expect anything different.

Rob gathers up my cash drawer and papers while Connor stares at the wall and pretends not to see me. The muscles working in his jaw and throat say otherwise. I look at the floor, then at the ceiling, then at the wall, then at a shelf full of Skywoman figurines. She's in various poses: one triumphant, her fist over her head; one fighting, her whip coiled in front of her; one pensive, staring off into the distance.

If Skywoman could go on after she discovered her beloved second husband was nothing more than the Blade's spy, if she could hold up her head and go about saving the world and the citizens of Silver City after she'd been so punched in the gut, I can manage to face Connor and Rob and the others.

Except Katharina, but I don't have to worry about that. Just the thought of her makes my jaw clench. "Is Katharina working in this area today?" I ask. My voice is rusty from disuse, but I have to know for sure if they know she's gone.

Connor's back stiffens like someone's shoved a poker up his butt. Rob stops mid paper shuffle and swings around to face me. "You haven't heard?" he says incredulously, his eyes wide, like he's forgotten he's supposed to be mad at and afraid of me.

"Heard what?" The more I speak, the easier it is, like the first words are battering down the path for the words tumbling after.

Connor and Rob exchange a *look*. "Katharina was supposed to work this morning," Rob says. "She never showed up."

So they know. "Is she . . ."

"We called the police when we couldn't reach her,"

he continues, as though I didn't speak at all. "Normally, we wouldn't call that quickly, but after Monica . . . well. They've been poking around. They can't find her."

I speak along with Rob. "She's gone."

Throughout the rest of the day I am a bird gathering bits of string and leaves and tinsel, building up a nest of all everybody knows about Katharina's mysterious disappearance. Evidently, word hasn't spread of what happened at our makeshift memorial service, because people are still willing to talk to me. Even Tina spares me a small smile as we pass on our way to and from the Canteen. Maybe Melody isn't the only one who didn't believe Katharina.

Today is Monday. Katharina worked the day shift on Sunday. Just like Monica, she waved goodbye to her coworkers, said she'd see them tomorrow, and disappeared into thin air. And, just like Monica, nobody's heard from her since. As Rob said, they usually wouldn't call the police after one day, but they called her house and her cell and nobody picked up. If she'd been taken like Monica had been taken, they didn't want to lose a second of time in the hunt.

Kyrsten in Merch swears she saw a mustachioed man in a black cape follow Katharina as she left for the parking lot, trailing after her close as a shadow. Marcus in Foods thinks Katharina mentioned taking off for a few days to visit her cousin in Florida and just forgot to register for time off. Sarah in Guest Relations says she saw, on the security camera, a blurry Katharina stealing off into the woods with Scott, the Merch supervisor, and that Scott must have killed her so she couldn't tell his wife and kids about their torrid affair.

One theory is conspicuous in its absence. Nobody mentions Monica. Nobody mentions that if two girls the same age go missing from the same place within a few weeks of each other, it's probably the same person who did it. Nobody mentions that Monica is dead, and that if they don't catch this guy, probably soon Katharina will be dead too.

Nobody mentions it, but I know they're thinking it.

Mayra in Merch has a fiancé who's a cop, and she says they don't have any leads. They scoured the security tapes and spent this morning tracing Katharina's last footsteps, but it's like she suddenly sprouted wings and took flight and is hiding up in the clouds, laughing every so often and shaking them and making them rain. They're scouring the woods near where they found Monica's body, in case he's keeping her nearby—because that's what the police think, that she was taken by the same person, even if nobody at Five Banners will admit it. They're talking to everyone who worked with Katharina during her final shift. Nobody knows anything useful. All they can say is that she's gone.

The police can't find her family. When they went to the address Katharina had listed on her employment forms, nobody was home, and nobody came home. They ran the address in their internal database, or whatever it is, and discovered that the house is vacant. Nobody is supposed to be living there.

All they have to go on is what Katharina told all of us at Adventure World. That she'd just moved to Jefferson at the end of the school year, the beginning of the summer. That she'd moved from somewhere in Ohio, or Iowa, or Idaho, or one of those states with lots of *i*'s and *o*'s. That she spoke of a cat. That she had a lot of old sayings with mysterious origins.

And all they know now is that she's gone.

At the end of the day, I expect Rob to bustle in, all business, to pull me off register and silence the hellspawn screeching over the speakers.

Instead I get Connor. He ambles in, hands in his pockets, shoulders sloped with a forced sort of casualness. I half expect him to purse his lips and fire off a whistle or two. "Hey," he says. I go to turn away, but he puts out his hand, and for some reason I stay. "Don't move. Please. I won't talk about . . . us. But I have to tell you something important."

I sigh. "Okay." I'm not really sure what else to say. We haven't really spoken since I told him to get away from me, and I'm not going to apologize for that. And I haven't seen him since I was accused of trying to kill his ex-girlfriend/ semi-girlfriend/whatever Cady is to him. I didn't do it, so I'm not going to apologize for that, either.

And I certainly hope he doesn't know about Katharina.

He licks his lips. I'm surprised to see how chapped they are. I don't remember them being that chapped when I had them pressed against my own. "Rob was going to come and take you off register," he says. "I asked if I could come instead."

Lips that chapped must be painful. I imagine them cracking, bleeding, every time he opens his mouth. "I just want to go home," I say, or plead—I'm not entirely sure.

He leans against the counter and sighs. "I think about you all the time. I wish things hadn't happened the way they did."

"Yeah, well, it still happened, and you still hurt me." I slam my hands against the counter, and he jumps. The Wonderkidz hellspawn screech out a particularly high note in the background. I can barely hear them. I can barely hear them in my ears, that is—I'm pretty sure that, at this point, their voices are etched deep into my soul. "Can you please just take me off register so I can go home?"

He doesn't move. "I tried to call you, but you didn't pick up. I wanted to tell you that I don't think you tried to push Cady off the Blade's Revenge. I think Katharina was lying. Tina and Cynthia think so too." I notice he doesn't mention Rob. That doesn't surprise me as much as his admission does. "I don't know why she would lie, but you couldn't have gotten at Cady at that angle."

I soften, just slightly. "Good. Because I *didn't* do it. I would never do it. Melody thinks Katharina was lying too. And they're friends." The fact of Katharina's disappearance hangs heavy in the air. "Well, they were. I don't know about . . . now."

He clears his throat, then blinks and runs his hand

over his face. "Yeah," he says. I've gone and made things more awkward than they already were. I can't even believe that's possible. I'm the champion of awkwardness. "Well, I just wanted to tell you that."

That strikes me as a funny thing to say. I laugh, and my laugh holds a tinge of hysteria. Probably not the best thing at this moment, when I want to look calm and cool and collected and definitely not crazy, but it spills out of me anyway. I can't stop. "I don't care what you think of me," I lie.

"I care what you think of *me*." Connor sounds genuinely wounded. I wish he *were* genuinely wounded. It would give me an excuse to rush over, to run my hands over his freckles in examination of whatever force tore them apart. "Scarlett . . ."

He looks at me, and inside I curse as I realize I'm caught up in the thrall of those half-golden eyes. My whole body tingles with the effort it takes not to touch him, to kiss him, to grind his belt buckle deep into the skin of my belly. "Don't," I say, tearing my eyes away, looking at the floor, the counter, anywhere but at him.

He doesn't say anything else, and I shift. "I really want to go home," I say. "Cady's probably looking for you anyway."

His hands, moving toward the cash drawer, stop when I say his ex's name. "Cady's furious with me," he says. "She's not looking for me."

I have to bite my tongue to keep from saying, *Good*. My

body tingles harder; I cough to try to shake it out of me. "My register?"

He coughs back, like we're speaking in a secret language. I wish I could understand it. "Sorry. I'm working on it."

"Work faster," I say. My cash drawer finally pops free of my register with a *beep*.

"Voilà." He sounds strangled. "Hey, I almost forgot. . . ." He reaches under the counter for the button that turns the speakers on and off, and clicks. The hellspawn cut off mid-screech, and the silence rings in my ears.

I just need time. A little bit of time.

CHAPTER FIFTEEN

I'm still hopped up on nerves when I head to work the next morning, and the nerves only jump more when I see the men in suits stationed throughout the park. It's a long walk today, to the north side, and so I see at least four of them. Men in suits, and cars, too. I've never seen a car in the park. A black car. So much black.

I make a note to ask the assistant manager what's up. But when I enter Dolphin Discovery—the north-side headquarters—I find Cady on her knees, folding shirts, her hair sticking up in little spikes all over her head. I stop short, and my heart plummets to my feet. She doesn't hear it; she's folding shirts as viciously as it's possible to fold shirts, snapping them out and shoving their sides together, then slamming them onto shelves. Her face is red and she's breathing heavy as a bull.

I stand there and watch. I'm afraid her head might explode if I speak. I'm not sure if it would explode into shrapnel or tears. I'm not sure which would be worse.

Maybe I should turn around and leave. If I miss another day, I'll be terminated, but that's the least of my worries right now.

Cady looks over as I'm trying to decide. "Oh, it's you," she says, her voice flat. "What do you want?"

I clear my throat. There's no blockage or rustiness to clear, but it just seems like something I should do. "They sent me here," I say. "For the day. Sorry." *No*, I tell myself, *don't apologize. You have nothing to apologize for.* It's too late to take it back, though, and it hangs in the air like smog. I might choke on it.

She rolls her eyes up at the ceiling, like she's expecting help from above—maybe a massive icicle that'll suddenly appear and detach and spear me through the brain—and then turns back to me with a heavy sigh. "I wish they hadn't."

My stomach clenches. I wish they hadn't too. "I swear I didn't push you," I say. "I wouldn't do that. I swear."

She stares at me for a second before brushing her hands off on her khakis and standing. "How about kissing my . . . Connor?" she says acidly. "Do you swear you didn't do that, too?"

I wish I had some tea I could offer her. Offering

someone tea is a very Melody thing to do, which means it's the right thing to do. "No." I figure now isn't the best time to go into how Connor is actually her ex-boyfriend. "Connor and I did kiss."

She makes a scoffing noise deep in her throat, like she's choking, or like she's going to throw up. "What happened?" she says, and she's looking at the floor.

I really wish I had some tea. "I should probably go on register. It's already almost nine."

She looks at me again, eyes blazing. "What happened? Tell me how it happened."

Should I hug her? Probably not. "I don't think that's a good idea," I say.

Her eyes blaze so hot and hard my polo might actually go up in flames. It's probably not flame-retardant. "No," she says, crossing her arms so hard the tips of her elbows go white. "I want to hear exactly how it happened. I want you to tell me every single thing that—"

The door opens, making us both jump. "Cade." It's Rob, staring at her with soft eyes. It hits me then: he loves her. She's not just his friend; he loves her, but she's his best friend's girl—well, kind of—and therefore off-limits.

It hurts, then, to realize how good he is. He's no morally ambiguous Blade, he's Wonderman through and through. He must want Cady and Connor to break up and stay broken up, yet he's been doing everything in his power to keep the breakup from becoming completely final. He's been doing everything in his power to give her happiness at the expense of his own.

He doesn't hate me because he hates *me*. He hates me because he's conflicted, because a part of him wants me to succeed in breaking them up and making Connor happy enough where he'd be fine with Rob swooping in on his ex.

I want to hug him. I wonder how it feels to hug such a good person. I wonder if goodness is warm or cold or soft or hard. Goodness has piercings and tattoos and tiny, tiny teeth.

"Cade," Rob says again, breaking me out of my reverie. "Cynthia switched us. She wants you in the south today."

Cady takes a deep breath. "But I was just—"

"She needs you right now," Rob says, his voice unfathomably gentle. I think I might love him. Not in a physical way—I'm certainly not attracted to him—but in a way you'd love your grandfather or a beloved pet dog. I want to cuddle him and treasure him and never let him go.

Cady's shoulders slump. "Okay," she says, her resolve clearly weakening. "But—"

"You should go now," Rob says. "Okay?"

She nods, sniffing hard. "Okay," she says, still avoiding my eyes, and darts out the door without looking back.

Rob watches her until she disappears behind a hedge. "I'm going to send you to Hormones," he says. Hormones is the park's supposed store for teens, full of hip clothes and groovy accessories and sticky massage chairs crusted in potato chip crumbs. "Let me get your cash drawer."

I wonder if Cynthia really switched the two of them of her own free will, or if Rob asked for the change when he saw the assignment lists for the day. Probably the latter, martyr that he is. I wonder if he'd throw himself on a plush sword for her. "Okay."

We set out. Hormones is a short walk away, but we still pass a few of the black cars and people in suits. Maybe they're here for me. The thought doesn't scare me as much as it should. In jail, not only would I be safe from Katharina and Melody. I'd be safe from myself. "What's with all of this?" I ask, trying my best to sound unconcerned.

"They're finally fixing *all* the cameras," Rob says, and gives a short laugh. "Two girls gone missing from the park isn't exactly good for publicity."

Cameras. Of course. I breathe a little bit easier. "Any word on who took Monica?" I ask.

Rob grimaces and shakes his head. "Rumors say they think it was someone inside the park," he says. "That's the only way somebody could have gotten her out without crossing in front of any of the working cameras or witnesses. Same with . . . Katharina. I hear they're going to start talking to all of us over the next few days."

My heart slows, then stops. Somehow I don't die. "*All* of us?"

"Yeah," he says. "I hope they find her. And not like they found Monica."

My heart hasn't restarted. I should really be dead. "Yeah," I say, and swallow air. "Me too."

. . .

I didn't sleep at all the night I gave Pixie the knife back. I closed my eyes, sure, and pretended, but I was too afraid I'd wake up to her poised above me, about to stab. Or worse, that I wouldn't wake up at all.

In the morning, I was still alive. I opened my eyes and yawned widely, pretending to wake up, and found Pixie on her side, staring at me. "Morning," I said. "Did you sleep well?"

"Sure," she said flatly. She was already dressed. I didn't ask, and I couldn't see, but I would've bet my breakfast that she had that knife clamped tight against her side.

I wondered why she needed it. What she planned to do with it.

My unease grew.

Was she going to stab Stepmother? Aside from Pixie, Stepmother was all I had. She fed me and clothed me and had taken care of me since my parents decided they didn't want me anymore. I made her think of her daughter. What would she do without me? What would I do without her?

And Stepmother's words from long ago still nagged at me. If Pixie escaped without my knowing, I didn't think Stepmother would take it out on me. But if I knew about the knife—and Stepmother would know I knew, she knew everything—and didn't tell her, she would kill me. I knew that.

Pixie and I chewed our sandwiches in silence over the

sink. Stepmother sat at the kitchen table behind us, her reading glasses on as she combed through stacks of paper. Pixie took small, quick bites and chewed with a rabbity sort of concentration; she stood stiffly, and I knew she didn't want to move lest the knife shift position. "Don't," I whispered. Pixie glared at me. I heard the papers shift behind me as Stepmother looked up, then the papers shifted again as she looked down.

Pixie set her sandwich on the counter and turned around, reaching for her side. I turned to follow her. She'd taken one step toward Stepmother when I shouted, "She's got a knife."

Time stopped, and it was as if the world around me crawled in slow motion. Stepmother's eyes narrowing as she hopped to her feet, her chair skittering over the linoleum behind her. Pixie's gasp of surprise, long and drawn out, as she reached for the knife. The knife itself, glittering in the kitchen light.

But in reality it all happened in a second. Stepmother's jump, Pixie's lunge, the knife cutting through empty air.

All I could do was stand and watch. I couldn't move.

Pixie, on the other hand, was nothing but movement. She let out a wounded cry when she saw she'd missed, but regrouped quickly and darted for the kitchen door. It was locked, as always, and the precious few seconds it took for Pixie to open both locks was enough time for Stepmother to catch up to her and yell for the girls to come help.

But Pixie wasn't having it. She snarled and swung the knife viciously just as the lock clicked open; Stepmother gasped and stumbled backward to avoid the knife slicing through her stomach. Pixie stood there in front of the unlocked door, panting, the knife held before her with both hands like a prayer. The girls stopped in the doorway and inhaled all at once. Stepmother eyed her warily, her hands on her belly. I saw a line of red drip to the floor, and it was my turn to gasp. She'd been cut.

Pixie's eyes flickered to me for a second, just for a second. I couldn't read her expression; she could've been pleading for me to come along, or angry that I'd betrayed her, or excited to burst out that door, or all three at once, I still don't know. I looked at the floor, and when I looked up again, she was gone.

Stepmother and the girls gave chase. I waited for them in the kitchen. I finished my sandwich and then finished Pixie's sandwich too, because why not? Even if she came back, she wouldn't be needing it anymore.

Stepmother came back empty-handed, breathing hard, her eyes slits.

It was good I'd eaten that extra half sandwich, because she stuck me back in the basement and didn't let me out for three days. It was okay. I hadn't told her about the knife beforehand. I deserved it.

When she did let me out, she was calmer, her eyes flat and placid. "I found your friend," she said in greeting. I stopped breathing. "I caught her and she cried and asked for forgiveness. I do not forgive. First I cut off her fingers, one by one, then her toes, and then I cut her throat and threw her in an unmarked grave. Let this be a lesson to you, Jane, if you ever should think to betray me."

I tried to curl around myself that night, tried to wish away my thoughts of Pixie, but my tears soaked the mattress, and I was cold, cold, cold.

I don't go home after work. I drive immediately to the dirt road in the woods, then walk from there to my cabin. My heart hasn't restarted. I am a zombie shambling in search of brains. A zombie carrying a Tupperware container full of bran muffins and three bottles of water.

I'm shaking as I unlock the cabin door. I worry for a moment that Katharina won't be there—not that she will have escaped, but that she was never there in the first place, that her entire existence was just a concoction of a fraying mind—but she's still there, slumped in the corner, hair hanging in dusty ropes over her face. She glares through it as I come in. "What?" she spits, voice rusty.

I'm shaking so hard she must be able to hear my bones clattering against each other as I set the muffins and water down in front of her and then jump back before she can grab an ankle. "I came because I had to say I'm sorry," I say. "I never said it, but I hurt you, and I'm sorry for that." I expect I'll feel better as the words leave my lips, that they'll become balloons and lift me off the ground, but I don't. If anything, I feel worse. Because I can only give her these words; I can't go back in time and stop myself from doing what I did.

Worse, I don't think I'd do that even if I could.

Katharina snorts and rolls her eyes. "You're not sorry," she says. Her eyes stop midroll and zero in on the fireplace, at the far side of the cabin. "What's that?" she says slowly, like each word sticks to the inside of her mouth.

I look. To my surprise, a laugh jumps from my throat. It's my knife. The same size and shape as the one we found under Violetta's mattress. "I bought it a few years ago," I say, and wander over to pick it up. It's hard and cold and feels like sadness made solid. It hasn't always felt that way. "That knife saved my life. I felt naked without one, especially out here. You never know what might happen out here." I've always felt relatively safe in the woods, but that doesn't mean totally safe. Pepper spray only slows someone down; it doesn't stop them forever. And out here, where it's at least a mile to civilization, slowing someone down might not be enough.

"I just want my life back." Katharina sounds like she's crying, too, like the words stuck so fast they clogged her throat all the way up to her tear ducts. "You took everything from me. You owe me this, at least." She's been shackled to the wall by a girl with a knife, a girl who's proven herself ruthless where she's concerned, and yet she's not backing down. I admire that.

And it doesn't surprise me. I would do the same thing. We were always so much alike, me and her. Her and me.

"I'm sorry," I say, and I really am. I don't know what's going to happen. I can't leave her here forever, but I know I can't let her free to ruin my life. I'm finally okay, or as okay as I can be. I have a job I like that makes me feel useful, and I need to find out what happens to Skywoman after the cliff-hanger of the last issue of the comic book, which left her now-Blade-allied self at odds with Wonderman on the roof of the Silver Corporation. If I let Katharina go free, I can never work to put people like Stepmother behind bars, where they belong.

I don't realize I'm staring at the knife until I blink and see silver dazzling on the backs of my eyelids.

"I'm sorry," I say. I seem to have gotten stuck. Katharina covers her face with her hair, maybe so she won't have to see what's coming, and I feel a twinge deep in my belly. She thinks me capable of murder. Which isn't surprising, given what she's seen of me.

My lip trembles—if you weren't looking for it, you'd miss it. "I'm sorry," I say, still looking at the knife, and then I hear the door open behind me.

"Scarlett?" Melody's voice cuts through the tension, and Katharina peers out through her hair. "Scarlett!" I swing around only to see that Melody isn't talking to me.

She's talking to Katharina.

CHAPTER SIXTEEN

Melody is talking to Katharina, is calling her Scarlett, but she should be talking to me. I drop the knife, feeling sick at what I almost considered doing.

Pixie is dead. I killed Pixie when I slashed Stepmother with my stolen knife and ran out into the sun and ran through the woods and ran until my feet bled and ran out in front of the truck that stopped so close to me I could feel its heat touch my arms. I killed Pixie when I walked through the police station, leaving a trail of bloody footprints all the way, and told the police lady who wrapped me in a blanket and gave me hot chocolate that my name was Scarlett Contreras and I was from Merry Park, outside Chicago, and that I had never had pet rabbits. I killed Pixie when I let Scarlett's parents hug me and bring me to Scarlett's house and put me to sleep in Scarlett's pink canopy bed, underneath Scarlett's sea of glow-in-the-dark stars.

I *am* Scarlett now. I *am.*

I made that choice. It was the first choice I ever made that meant anything. I could have chosen to tell the police lady that my name was Pixie Lopez and I was from San Antonio and I had no parents, and I could have chosen to let her send me back into the foster system to people who thought of me as a living, breathing check. Instead I chose to become Scarlett, because Scarlett clearly didn't want her life anymore, not if she'd chosen to stay behind and die when she could have run with me. She was dead. She wouldn't need her old life anymore.

I knew I was killing her. I knew Stepmother would kill her for letting me run. And I ran anyway.

It wasn't an easy choice. My real name was on the tip of my tongue the whole time, every time a teacher called me Scarlett or when I lined up at the beginning of the alphabet instead of in the middle, but it got easier. It got easier every time I fell asleep in my warm, safe bed and smelled the soapy smell of my baby brother's head and went to a real school where there were kids who went off to college instead of kids who tried to stab each other between classes.

But Melody is still talking to Katharina. "Scarlett, did . . ." She glances at me, glances longer at the knife on the ground. She's not sure what to call me. "Did she hurt you?"

Katharina . . . Scarlett—no, I can't call her Scarlett, she has to stay Katharina or I'll break right in two—*Katharina* doesn't reply. She has eyes only for me. "I trusted you, Pixie," she says. "I wasn't mad when you ran and left me behind. Stepmother didn't care about you the way she cared about me." She stops and blows out a deep breath. "Okay, so I *was* mad, but I understood. You had to do what you had to do. I couldn't forgive you for it, but I understood."

"I'm sorry," I say helplessly, because it's all I can do. I can't, and I won't, go back. I can't, I can't, I can't, I can't, I can't. I *can't.*

"Stepmother got sick, and she told me to go before she died and someone else took over the business," Scarlett— no, Katharina!—says. Her voice is the same monotone as the Blade's voice actor. She sounds almost like she's bored. "I knew my parents didn't want me back, so I asked some-body if I could borrow their phone, Google my name, see what was out there."

Now it sounds like something is rising in her throat, like she's going to spit it on the floor. "Only it turned out I'd already been found." She looks at me hard, and I have to look at the floor. "I had to talk to you, Pixie, before I went to the police."

It hits me like a punch to the stomach. "That's why you drugged me," I say, and look at Melody. It's her turn to look at the floor. I turn back to Katharina. "After you guys talked at the vigil, you wanted to prove to her that I didn't have the scar. That *you* did. But there were people around.

And so you decided to drug me at home, in the kitchen, Melody." I remember the cool hand slipping under my dress, her voice yelling for my father. "You tried to show Dad. To prove I wasn't really her."

Melody's voice shakes. "I always knew," she says, and suddenly her behavior throughout the years makes sense. Her constant cold stare. The hatred that simmered just below the surface. "But when I told Mom and Dad right after you came home, they told me to stop it. To stop lying and to welcome you back home.

"When I showed Dad you didn't have that scar, I expected him to be shocked and furious," she says. She looks up, and her eyes are shiny, her lower lip trembling, her voice foggy. "He sat me down and said he knew. That of course he knew. He knew his own child and he knew you weren't her. I didn't understand. Why didn't he ever look for Scarlett? Why did he keep you?"

Katharina doesn't say anything. I hear her breathing fast, so fast her chains rattle. She doesn't want to tell, and I know why.

"It's because Mom sold Katharina," I say for her, because I can't change what happened, but I can give her this one tiny gift. I can feel Melody's shock in vibrations in the air. "Mom was an addict, and she was strung out, and she owed a lot of people a lot of money, and if the police had found out, they would've taken us all away. You and Matthew, too. That's why Dad didn't expose me. Mom couldn't live with the guilt after I showed up, and she ran."

Melody is shaking her head before I'm even done. "No," she says. "No, you're lying."

"It's true," I say. I don't look to Katharina for confirmation. She doesn't owe me anything.

Katharina speaks anyway. "Stop calling them Mom and Dad," she says. "They're not your parents. They're *mine*. And Melody is *my* sister."

"Scarlett," Melody says, but she's looking at the floor, and I don't know which one of us she's talking to. I hope it's me. I want it to be me.

Tears rise in my throat, but I don't let them out. Skywoman didn't cry when her world cracked around her and came crashing down. I won't either. "Melody, please," I say. "I am your sister. I *am*."

She shakes her head. She's still looking at the floor. I don't know if she's shaking her head at me or Katharina or the unfair world or her shoes. "This is too much," she says. "I can't . . ." She backs away and hits the wall, shaking her head the whole time, burying her face in her hands.

Melody has to understand. She has to understand there isn't any other way. I am trapped in a corner, in a basement, and Katharina is blocking the door. The only way out is through her. "Melody—"

"Scarlett?"

My heart thuds to my feet. Melody must have brought Matthew with her when she followed me, because our dad wasn't home and she couldn't leave him back at the car, but he can't be here. I can't lose Matthew.

He's standing in the doorway, looking suspiciously from Katharina to me to Melody, who's shrunk so far back into the wall she may actually be turning into wood. "Scarlett?" he says, and he's talking to me, and it's that more than anything that gives me strength. "Scarlett, what's going on?"

I could grab him and run. I could tuck him under my arm like a football and take him away, away, away.

My cheeks tingle with nausea. No. I could never do that. I could never do to him what was done to me.

I need to think. I need time to think. I can't hurt Melody. I can't hurt Matthew. But I can't—

"Scarlett?" Matthew is tugging on my sleeve. "Scarlett, what's going on? Why's that girl have handcuffs on? Why's Melly crying?"

"It's a game," I say, and it kind of is—a mind game. "Matthew, shhh. Let me think."

"Hey," Katharina says to Matthew, trying to reach for him. Matthew shrinks away. "Hey, do you know who I am?"

"No," he says. I drape my arm around his neck, my flesh a gorget. I want to tell her to shut up, to stop talking, but I know she won't listen. I wouldn't listen if I were her.

Katharina juts her chin at me. "That girl isn't Scarlett. She isn't your sister," she says. "I am. I'm Scarlett."

Matthew shakes his head, slowly at first, then so fast I think his head might fly right off his shoulders and sail out the window. "You're not Scarlett," he says, and the certainty in his voice fills me with another shot of strength. "You're not."

"I am," Katharina hisses. "I am, and you need to let me out of these chains."

"No," Matthew says, his voice trembling. "Scarlett, let's go home."

Home. I don't know what home is anymore. I don't know if I have a home anymore.

I need to think, and I can't think here, not with Melody crying in the wall and Matthew tugging at my sleeve and Katharina hissing and spitting from her corner like a soaked cat.

"Melody . . . ," I say, and my words stick in my throat. She doesn't look over anyway. I want to know what she's thinking, and I don't want to know what she's thinking. Her thoughts could burn me.

"Melody, I'm going to take Matthew home," I say. Home. For now. I know when Melody gets herself home, Katharina in tow, I'll have to leave. I'll have to go somewhere. I don't know where. I don't know what will happen. All I can do is focus on my brother.

I turn and leave, Matthew's hand hot in mine. I leave the knife in the cabin. I don't need it anymore. I don't want it. I never wanted it. It was never going to keep me safe.

Melody lets me go. I don't think she even sees me leave.

But she must, because I hear the clanking of chains just as I step out the door, hear the sigh of relief whoosh out of Katharina's throat. Melody's let her go. I walk faster. "I just want to talk right now," Melody is saying inside, and then she yelps. My steps still, but then I speed up. Whatever's happening, I need to get Matthew in the car. I need to get Matthew safe.

I'm still focused on the thought of the car, still focused on Matthew, when Katharina tears out the door behind me and rips him away from me. I turn and freeze when I see Katharina holding Matthew tight. Over her shoulder I meet Melody's eyes, horrified as she stands frozen in the doorway.

"You both need to listen to me," Katharina says, her voice high and thready, and then I see the knife.

My time with Stepmother was divided into two parts: Before Pixie left and After Pixie left. B.P. and A.P.

Objectively, A.P. wasn't all that different from B.P. During both eras I lived according to Stepmother's whims, and came upstairs and went downstairs at her call. I ate food over the sink and showered when she told me I was starting to smell. I slept on the same mattress, still curled in the shape of a comma around the hole where Pixie should have been.

I didn't get another companion. After Pixie, after what she did and what she said, I knew better than to ask for someone else. I did the work of two people, scrubbed thoroughly and silently, and resigned myself to the loneliness.

I thought about Pixie all the time. I scrubbed harder

when I thought of her, scrubbed fiercely at the wet streaks on my face.

B.P. was four years long. A.P. was another three years. I was eight when the man scooped me into his car and deposited me in the basement. I was fifteen when I left.

I knew something was going to happen a few months before it actually did. Stepmother's skin was slowly turning gray, as if she were hardening into stone, and her hair was thinning out and then finally gone, her patchy scalp covered at all times by one of the girls' colorful scarves. One morning, just after my fifteenth birthday, I was sweeping the living room when a man showed up, one whose pencil-thin mustache and greasy hair made the hairs on my arms rise straight up.

She called me into the kitchen as soon as he left. "Jane," she said. "The door is unlocked. Go."

I looked at the kitchen door. It was indeed unlocked. I looked back at her and didn't move. This had to be some sort of trick.

She sighed. "Go," she said wearily. "I'm going into hospice at the end of this week, and that man will be taking over my operation. You don't want to be here for that. This is a kindness, Jane. Take it."

I took a hesitant step toward the door, then looked back. I didn't know what I was looking for. If she was telling me to go, I was going to go. I had never disobeyed her before.

"Don't tell anyone about us, of course." Stepmother's

voice was still strong, even if her body wasn't. "I may be dead, Katharina Svecova may no longer walk this earth, but you wouldn't want the girls to get hurt."

Katharina. Stepmother's name was Katharina. I nodded at Stepmother, at Katharina, and I fled.

I didn't tell on her, and I didn't forget her. I borrowed her name when I needed a new one. I borrowed her name when I needed to be as hard and cold as she was.

I borrowed her name when it came time to make Pixie pay.

CHAPTER SEVENTEEN

The seconds tick by so loudly it's like I'm trapped inside a clock. Wind rustles the branches above but flees when it sees the scene below.

Katharina is holding a knife to Matthew's throat. She's holding. A knife. To my little brother's *throat*.

I've never seen Matthew so still. He stands rigid, pressed against her stomach, his eyes so wide they might pop out and roll away on their own. The metal of the knife must be cold against his skin. "It's okay," I tell him, but my voice shakes. "It'll be okay. Don't move."

He doesn't move. *Good boy.* I turn my attention to Katharina. "Let him go," I say. This time, my voice is deadly calm. I search my mind for other things to say, for threats, promises, pleas, but I come up blank. She has a knife against my little brother's *throat*. "Let him *go*."

Katharina is seething, spit practically frothing on her lips. "I will cut his throat." Involuntary yelps escape my and Melody's throats at the same time. "I swear to God, I will cut his throat if you don't give me my life back."

"He's your brother," Melody says. Her voice is shaking. "You can't hurt him. He's your *brother*."

Katharina doesn't listen. It's like she doesn't even hear her. She's focused on me, eyes shining, and I notice her arm, the arm holding the knife, is shaking too. "I will cut his throat if you don't give me my life back," she says, and her voice is steady, and I don't doubt her for a second. I don't even need to hear what she says next. "I did it before."

A breath stops halfway to my lungs. "Monica . . ."

Katharina barks a laugh, but she doesn't sound angry. Just sad. "She found out I was living in the storage building. She found out what I was. I had to stop her. I couldn't let her tell."

The breath charges in, hits my lungs so hard I feel sick. "She was innocent."

Katharina spits out another sad laugh, and somehow I find myself feeling pity. She isn't a psychopath. She didn't enjoy killing Monica, and she doesn't enjoy the thought of hurting Matthew. She's warped. She's made too many choices in the wrong direction.

Nobody can come back from that.

"No," Melody is saying behind her. "No, no, no, no, no,"

and it sends me right back to the basement, to the flow of words I couldn't stop, to the feeling of Scarlett's shirt damp against my cheek.

I can't focus on Monica now. She's already dead, and there's no coming back from that, either. "Let Matthew go," I say, and sorrow cuts through me. "I will give you your life back. You can be Scarlett again. I swear." I swallow hard, rocks cutting into my throat. I've lied before. I'm not lying now. "I will do anything, anything, to keep him safe."

Melody is sobbing, the "no's" dissolved into tears. She is useless right now. I can't depend on her, so I zero back in on Katharina. "I swear," I say, and I'm looking at her and she's looking at me and her arm is shaking and my throat is gulping and her face shifts and something in my face or my voice must convince her, because she drops her arm and lets Matthew run to me; he buries his face in my shirt and I know he's getting snot all over me and I don't care.

"How should we do this, then?" Katharina says, and she sounds calm, like ten seconds before she'd been ordering a sandwich or processing a return, not holding a knife to a little boy's throat. "Make the switch? Obviously, we'll have to go to the police."

"Obviously," I say, pushing Matthew behind me and moving closer to her.

"I'll ask them not to be too hard on you," Katharina says. "Even with all you did. You'll probably get sent to juvie or a state facility or something. You'll get out and get to have a normal life after a few years."

"Sounds fine," I say, moving closer, slipping my hand into my pocket.

She's gazing off into the distance, eyes dreamy, like she's visualizing her pink canopy bed, the glow-in-the-dark stars spotting her ceiling. The new pink sneakers sitting untouched in her closet, way too small now for her feet. "I can't wait to be back in my old room," she says. "I can't wait to——"

She doesn't see me—or the pepper spray—coming. Melody does, though, and jumps out of the way just in time for me to slam into Katharina, who's doubled over wheezing, and push her through the door of the cabin, then pull the door shut and snap the padlock closed. She shrieks in surprise and then pounds on the door, still coughing. The door won't open as long as the padlock is closed, but it won't take long for her eyes to clear and for her to climb out a window or something. One is already broken. This is a temporary measure only.

"She had a knife," Melody says. Her tears have dried up, leaving shiny trails down her cheeks. "What if she stabbed you?"

I didn't even think about that. I just shake my head. Even if I had thought about it, I don't think I would have cared. "I'm going to take Matthew home," I say. Let her try to stop me. I dare her. I don't want my baby brother to remember me like this; if I'm going to have to run, I want him to have a good memory of me as his last one. This car ride is all I have. "And then . . ." I stop. I don't know what comes after the ellipsis. I just know I'll have to get away before Katharina gets out, before Melody tells. "I don't know. I just need to take him home."

Melody nods, but she doesn't move. I don't know if she's in shock or if she's waiting for me to leave so she can let Katharina back out, usher her back into her old life. It doesn't matter; I can't do anything either way. I leave her behind, glancing over my shoulder once. She's watching us go.

I spend most of the car ride home trying to make Matthew feel better; he's panicked, quite understandably, about having a knife held to his throat, and stops shaking only when we're almost home. I also tell him I love him approximately five hundred times. When he thinks of me, I want that to be what he remembers: that I love him. That I love him more than anything else in the world.

"You okay?" I ask as we pull into the driveway. My dad's car is there. My heart twists and squeezes, a piece of wrung-out laundry.

He nods, but tears carve a path beside his nose. I pull him close to me and kiss his head. "I love you, and I am your sister," I say. "That's the truth."

He nods again. "I know."

I pat him on the shoulder. "Listen," I say. "Dad's home, but you can't tell Dad what just happened. Not until Melody gets home. Okay?"

He nods. He trusts me. I love him for that. "Okay."

"Good," I say. I close my eyes and brace myself. "Go ahead. Go inside. And remember I love you, okay?"

He doesn't move. "Where are you going?" There's fear in his eyes. "Are you coming back?"

"Of course," I say, but the words feel heavy. I want them so badly to be true, to be light and carefree and melt on my tongue like Adventure World's fly-riddled cotton candy.

"Good," he says. "See you later." And he hops out and charges inside, without even looking back. Like he's so confident I was telling the truth he doesn't even worry about taking a last look.

I watch him until he disappears from view, even leaning forward for that last split-second glimpse of him as he shuts the front door behind him. I am not so confident.

I do know where I'm going, though. I drive by pastoral fields of hay waving in the breeze, past cheerful red barns and even more cheerful white picket fences and horses so cheerful they might as well be braying music, to Connor's house. I park a little ways down the street and sneak through his backyard to the barn. I slip inside and sag against the wall and nod a silent hello to Ernesto and Bessie, who might not even be there. They might be dead, for all I know, ground up and jammed into cans of cat food. But the barn smell is calming, and the hay in the air and the nails in my back and the thin threads of light trickling in through the slats of wood remind me of the last time I was really, truly happy. I'm going to need this memory for whatever happens ahead.

I don't know how long I sag there before I hear Connor say my name. I stand up straight, blinking in the sudden influx of light. "Scarlett?" he says again. "My brother said he thought he saw a girl in the barn."

Despite myself, despite everything that's happened, I still feel a rush of pure, hot want when I see him in the doorway. "I'm sorry," I say. "I just . . . needed to hide for a little while, and this is the first place I thought of. I'll go."

He steps inside and closes the door behind him. I tense, but mostly out of reflex. I am no longer afraid of the dark. There are worse things to be afraid of. "Don't go," he says. "I mean, it's amazing. I was just thinking about you and now here you are."

"It's like I'm a figment of your imagination."

"No," he says. "No, I could never imagine someone quite like you."

Somehow he's there, in front of me, so close I can feel his heat. It stokes the want, and I have to press my hands against the wall behind me to keep myself from lunging at him. "Why were you thinking about me?"

"I talked to Cady. I made it clear I would always be there for her as a friend, but that I liked you and I wanted to be with you," he says. "I wasn't being fair to anyone. It took me a while to realize it, but I had to do the right thing."

I answer him with my lips, and then my back is up

against the wood, the nails digging in. I welcome them into my flesh. I missed them.

He pulls away after a minute. "I thought you hated me," he says huskily.

"No," I say. And it's true. It just took me some time to realize it, and for the want to wash it away. Because haven't I done so much worse than be confused over my love life? And if I've done so much worse, and if Skywoman has done so much worse, does that mean we don't deserve to be loved?

"But . . ."

I silence him with another kiss. "I like you more when you don't talk," I whisper. It's not true, and his laugh tells me he gets it. He gets me. I press up against him and let the want carry me away.

My phone vibrating in my back pocket, buzzing angrily against the wood of the wall, yanks me back to the present. Yanks me back to Pixie. The nails in my back no longer feel quite so welcoming. "Wait," I say, and pull out my phone.

It's Melody. My stomach fills with dread and I'm tempted not to answer, to push off the inevitable just a little longer, but something makes me click the green light and press the screen against my ear. It slicks with sweat. "Melody?"

"Scarlett," she says, and that one word evaporates the dread, makes it rise through my skin and dissipate into the air. "Scarlett. I need help."

"With what?"

Connor backs away, hearing the urgency in my voice, but I motion for him to stay. If he leaves, he might never come back. "Melody?"

Her voice cracks in a sob. "Katharina," she says. "I . . . I was trying to . . . she tried to . . . after what she did, she . . ." She falls silent for a moment, then adds, "It was an accident. . . ." I don't know if she actually sounds completely and thoroughly unconvincing, or if it's all in my head. "An accident, I swear." And then she stops, haltingly, and takes a little gasping breath. Like she's trying to hold in something horrible.

The fifth choice isn't mine. It's Melody's.

All I need to know now is that she used Scarlett's name. That she used *my* name. "I'll be right there," I say.

"Thank you," she says, and her voice breaks again. "Scarlett."

THREE MONTHS LATER

Melody is teaching me how to make banana muffins. "Mash the banana in, but leave some chunks. You want chunks," she directs, watching closely as I smash the fruit with my fork. "Then mix in the melted butter, the egg, and the sugar, and mix, but not too much. Okay, that's good."

We've already mixed the dry ingredients—the flour, baking powder, baking soda, cinnamon, salt, and nutmeg—and so she has me mix everything together now. "Don't mix it too much or the texture will be weird," she says. "Like I said, you want chunks. Chunks are good."

I mix it carefully and present it to her for her approval. She peers down her nose at it, then gives a regal nod. "Good. Now put it in the muffin tin. Make sure all twelve are equal. I'll make the crumble." I guess the crumble isn't quite up to my skill level yet. I'm okay with that. "Make sure you grease the muffin tin first, just rub some butter in each of the holes."

A few months ago, I would never have expected to spend a day in the kitchen with Melody, having her help me with something completely and totally voluntarily. I would have wanted it, yes, wanted it so hard my chest hurt.

She told me it was an accident. That's what she said. She'd been horrified by Katharina's willingness to scare Matthew, maybe even hurt him or kill him, and so when Katharina lunged at her as she was leaving the cabin, Melody grabbed the knife on impulse, to protect herself, and Katharina lunged too close. She didn't mean it, not really, but as she stood there, watching Katharina gasp and bleed on the dirt, she didn't feel sorry and she didn't call for an ambulance and she didn't try to stanch the bleeding. She felt shocked, yes, and gutted, and she cried in great, gasping sobs even as she couldn't breathe, but she couldn't bring herself to feel sorry.

"The crumble's done," Melody says, and our eyes meet over the muffin tin. She smiles grimly at me. She's changed in the last three months; her cheeks have thinned, she cut her hair short, and she has permanent dark shadows under her eyes. She looks older. That's what happens when you have dark secrets. When you make the darkest of dark choices. When you do what's necessary to protect your family from someone who is, at once, a loved one and a destroyer.

I would know.

I smile back. I think we're friends now. We haven't braided each other's hair yet, or painted each other's nails, but we've told each other our secrets. Everything is out in the open, and now we share the biggest secret of all, the secret that points back to a patch of disturbed earth deep in the woods, a patch that by now should be covered in dried brown pine needles and squirrels hiding acorns for the winter. "Can I bring a few to Connor?" I ask. "I'm seeing him after school on Wednesday."

"Of course," she says, sprinkling the crumble on top of the batter. "They're yours, too, you know." Her smile twitches, turns into something more genuine. "That is, if you can keep them from Matthew. Three days is a long time for anything to last in this house."

As if on cue, right as the muffins start to become fragrant in the oven, giving off clouds of banana and cinnamon, Matthew races into the kitchen. "Oh, are you baking something?" he asks, like he hasn't been lurking outside the door, waiting.

Melody rolls her eyes. "I don't know, what do you think?"

"I think yes," Matthew says, and beams, pressing his face up against the oven's glass front. It must be hot, but it doesn't seem to bother him. It's clearly not hot enough to burn him, so I let him be.

"You okay?" I ask Melody—quietly, so Matthew doesn't hear. "I heard you yelling again in your sleep."

Her lower lip trembles, but only once. She is strong. She will be okay. "When will it stop?" she asks.

I swallow hard. This isn't the answer I want to give her, but it's the truth. "It will never stop, not really," I say. "But it will get easier."

I grab her hand and squeeze. She squeezes back. She is strong, like me, and she will be okay, like me, because we are sisters. Sisters by choice. We might not share blood, but we do share a secret, and secrets are stronger than blood.

ACKNOWLEDGMENTS

This book was informed by the two summers I spent working at Six Flags Great Adventure. Thank you to the park for such a memorable first job and to the people with whom I worked, played, and fell in love during the summers of 2007 and 2010. We had a wild ride, and I could not have asked for more.

Thank you, as always, to my publishing team: Merrilee Heifetz, Sarah Nagel, Allie Levick, and Michael Mejias at Writers House; Chelsea Eberly, Michelle Nagler, Jenna Lettice, Aisha Cloud, Jocelyn Lange, Nicole de las Heras, Alison Kolani, and Barbara Bakowski at Random House; and Kassie Evashevski at United Talent. You are all the best, and I feel lucky every day to have you on my side.

Jeremy Bohrer, thank you for supporting me and brainstorming with me and making my life better—I love you. Fearless Fifteeners, Lippincott Massie McQuilkin, Twitter community, friends, and extended family—thank you for your cheerleading, your help, your friendship, your love, and/or all of the above. My friends and critique partners Annette Dodd and Alix Kaye—thank you for helping make my writing better and my stories stronger.

Thank you, finally, to Beth and Elliot Panitch. I would publicly apologize for making all the parents in my books terrible people, but maybe they're only that way because it would be impossible to write parents better than mine.

ABOUT THE AUTHOR

AMANDA PANITCH grew up next to an amusement park in New Jersey and went to college next to the White House in Washington, D.C. She now resides in New York City, where she works in book publishing by day, writes by night, and lives under constant threat of being crushed beneath giant stacks of books. Visit Amanda online at amandapanitch.com and follow her on Twitter at @AmandaPanitch.